Gabriella

Carl Facciponte

ISBN: 978-0-9961648-2-5

This book is gratefully dedicated to my wife, Ellen, who put up with my nose buried in my ever-present lap while I pretended to be watching movies with her on TV. I appreciate your patience, understanding, and especially for you keeping the coffee flowing

A special thanks to all of my fellow authors who advised me on the tenants of the English language and who gently redirected me to safety when I wandered off the path.

Preface

To be human...

... does it require blood and bones?

Gabriella West is an android, but she's special. She lives on her own, she falls in love, and she even searches to find God.

But there's a catch: no one, except for her creators and the government, are aware she is a machine.

As she searches for a pathway that leads her to become more human, she finds something interesting.

And the revelation blows her mind.

When she was created, a switch was implanted in her, and its purpose isn't a good one. Can she discover the trigger before she gets shut down?

Will she be able to become "human" and find love, or will she be forced to comply with her main objective, and lose everything she treasures?

How thin IS the line between human and machine?

Chapter One

Congratulations, everyone," Jim said at the activation milestone ceremony. He lifted his champagne glass high. "It may be late winter outside, but the sun is shining warmly inside for us! We've completed the first stage of Project Lincoln! Ladies and gentlemen, Artificial Intelligence Concepts Incorporated, and this team of the best scientific minds in the field have made science fiction come alive! Today, science, technology, and life have changed forever. The world will never be the same from this point on."

Jim paused for a moment. "And a big thanks to AI Concepts for turning the entire tenth floor of this Midtown Manhattan building into a stand-alone, state-of-the-art, secure research and prototype facility just for us. Salute!"

The joyful sound of clinking glasses filled the room. Cheers went up from the staff of engineers and technicians. Hands shook. High-fives slapped. Some people hugged. Gabriella stood next to Jim and raised her glass high to join in the toast.

***

Two months earlier, Jim and Francine discussed the rewards a successful animation would bring. Jim whispered as he drew Francine close and felt her warmth. "If the animation of our android goes well over the next few weeks, there will be no shortage of project cash and some outrageous bonuses for us and our people. No one on the planet has ever done what we have. You and I need to have our own private party before the official one," Jim said, winking. "Want to work late tonight?"

Jim Arnold was the clean-shaven, handsome, early middle-aged AI Lab Director. His Ph.D. in Advanced Artificial Intelligence and Biosystems earned him his directorship. The fifteen-year childless marriage to his wife, Alice, had cooled off over the five-year life of the project. Jim's job demanded long hours, but that wasn't the sole reason he was often late coming home to their small Park Terrace West apartment.

"Look at her," Jim said about Gabriella, who was lying on the animation table, all the while admiring Francine. Jim pulled Francine even closer to him as he allowed himself to become intoxicated by her perfume.

"It's beautiful," Francine said as she pressed her body into Jim, "and anatomically perfect in every detail, right down to small body hairs. The look. The feel. Everything. I love what the cosmetics engineering team did with her green eyes and curly honey-colored hair. But, Jimmy, there is no 'her.' It's only a machine." Francine smiled as she noticed the lingering trace of Jim's morning aftershave. She rocked her hip against him, promising future delights.

Jim smiled, "Unless someone attempts to monitor its vital signs, Gabriella will be indistinguishable from a living human being. We've done it, kiddo! Now, about that working late together thing..."

***

Two weeks before the victory celebration, the Cray XC40 supercomputer downloaded the android's operational programming, activating Gabriella's other systems. Linguistic, scientific, and cultural data followed. Gabriella was 'born' a fully functioning adult. The engineering staff gathered around to observe the system initiation. One of the very few religious engineers at AI Concepts compared her to Eve, of Biblical fame. Unlike Eve, upon animation, Gabriella sat up on the lab table, looked over the spectators, and asked, "Why am I the only naked person in the room?"

"May I have some clothing, please?" she asked, the faint hint of an accent adding richness to her voice. Although her speech was flawless, the almost musical inflection suggested that English was not her native language.

"Jim," Francine whispered as her eyes widened in surprise, "she asked for clothes. Is that part of the programming or an unexpected bit of code cross-talk? She can't be reasoning on her own already, could she? Are the silver strand nano-machines configuring on their own this soon?"

"I'm pretty surprised myself, Francine. I reviewed the programming specifications with the code designers only a month ago, and we didn't predict this to happen yet. Sure, we designed her brain to self-adjust its nanowire configurations to mimic neuron functions in the human thought process, but we calculated it would take a longer time than this to kick in and produce results. This is intriguing."

One of the young engineers brought a white lab coat for Gabriella. She slipped down from the table and put it on.

"Jim, why are you so surprised?" Gabriella asked in a low, calm voice which hinted of belonging to a cultured family. Her slightly olive-tinged skin would make one assume she was of Mediterranean descent. It would be easy to envision her sliding her long legs out of a limo and attending the opera with foreign friends or dignitaries.

"Your team designed me to think beyond my initial programming, and here I am, doing exactly that. Wasn't it included in your design?"

The team turned to Jim for an answer.

Startled, Jim muttered, "Yes, yes. That's aligned with our expectations. Good job, team."

Recovering from the question, he continued, "Okay, gang, let's recheck to see if there are any differences in Gabriella's brain operation compared to the base systems programming data."

Frank Wright, the president of AI's Research and Development business unit, motioned Jim over to his side.

"Jim, I didn't expect Gabriella to know she was naked and certainly didn't expect her to ask for clothes. Was this part of the programming design?"

"Truthfully, Frank, no, it wasn't. Beta versions of the brain didn't show it would self-actualize this soon. I'm surprised, but consider it to be a bonus."

"Well, I guess that's good in this case. I'm uncomfortable when things we didn't design for, happen. Keep me informed on any other surprises, okay?"

***

There were no more surprises before the official activation ceremony. Gabriella's operational testing continued over the next three weeks. Speech, recall, cognitive ability, fine and gross motor skill tests were all passed as expected. A brain scan followed each successful completion.

"How did Gabriella's daily scan go this morning, Francine?" Jim asked on the morning of the ceremony.

"Pretty good. We mapped out her neural networks and found new ones are forming themselves at a rate exceeding initial projections. The Deep Base programming recognizes patterns effectively and is reforming her neural networks to simulate our brain functions. She is thinking as an enhanced human. Her internal systems are looking up data on the internet and including it in conversations with lab personnel. What a billion-dollar idea if we developed a chip and implanted into people to allow personal internet access! Yes, chip the planet," Francine said, "that would make us richer than God."

Chapter Two

Lance Coopers wanted to be an army general since, well, since before he could remember. He grew up in the Liberty, Kentucky, countryside.

From the early age of six, Lance enjoyed war stories. He would crawl upon his father's lap and say, "Hey dad, can we watch an army movie?"

"Sure, son, I have just the one here. I'll make some popcorn, and we can cuddle up on the couch and watch it together."

It was watching those old World War II movies with his dad which first ignited a little boy's imagination to advance his troops into a noble battle. He and the other boys would play cops and robbers on sunny summer days. Lance, however, always took the role of a general deploying his troops against an entrenched, sinister enemy.

"Okay, men, let's storm that hill," Lance shouted as he led the latest charge up the treed hill in the town park. "Follow me!" was his impassioned cry as he raised his stick gun over his head and rushed headlong into victory after victory. He was General Lance, and it didn't matter at all to the boys that Lance was always leading the heroic charges. As long as they were fighting for a cause, the other details were insignificant to them. They were little boys running through the weeds and woods, fueled by imagination on carefree summer days.

On a cold March day marking his seventeenth birthday, Lance asked his parents for their signature on the DD-1966 form to allow him to join the Army with parental consent.

Lance's father was an air force retired Lieutenant Colonel from a three-generation line of air force men. "You mean air force, don't you, son?"

"No, sir, I mean army!" No matter the number of grand, if somewhat inflated, stories outlining how exciting a career in the air force could be, Lance set his face like flint to join the army and become a general.

"Lance," his father continued, "you're only seventeen. Wait a couple of years, and let's talk again."

"Dad, I'm old enough to know what I want in life," Lance shouted back, his arms flying into the air. "I'm not stupid, you know!"

"You're not stupid, but there are things you still don't understand. We're trying to protect you from getting hurt, son," his father said with the voice of a parent trying to save their child from making an unwise decision.

"I don't need your help. I understand everything! You're the ones that don't understand. I'm asking you to trust me on this!"

"Don't you dare raise your voice to me, young man! No, you are the one that doesn't get it. You understand one hundred percent of what you understand, but you don't realize it's only about twenty percent of what you need to understand. You think you see it all, but you see almost nothing!"

"I've had it. You're calling me stupid. I'm not! You don't understand. To hell with this conversation! I'm going to Dot's."

"Hold on, son. Don't go anywhere like this. Let's talk more."

It was too late. Lance marched out of the house as his father was still speaking. He bicycled towards Dot's Pizza Palace on Old Middleborough Road. He hoped to run into some of his friends for comfort and companionship. They often met at Dot's to discuss life plans, their favorite sports teams, and girls. The rustic, familiar place had become their unofficial headquarters.

"Good. There's no one sitting at my table," Lance slid into the booth in the corner by the kitchen. It was an old wooden booth whose solid wood seats had seen many high-level strategic meetings conducted by three generations of teenagers. Although the owners of Dot's Pizza Palace had changed several times over the years, the interior had not. Lance smiled. Even after cleaning, it had a perpetual faint smell of sauce and pepperoni embedded into the wood.

None of his friends were there. Lance came for the comfort of being in 'their' special booth for a little while. He had seen his father retreat to the den when he was upset and wanted to get away from it all. Lance's man cave smelled of pizza.

The lone waitress walked to the booth, and in a very lackluster voice, asked if he wanted anything.

This is exactly the type of person I don't want to become like. A zombie at work. I'll bet her parents didn't let her do what she wanted after high school either, and here she is.

"Just a coke. No ice, please." He dismissed her with a wave of his arm.

"I can't see why they won't let me enlist," he spewed under his breath. "I'm old enough and ready for it. Why can't they trust me on this? What the hell!"

"Here's your soda," the waitress said, plopping the glass on the table as Josiah walked through the door.

Lance saw his friend and waved him over. "Hey," both boys said to each other in unison, "what's up?"

"I'm glad you could make it here, Lance. You're probably wondering why I called this meeting."

"Huh? What?

"Nah, just screwing with your head, Lance. But if you fell for that, you must be into something heavy. What's up?"

"Parent crap again," Lance admitted. "I want to go into the army after graduation. They're against it. It doesn't make any sense to me."

"What do they want you to do, go to college?"

"Yeah. It's not that I'm so much against it, but I tried to explain if they let me enlist now, I can serve four years and then have the Army pay for my college anyhow. I'd save them a bucket full of money. They don't get it! It's so obvious I'm right."

"Hmm, see what you mean," Josiah answered in his best sage-like voice. "What are you going to do? Where do they want you to go?"

"Kentucky State, but I'm not ready. I don't know. Crap! Screwed in every direction. I can't enlist without their permission and don't want to go to college this fall. It would be great to take a year off and sort it all out, or at least until I get old enough to enlist by myself. Is that such a bad idea? Lots of people do it. Why do they have to pick on me all the time? It's like they don't think I'm old enough to make my own decisions, for cripe's sake."

"I feel you, man. What would you do until you could enlist if you didn't go to college? They aren't going to let you sit home, that's for sure."

"Well, I've already talked to Ed Michener at the Tractor Supply Company. He says he could get me a job there until I figure things out. It wouldn't be much, but he said they are always looking for someone to work in the stockroom."

The waitress walked over to the table, carrying a large, square box with greasy fingerprint stains near the flaps. She looked in Josiah's general direction and mumbled with no feeling, "Here's your takeout. Enjoy."

"Thanks," Josiah responded. "Look, I've got to go. This greasy thing will coagulate soon, but let's get together and talk things out more. Good luck with your folks. See ya."

"Been real, Josiah. Catch you later."

Lance sat there nursing his coke for a while before muttering, "Life sucks! What the hell am I going to do anyhow?" and then stomped off in a deep dark funk for the bicycle ride back home.

A few patrons turned to glance at him after his exclamation. "Kids," one of them said to his dinner partner. "They're all the same. All confused know-it-alls. Not at all like us when we were young." His partner nodded.

Lance applied to Kentucky State College in June. A letter arrived from KSC before the end of the summer.

"Lance, you have a letter from Kentucky State!" his mother shouted up the stairs.

"I'll be down in a few minutes," came the half-hearted reply.

"Come on down here this minute, mister. I'm excited and need to see what it says."

"You have my permission to open it yourself, Mom."

"Lance, get down these stairs and open your mail for your mother!"

"Okay, okay. Here I come, mom." Heavy, protesting thuds from man-sized feet filled the stairwell as Lance thumped his way down the stairs, hoping it was a rejection letter with all his might.

"So, let me have it," he said as he stretched an arm out to her. Lance opened the envelope with resignation.

"Damn!"

"What is it, son? You didn't get in?" came the concerned response.

"Worse. They've accepted me." His mother squealed with joy and threw her arms around him. "Stop it, Mom. Someone might see through the window!"

"I don't care! My boy is going to college! I'm so proud of you."

However reluctantly, Lance was college-bound.

Lance spent a listless summer at the Tractor Supply Company as the specter of the coming Fall loomed over him.

***

The first two weeks of college were hectic and frustrating.

"These basic English and math courses make me feel more like I'm in a glorified high school. Except Kentucky State is bigger than our whole town of Liberty. This is crazy. I want to go home," Lance moaned to his shadow as he walked from one building to another. A passing student responded, "Right on, Bro," and raised a fist in solidarity as he kept walking.

Lance did a slow slide into depression. *There has to be a legitimate way of dropping out without my parents coming down on me.*

"Going to the Freshman Mixer, Lance?" asked a freshman girl as she worked at qualifying for her 'ring by spring' status by becoming engaged before the end of the school year.

"No, thanks. I'm not much of a mixer."

It hurt the girl for only a moment before she noticed another young male freshman to hit on. Her smile returned as she rushed off to intercept her new target.

Two weeks later, Lance walked into one of the campus cafeterias and noticed a small poster advertising the Reserve Officers Training Corps. The sign promised not only would ROTC pay for his college and give him a monthly living allowance, but he would also graduate as an army officer.

"Hell yes! Now, this is what I'm talkin' about," he said aloud. The world brightened. Lance's pulse raced as the implications formed themselves into visions of his glorious future. *If I stay in this college for four years, I'll be in the army as an officer and on my way to becoming the general I know I am. Life is finally getting better!*

Lance pushed his studies hard. The rest of his college career was a blur, except for those portions about ROTC.

"Lance, how are your courses coming?" his father asked during one of the rare weekends at home.

"I love it, Dad. Especially the ROTC Army Leadership and Operations and Tactics courses! They have me thinking about declaring a major in Computer Information Systems."

"That's a difficult field. Can you stick it out, son? It won't be easy. Studying was never your strong point in high school."

"Got it covered! ROTC has a course in Goal Setting and Accomplishment that will whip my butt into shape to study. I can do this! I know I can!"

"Then go for it with all the focus and fight of a drowning man fighting for air, kid. I think you can do it too."

A small tear formed in Lance's eye. *My dad finally approves of me! I don't know how to feel about it.*

Lance volunteered for every extra assignment, every challenge, and attended every meeting. He rose through the ranks as a natural leader. In what seemed to be a few months, the four years passed. He graduated with a BS in Computer Information Systems. *Life is good. I'm on my way!*

The CIS degree smoothed the way for him to get into the Army Military Intelligence Officer Basic Course to begin his career as a Military Intelligence Officer (MIO).

As far as I know, there are no snipers in a computer lab, he mused, *and Military Intelligence is the perfect place to start my career.*

Chapter Three

Holy crap!" Martha Robinson exclaimed one afternoon when an unsolicited offer came in the mail from AI Concepts, Inc. It offered her a job in Manhattan, working on an AI project. "They will give me how much money? Plus a signing bonus?" she half-shouted to her apartment, holding the letter over her head, both hands waving in the air as she twirled around the living room. "I love university life, but I can learn to love other things, too. A lot of other things. Like having a solid bank account and a ton of designer shoes! New York, here I come!"

With a 3.98 GPA, Martha had had no trouble pursuing a doctorate in clinical psychology at UCLA, nor in winning a position as Associate Professor at UC Berkeley. She achieved fame by publishing articles in the *Psychological Bulletin* and in *Psychology Today* magazines. Martha's reports linked human psychological processes with advances in artificial intelligence. That gave her a national presence, leading to being featured in *Black Enterprise* for her work. AI Concepts noticed her.

***

The team was in the latter portion of the android debug and primary evaluation phase of the project when Martha came on board.

Martha's heart was full of excitement and expectation on a cold, rainy late winter Wednesday morning as she arrived in New York and checked into the Grand NYC hotel.

Martha spent the next two days in the AI Concepts headquarters with Human Resources. They were full days of filling out employment paperwork, including permission for AI Security to conduct detailed background checks and contact family and friends for references.

Security asked for DNA cheek samples. A scanner recorded her fingerprints. An almost friendly security woman taking Martha's photos and video explained the need to identify her from the security camera footage from any perspective.

The psychological testing administered by Human Resources amused Martha. *Have they not read my resume at all? Giving me these tests is like asking a professional chef if they can cook a burger. Seriously?*

The corporate live orientations and overviews were fast-paced. Presenters spoke of great accomplishments and the fantastic future to come, addressing no specific projects from the AI Concepts Research and Development Lab.

These talks have a lot in common with politicians delivering campaign speeches. Lots of chatter and excitement, but no usable data.

A plainclothes armed security guard escorted Martha to the 10th-floor research lab two blocks away after her processing.

Jim and Francine met Martha at the elevator, welcomed her warmly, and dismissed the guard.

Jim took the lead. "Martha, before we fill you in on your job details, let me show you around the lab. You'll love meeting our staff. Like you, they are the best people we can find in their field."

Francine rolled her eyes and sighed at Jim's not-so-concealed attempt at schmoozing the new girl.

"Thank you, Mr. Arnold," Martha said, "I can't wait to meet my coworkers and see your android."

Jim smiled. "Please, it's Jim. We don't address each other by titles or our last names. I'm simply Jim. Let me introduce you to some of our department heads before you meet our android. You'll get to meet everyone, but for now, let's not overwhelm you with names. We work long hours, so you will get to know everyone."

"I'm excited," Martha said with anticipation as she glanced across the lab with all of its complicated looking equipment.

Martha was escorted to a cluster of five desks arranged in a semi-circle. Each desk had six computer screens, mounted two-high and three-across.

"Martha, I would like you to meet Aki Gua. She is in charge of the Base Programming for the android."

Martha extended her hand in greeting. Aki shook her hand and gave a short bow. "Welcome to the group, Martha. I'm pleased to meet you. Our job here is to monitor the base information programming to allow it to facilitate the nano-rod gel technology in the android's brain to learn on its own. Our programming not only provides for data most people would call 'general knowledge' but also contains the algorithm which allows the brain to classify information on its own."

Francine explained that Aki graduated, with honors in her doctorate program, from Tsinghua University in Beijing. AI Concepts found her working as an AI programmer at Alibaba in China. "She was too good of a programmer not to convince her to come over to us."

Aki smiled at the compliment. She bowed to thank Francine.

"So tell me more about this 'base programming' thing. It sounds fascinating," said Martha.

"Much later, Martha," responded Francine. "Let's not overload you right off the bat. Let me introduce you to T'quan Taylor in Hydraulics and Servos."

Martha looked around the Hydraulics and Servos development area. "I thought it would be a bunch of tubes and big motors, but this is delicate stuff," she said, running her hand over one servo on the prototype board.

"I'm happy you like it," T'Quan said. His South African accent made Martha smile. "We do our best to make it so. All the components are tiny and run at high pressure. The pressure, combined with special electrical servos, allow for smooth, quick movements."

Jim spoke up, "T'quan received his doctorate in hydraulics from MIT."

"You have an accent. What's your country of origin?" Martha asked.

"Well, I was born in Uganda. My mother was from there, but my father was from the States. He was the one that named me after a favorite uncle. After completing high school in Uganda, I went to university at MIT."

"You can brag a little about MIT, T'quan," said Francine.

T'quan's almost pure black color turned even darker as he blushed. "Okay, so I got a full-ride scholarship to MIT. It was nothing."

"Indeed," responded Martha. "That's no small achievement. Congratulations!"

"Thank you, Martha. I'm sure we'll enjoy working together. It was nice to meet you."

They moved on to the electronics area of the floor.

"Martha, this is Fred Jensen. Fred comes to us from Aalborg University in Denmark, where he received his doctorate in electronics, with a focus on interfaces for advanced AI's. Fred, can you tell Martha a little about what you do?"

"Absolutely. Well, as Jim said, my group designs the electronic interfaces allowing the android's nano-gel brain to send messages to the rest of her system. It works much like the way your nerves carry messages from your brain to all of your parts. Make sense?"

"Well," said Martha, "I understand the concept. But how does it actually work?"

"Therein is the magic, Martha. To go any deeper would take a ton of time and a raft of drawings. We've had people fall out of their chair in a stupor from PowerPoint Poisoning when we give a more in-depth explanation." The four of them laughed.

"Then thanks for having mercy on me on my first day," Martha quipped back.

"Two more quick stops, Martha, and then we can grab some lunch. How does that sound?" said Jim.

"I'm game. Where to next?"

"Now for the real magic," teased Francine. "We'll talk to Dr. Alex Ortiz next. He comes to us from the University of Texas at Austin. Alex and his team are responsible for developing the nano-gel brain. It's the only workable one on the planet. We're thrilled by his work."

Martha gave a low whistle. "The only one, huh? Man, that's amazing."

"I'm so glad to meet you, Martha. You and I will work closely together in your socialization processes. I always like to start an overview by asking what questions need answering, so... what questions do you have about an advanced android brain?"

"Only the obvious, Alex. What does it do and how does it work?"

"Sure thing. A short answer is, it does what the human brain does. Our silver-carbon nano-rod machines can move around to some extent in the special gel. It gives them the capability to form their own neural pathways. It can think and learn. How's that for starters?"

"It seems impossible! How did you do it? I can't even begin to imagine it!"

"Well, first, we start with a package of lime Jell-O." Martha's eyes widened. "No, seriously, it's an extremely complicated chemical and engineering process. It would take quite a physics and chemistry background to grasp the details. Sorry for screwing with your head, Martha. We mess with each other a lot around here."

Alex glanced at Jim and Francine and winked.

"Shall we leave Alex to his work, Martha, and move on?" Francine asked.

"Sure. I'm loving the tour so far, but I have a couple of questions. What exactly is my job? The job description said it was to socialize the android. Not very descriptive at all. How do you socialize a machine? Don't the programmers build all that in? I can provide significant input, but it's not clear what you had in mind. Is the android tethered to a computer? From what kind of database does it draw its information?"

Francine answered. "Let me try to address the issue for you. The questions you pose are good but are based on the current state-of-the-art androids. You noticed security is extremely tight around here. There is a reason. The people you met on this tour are the tops in their fields. I assume you are familiar with the AI research DARPA is doing?"

"Yes, of course I am."

"Great. Well, our android is far beyond anything DARPA, the public, or even other artificial intelligence companies can imagine."

"Wow, an impressive statement!"

"We're proud of our work. But programming can only go so far. Our android has true artificial intelligence in every sense of the word."

Jim interrupted, "I'm in favor of dropping the 'artificial' designation. Our android needs a top-notch person to develop its social and communication skills to allow it to communicate and integrate into society. Programmers can't do that. We need you to make it happen."

"That's a huge statement, Jim," Martha said. "I guess I'll understand more when I have time to poke a couple of wires." Martha laughed.

"Yes," Jim replied, chuckling, "poke a couple of wires."

The trio continued to the skin covering development area. Francine introduced Martha to Gabriella as part of the staff.

Martha did not notice several lab personnel who were watching them, smiling from their work areas.

"Hi Martha, I'm Gabriella. I'm working on a skin texture and durability project."

Martha held her hand out for a handshake.

"Hi, Gabriella, I'm pleased to meet you."

Gabriella explained some of her objectives and design processes to Martha. "We need a covering with more cut resistance. Our current product is tough, but the new one will be even better." The two conversed for a while at the workbench.

Francine and Jim stepped back to allow Gabriella and Martha to get to know each other.

"You're very easy to talk to, Gabriella. Jim and Francine are allowing us to talk longer than I did at the other stations. In my experience, it means the new person is getting assigned a mentor, namely, the person they are talking to the longest. Is it true in this situation as well? I wouldn't mind at all." Then added in a low whisper, "You seem to be more sociable and less geeky than some other people here. I think we'll hit it off. What's your background?"

"I'm an engineer. And yes, I can tell we will hit it off."

"Fantastic. It was great meeting you," Martha said. "I'm sure we'll talk much more. Mr. Arnold... err, Jim, I'd like to see the android now, if it's okay."

Gabriella reached out with her right hand, took Martha's hand into hers, shook it again, saying, "Hi Martha, I'm Gabriella."

"Yes, Gabriella, I know. Besides, I can read your name badge," Martha said with a puzzled look. "Wait... what... what the... you can't mean that..." Martha stammered and looked disoriented. "No, it's not possible. No freakin' way! Hold it! I get it; you guys are screwing with me because I'm the new kid on the block. Gabriella, you can't be... I... I can't even say it."

The lab onlookers chuckled. Some men punched each other on the shoulder and laughed.

Gabriella reached out and gently held both of Martha's hands. Smiling, she said, "Let me say it for you. Yes, I am the android. It's true. Welcome. I'm happy to meet you, Martha. Here, you look like you need to sit down."

Gabriella slid her chair behind Martha and encouraged her to sit for a moment.

"You can't be an android. Your skin is soft and warm. You're alive and talking. No wires, no tethers. How...?"

"All in due time. You look like you could use a coffee. Let's go get some."

Gabriella helped the somewhat bewildered Martha out of the chair and led her to the coffee pot in the cafe. "I like coffee, Martha. I hope you do too. Let's sit and talk for a while. I have a lot to learn, and you have a lot to teach me."

Chapter Four

It was early evening on Friday two weeks later when Francine Drakus strolled through the door of Jim's corner office, imitating a streetwalker approaching a John. Her perfume permeated the air around her like a scented rose garden in the summer sun. He looked up and smiled at her. She reached out and ran her fingers through the hair on the back of his head.

"Is this a special perfume?" he asked, knowing precisely why she wore the brand.

"Could be," Francine whispered as she continued to stroke his hair. "Jim, you should save your computer work more often than you do. Here, let me help." She leaned from the waist across Jim's keyboard and clicked the save icon. "There, much better, isn't it?"

Jim peered past the open top three buttons on her blouse.

"Oh, to snuggle up between them, but it will have to wait until a little later," Jim whispered. His hand reached out to touch her, but he summoned it back through force of will.

Several people on the lab floor noted their brief exchange. Most averted their eyes in quiet support of their own affairs with co-workers. Martha was not so shy.

"So what's the story with Jim and Francine?" she asked a nearby engineer.

"Everyone in the lab knows that they are occasional lovers."

"Yeah, but she's the Associate Director under him. Isn't there a corporate rule about becoming too familiar with a direct report? Coercion, or conflict of interest, or something. Can't they get into trouble?"

"Sure, at least technically they can. Who will tell, though? No one would snitch on them. Besides, who doesn't hook up with a coworker once in a while? We spend a lot of time working together and have tons of deadlines to meet. It's only natural to relieve the tension so we can get back to thinking. No big deal."

"But where...?" The engineer cut Martha's question short with his curt answer.

"On the couch, mostly. We all use it."

Martha's brow wrinkled in disgust. "Ewwww! I sit on that couch!"

After a few moments, Martha shrugged her shoulders in silent resignation. "Well, I'm too engrossed in my work to worry about office romances that don't concern either myself or Gabriella. Damn, it's a lot like growing up at home watching mom and dad's 'special friends' come and go."

"Your folks had an open marriage?" asked the engineer.

"You know how it is around Berkley," Martha answered matter-of-factly.

***

The lab was empty for the day. "Let's hang around after work tonight and relax for a change," Francine whispered.

Jim grinned as he let his eyes roam over her shape. She was attractive but not beautiful. Her nose was marginally more aquiline than the average woman's. Long black hair and dark almond eyes kept a persons' gaze away from her somewhat thicker hips. Her appeal was based on some undefinable quality, which gave a man the general feeling this was a woman who appreciated the sensual side of life. A wife would feel safe with her husband working alongside Francine. A husband would know he was not.

"What a delight you are. Love that perfume," Jim mumbled as they snuggled.

"It's similar to Joy." Francine sighed as they caressed. "Jasmine and roses, as if you actually cared. Like it?"

"A whiff and I want to stroll through your well-groomed flower bed."

"You have the key to the garden gate, Jimmy."

"Gardens are beautiful things," he whispered, becoming intoxicated by the heady scent of the perfume and the faint, sweet smell of Francine's warm skin. He drew her closer and buried his face into her.

Gabriella looked on.

Curious. They seem to enjoy having sex with each other. There must be significant amounts of dopamine and oxytocin released into their brains. I'd like to try it myself to see if it does anything for my systems.

If Gabriella stood motionless in the lab's corner at day's end, a casual observer would get the impression she was deactivated for the night. Jim and Francine knew she never powered down. They continued on their pleasure cruise. Gabriella watched with interest and learned.

Chapter Five

Martha raised her arm and waved it above her head at the key lab personnel weekly staff meeting. "Okay, gang, it's Tuesday, and the socialization chart says we're scheduled to test Gabriella on higher-order tasks beyond walking in public and not being recognized as an android. It's time to go to a restaurant for lunch!"

A cheer went up from the core group. "Engineers are always ready for lunch," shouted Gary Barker, a materials stress engineer from within the group.

"I've picked an upscale burger place on East Fifty-Seventh Street. They're reserving some tables for us."

The team agreed that it was a good choice. Martha turned to Gabriella. "Yeah, like a group of hungry engineers would turn up their noses at any a free meal." Gabriella understood the humor and grinned.

On the walk to the restaurant, Martha talked shop with T'quan Taylor. "I'm curious. How does the digestive system you guys designed work?" Martha said. "Gabriella eats and drinks. What goes on inside?"

"Glad you asked. It's basic, but the team and I are proud of it. We designed an elegant pseudo-digestive system to simulate eating when she's in a social situation. Food is held in a flexible internal chamber and eliminated at her convenience in the usual human fashion."

"Graphic! That's almost too much sharing. But Gabriella always smells so fresh."

"She drinks three ounces of mouthwash every day or so to prevent odors. You couldn't very well pass for human if you couldn't eat or drink in public. And you don't want to smell like you have bad breath or a gas problem, now would you?"

"Certainly not! Wouldn't want an android with gas problems," Martha replied, her eyes crinkling from the humor.

"Thanks, T'quan. And speaking of eating, we're here, everyone." Then added in a hardly audible voice, "and just in time." *Note to self: don't ask engineers too many questions that may go down the gross-trail. They have no real filters.*

The small crowded restaurant prepared their reserved tables. Larry, from Base Programming, slid up next to Gabriella at the bar. "So, what do you think of this place?"

Gabriella instantly checked the restaurant's web page. "I like it. It has such an organic atmosphere using natural materials and plants."

"Perfect, Gabriella. You're doing great with casual conversation. Most excellent! Our table is ready. Let's grab some seats."

Jim chose the critical seating. "Gabriella, sit here next to me on my right side. Martha, could you sit across from us, please?" The team left the chair to Jim's left empty for Francine. They understood that Francine always sat next to Jim.

"Thank you for saving a seat for me, Jim," Francine said as she ran her hand across his shoulders, appearing to steady herself as she sat.

"Okay, everyone," Jim raised his voice so the team could hear him over the din of the other patrons. "We agreed part of the experiment was to see if we could avoid talking shop while we are here."

The team stared at him.

"Yeah, I know," Jim replied to their looks, "Please try it, though, for Gabriella's sake." Chuckles and nods rippled around the table.

Martha leaned across the table to Gabriella. "This is a huge challenge," she whispered with an exaggerated grin. "Telling engineers not to talk shop as they are having lunch in a Manhattan burger bar with you is next to impossible."

"Why would it be a challenge?" Gabriella asked, and then added, "Never mind. You can explain it to me later. I need to focus on casual, conversational cues from people and how to flow with the topics."

The engineers discussed sports and then had an enthusiastic exchange on which of their favorite video games were the best. Gabriella picked bits of information from the net and wove game tips and strategies into the conversation.

"I didn't know you knew so much about video games," Alex Ortiz said. "Impressive."

"One tries," Gabriella responded.

"Sounds like she is becoming an integral part of the team," said Aki Gua with admiration.

Martha was taking notes on Gabriella's conversations and her reaction to the surrounding people. She also documented the responses of people to Gabriella. Martha noticed the two young businessmen at the counter watching Gabriella as she walked into the restaurant. Their eyes followed her to her table.

"Martha," Gabriella asked, "why were those two men at the counter watching us walk in?"

A small smile spread across Martha's face. "Honey, they sure weren't interested in the New York Yankees baseball highlights we were discussing. We can discuss more back at the lab."

Gabriella observed, "There is a growing list of things to talk about when we get back to the lab." Martha nodded in agreement.

Martha's job was to notice everything happening near their android and to design role-playing exercises to help Gabriella mimic a human. *I can't help but wonder why Corporate is so intensely interested their android could pass. Sure, it would be a ground-breaking event, but I have a feeling there is more to the request than what's being revealed. What is their end-game? I'll have to wait and see.*

Her mind wandered from crazy government conspiracy plots to the very high-end adult toy market. Martha dismissed them. *I'm afraid I'm becoming 'one of those people' who see conspiracies in every bowl of Corn Flakes they pour for breakfast. If I keep this up I'll end up wearing aluminum foil on my head to block alien mind probes;* she told herself smiling, *and own six cats.*

"Gabriella, you're becoming very adept at mimicking some social styles and laughter you observe around us," Martha observed.

"I'm trying to. I'm pleased you think I'm doing so well." Martha entered a note into her pad about Gabriella, including more feeling words in her speech.

The waiter came and took their food orders. After a time of conversation, the lunches appeared. Gabriella flagged the waiter and ordered a coffee with a shot of espresso. The team encouraged Gabriella to sample some of their food. She said the burgers and bacon-cheddar soup tasted better than the rest of the fare.

"Let's all take a short walk through Central Park to work off those calories," Jim suggested at the end of the meal.

"I think it's a marvelous idea," Gabriella said, reaching out and lightly stroking Jim's bare arm as she had seen the brunette woman at the next table do to her lunch partner.

The touch startled him. He tried not to react. Her hand was soft and warm. The engineering side of his mind told him her skin was fibrin-agarose biomaterial, protein, and seaweed/sugar substances, all combined with a multiferroic alloy that could absorb heat from the environment, giving the surface a soft, warm feel. His emotions only noted the beautiful green-eyed, honey-blond woman sitting next to him touched his arm with her warm and gentle fingers.

He smiled and took a long sip of his coffee. Martha jotted down another note.

Chapter Six

It was one-thirty on a sunny late-spring New York afternoon. "Gabriella, let's go for coffee. You're working your fingers to the... ah... titanium rods," Martha said, laughing. "It's a nice day for a walk."

Gabriella smiled. "Be right there. Give me just a second to finish these calculations." A moment later, she wrote some figures in the Skin Covering Design and Development Project logbook.

"You're doing well with your social interactions. What do you think about it?"

"I think I'm doing well, but how would I know? You're the one to tell me how I'm doing. I'm too close to myself to make an accurate assessment." Martha's eyes widened for a second at Gabriella's insight on judging her own progress. *Very good. She's got it going on.*

"Gabriella, I feel like we're becoming real friends. The logical side of me thinks it can't happen, but the emotional side likes these walks to the coffee shop and our chats very much. How do you feel about that?"

"Oh, I feel the same way. I like you a lot, Martha. I thought you could tell. Why do you ask?"

"Simply wanted your thoughts."

"Becoming friends is interesting," Gabriella said. "Are you wondering if you like me as a person, like me as a pet, or a little of each? Do you think that's what's happening?"

Martha was quiet for a moment, surprised by Gabriella's train of thought and conclusions. *She's reasoning way beyond what we had calculated for this point in time.*

"Yes, I guess I feel both, but much heavier on the friend part. How does that make you feel?"

Gabriella smiled. "It doesn't bother me at all. You'll come to realize I'm a thinking, feeling woman much like you, even if my insides don't match yours." She chuckled and winked at Martha. Martha's brow rose in a micro-expression of surprise.

The New York street was bustling with cars lurching and breaking as they started and stopped in the congestion. Automobile horns punctuated the molasses ballet every few seconds, their drivers hoping that by adding to the overall din traffic would move more efficiently.

Neon signs everywhere blazed that each establishment had the answers to all of your worldly dreams and desires right inside their doors. The sign in Pat's Eatery window boasted Pat's had the best coffee in the entire world, as did the posters in the windows of the other two diners on the same block.

A small family of tourists, each clicking away on their cell phone camera, passed on the busy sidewalk. Martha said it was nice to see a group of people who were not rushing to get from point A to point B. "I wish I could be like them more often. Walking around at my own pace. Must be nice."

"They are blocking the sidewalk and the flow of pedestrian traffic," Gabriella said. Martha noted the irritation in her voice.

Food vendors under umbrella-topped carts dotted the way to the coffee shop. Smoke from a green and yellow Salvatore's Hots cart spread the aroma of cooked deliciousness throughout the area.

"I love the smell of the food, Martha, specifically the spicy smell of the sausage."

"Why do you think the sausage smells good?" *Can she quantify the difference between a smell and a pleasant smell?*

"I like the smell of the sausage because I can taste it too. It has a stronger, spicier flavor than hot dogs. Smells good."

"You can taste it from the smell?" Martha asked.

Gabriella gave another grin and said with an impish tone in her voice, "Yes, of course, I can. Can't you taste it from the smell too? I thought we all could."

Martha noted that Gabriella again classified herself as part of humanity. *This is quickly getting interesting. What on earth is going on in that gel brain of hers?*

"So, socialization is going well for you? You know, being out in public and all?" Martha probed again.

"I'm becoming more comfortable with it," replied Gabriella. "It was awkward in the lab, but it seems so much easier when we are out on the street, or at least in other surroundings." She put her arm around Martha's shoulders.

"Thanks for the hug, Gabriella, but can I ask you why you did that?"

"Certainly. You're my friend. I've seen Jim do it regularly to the women in the lab who are his friends. He's done it to me too when we're working on a problem at my lab table. I rather like it."

The wind blew a strand of hair across Gabriella's cheek. Martha brushed it slowly back over Gabriella's ear.

"Gabriella, honey, you can be so smart about some things and so naïve about others. Anyhow, keep your eye on Jim. He's a bit of a horny-toad. He's a great guy and a skilled lab director, but he sure likes the women, even though he's married. Just keep an eye on him."

"Well, I looked up the idiom 'keep an eye on' and found it means to watch or give your attention to someone. It makes some grammatical sense, but I can't see why anyone would apply the phrase to Jim. I can't find any explicit reference for horny-toad that makes any sense at all. A search pulled up an obscure restaurant, a clothing manufacturer, and a photo of a horned toad, but none of those seem to fit your inference. Explain those terms, please," Gabriella said. "I'm not processing them properly."

"Sweetie, first of all, you shouldn't use the word 'processing' when you're in public. It will only point you out as being different from everyone else. You can say it in the lab, or a university or someplace, but let's not do it on the street, okay?

"Secondly, most people understand the word 'horny-toad' even though it isn't in the dictionary. Let me back up a little and explain. You touch things and feel the same sensation as I do. This is true for normal touching and, let's say, closer contact. I think Jim is getting interested in that 'closer contact' part. Remember, he's a married man and a bit of a letch. Okay, don't look it up. I can tell you were going to. It means he is erotically suggestive and lustful. More than likely, he wants to get into your pants."

"Is that a bad thing?"

"Girl, do I have to explain everything to you?" Martha faked exasperation as she threw her hands up. "Yes, I suppose I do. Listen, in our society, it is generally seen as bad form for a married person to have an affair. Most men and women prefer a rule discouraging their spouse from having sex with someone who isn't them."

"So are you saying having sex is a bad thing? Several of the people in our lab are having sex together, and they aren't married. I've often watched Jim and Francine have sex on the couch. It would be fun to experiment with it to see what the fuss is all about."

"You watched Jim and Francine have sex? Did they know you were watching?"

"Yes, they did. It didn't seem to bother them. It was much more interesting than watching the same things on those internet videos. I don't think all the shouting and moaning on the internet is real, do you?"

"Whaa? They let you watch! Somebody needs to do something about them. That's just wrong!" Martha sighed as the two of them arrived at the coffee shop. *This girl is too, too much.*

"I'll have to have a priest or someone explain things to you more," Martha said. "Let's get our coffee and get back to the lab."

Chapter Seven

It was early June, eighteen months before Gabriella became animated. Major General Brian Cunningham summoned Lance to his Pentagon office.

Lance had spoken to Major General Cunningham at various military functions. It never failed to strike him that Cunningham looked so little like a stereotypical square-jawed Army General figure. His rounded face and mild wrinkles conveyed the image of a gentle, elderly uncle. His short white hair fenced in a broad expanse of skin on the top of his head. Every article of clothing was razor creased. But it was his eyes that revealed his true determination and strength. General Cunningham was not a person to trifle with.

I'm intrigued, Lance thought as he made his way down the halls to the General's office. *Why would General Cunningham call me in? He should go through my boss, General Moorhouse. The Army always follows the chain of command. Interesting.*

An attractive blonde major in her mid-forties greeted Lance as he entered the office. "You must be Colonel Coopers," Major Kim Allen said with a friendly smile and a firm handshake. "You're a couple of minutes early. Very good. Please have a seat. I'll let him know you are here."

He declined the seat. After a moment, Major Kim's phone gave three soft beeps. She ushered Lance into the Major General's office.

"Glad you could come, Colonel Coopers," Cunningham said. He remained seated. "Have a seat," he said, gesturing to the red leather-covered chair on the other side of his desk.

"Yes, Sir," Lance said as he took the seat.

"Colonel, I'd like to make you an offer you may find interesting."

"Yes, Sir. I'm listening," Lance replied, knowing there was little difference between an offer and an order in the Major General's office.

"I'll come right to the point, Colonel. I've been watching your career and evaluations for quite some time. I like what I see. I like what you've done with your intelligence group."

"Thank you, Sir," said Lance with a nod.

"You understand our country has enemies. Some are overseas. Some are within our borders. Their top leaders have protective layers of terrorists around them. It's dangerous to risk sending in our best undercover people to infiltrate their organizations. A captured and agent could divulge far too many secrets under torture; secrets which could impact national security." The general then continued in a hushed tone and leaned forward on his desk as if to take the Colonel into his confidence. "Follow me so far, Colonel?"

Lance thought for a half-second. To be presumptuous in what the General was thinking could be reckless. *Answering a question with a question is a safer course of action.* "Yes, Sir. I hear what you are saying; however, what does it have to do with what I do for the Army?"

"Good, Colonel. Right to the point. I'll be direct too. We are financing a top domestic artificial intelligence engineering firm to design and develop an android that will be indistinguishable from a human being."

Lance stared intently at General Cunningham.

"In effect, they are building us a machine to infiltrate the most dangerous circles without the risk of sacrificing our top operatives. If it's exposed, they could not force it to talk. The enemy might disassemble it, but there is no way to make it disclose any classified information."

"Couldn't they remove and read its drives?"

"No, Colonel. If they captured it, we could obliterate all its memory from the States with the push of a button."

Lance nodded his understanding.

"I would like to assign you, and a team hand-picked by yourself, to perform remote surveillance on the construction of this android to ensure it meets military specifications. The engineering team has been working on it for several years and is getting close to putting a prototype model together."

"Yes, Sir. I understand," said Lance, steepling his index fingers to his lips, considering the implications.

"The only caveat, Colonel, is the development team can't know the Army is involved. They can never suspect they are developing a national defense weapon straight out of science fiction. Only the Corporate Research Director knows about us. You will monitor their every action and send encrypted reports only to me every week. You will also oversee their functional experiments and ensure they include every aspect of human interaction." The General put heavy emphasis on the word 'every.'

"Do you understand me, Colonel?"

"I believe I do, Sir," replied Lance, more sure of the correct answer this time. "You are also referring to both physical and sexual contact."

"That is correct. It must be capable of sleeping its way into enemy leadership circles. When you take the assignment, you will move to Manhattan. If all goes well in your execution of this project, I can see you make Brigadier General."

Lance sucked in his breath. The general continued to explain additional details of the assignment. Lance lost most of what the Major General said after he heard "... make Brigadier General."

Who do I have to kill to make that happen?

"Are you in, Colonel?" asked Cunningham.

"Yes, Sir, I'm in!" Lance said with snap and determination in his voice. "I am most certainly in, and will execute the mission completely, Sir."

The Major General smiled. Although Lance had his character flaws, everyone knew Colonel Coopers was always faithful to his word. If he said he would do it, it would happen.

"Very good. I was hoping you would take it. I'll have a more detailed meeting with you to discuss the details. Thank you for coming in."

Lance left the office feeling taller. He took inventory of his best people to bring to New York with him. "Yes, I will definitely make it go well." he said aloud as he walked back to his car, "Nothing will stand in my way!"

Chapter Eight

She brushed her right breast across his arm. Her perfume filled the surrounding air. "Jim, how's Gabriella doing?" Francine asked, the undertone in her voice suggesting the question was only a pretext to her real intent. "Will she be able to pass on the street?"

Jim glanced down at his arm and hesitated. "She seems to be coming along very well, but more task observations need to happen in public arenas to validate any conclusions."

"What's going on, Jim? You're talking pretty formally. I know things at home haven't been great for you, but I get a sense there's more than just home on your mind. Am I right?"

He exhaled while looking in Gabriella's direction. "Well, it's strange, but as I work with Gabriella, I'm thinking of her more and more like one of the team members."

Francine took a step backward. She watched Jim with a questioning expression on her face as he gazed at Gabriella's five-foot-eight curvaceous figure undulating under her white lab coat as she walked across the lab.

"What?" Francine hissed at him in a whisper. "You're attracted to our machine? I can't believe what I'm seeing! Am I not enough for you anymore? Are you thinking with your crotch again? Do you want to boff our android? Pig!"

Francine pivoted on her heels and stomped toward her office.

People in the lab, including Martha, watched Francine march away from Jim. They decided not to ask what was happening. When Francine was in one of her moods, the men called her Dragon Lady. The women called her Bitch.

Damn, I shouldn't have been that transparent with her. Why did I think she might understand? Why don't women just get it?

He tried reasoning with himself again by logically reviewing the facts. *Gabriella is an android. My team and I built her. She isn't a living, breathing human being. Nothing more than wires and simulated skin.*

Jim's intellect agreed with what his motivational self-talk was proclaiming, but his libido laughed at him and rebutted, *Get real, horny-man! You just want to screw Gabriella. At least be honest about it!*

He kept staring at the way she moved under her lab coat, and his heart pounded.

Chapter Nine

Gabriella was allowed to walk Manhattan streets alone by early June. The lab monitored her remotely, but she no longer needed a co-worker to accompany her.

She enjoyed exploring, observing, and learning from the people she encountered, following the lab rule of not walking down empty streets alone.

"Gabriella," Martha warned her, "You might outmatch most attackers, even if they have a weapon, but it would be best not to draw any attention to your speed and precision. It would be a dead giveaway if a mugger cut or shot you and didn't even bleed. Nope, it wouldn't do at all to attract such attention. Be careful, sweetie, okay?"

One exploratory trip led her down Thirty-Seventh Avenue.

She walked past the Christian Fellowship Church. *Martha said I should talk to a priest to have my faith and morals questions answered. Why not now?*

Gabriella tugged at the front door handles on the church doors. The doors were locked. She read the plaque on the right side of the door listed daily and Sunday service hours. *Who on earth would get here at 7:00 AM on a weekday?*

There were also Wednesday night services listed at 7:00 PM, and a Sunday service at 10:00 AM. *What a crazy schedule. How can they get any customers with hours like that? They must know nothing at all about marketing.*

Gabriella tried all the doors with no success. *Perhaps in the back.*

She walked gingerly around the church to the attached building in the rear. This sign said it was the rectory. She stepped up and rang the doorbell.

It surprised Gabriella when, after a few moments, the door opened, and a blue-eyed little blonde girl stood there. "Hi, I'm Alexi. I'm six, and I'm in first grade. What's your name?" the little girl asked.

"Hello, I'm Gabriella, and I'm not telling you how old I am," Gabriella said, smiling brightly. Alexi smiled back. *I've wanted to meet a child. What a charming little person.*

"Alexi, who's at the door?" came a masculine voice from the next room. The speaker's voice became louder as he approached. "I told you never to open the door without me!" the voice chided.

"Oh, hi. I'm Pastor Paul Maxwell," the young man sporting a trimmed beard and a friendly smile said. He patted Alexi's head, "I see you've already met my daughter, Alexi. Can I help you?" Paul extended his hand in a welcoming handshake. Gabriella returned a firm but gentle shake. Paul's smile broadened.

"I don't know," said Gabriella, "I'm not sure where to start. I guess I have some questions about God and decided to check with an expert on the subject. Do you have any time to talk, or should I make an appointment?"

"No, no, it's fine. I've about an hour free. Would you like to come in?"

"Yes, thank you." Paul stepped aside to usher Gabriella in. She took in her surroundings.

Several doilies sat askew on the two end tables on either side of a worn brown leather couch sagging between the two windows on the outer wall. A dark brown satin throw pillow nestled up to the armrest on the right. The opposite armrest sported a rougher textured dark brown fabric pillow, which stopped just short of being burlap. Crudely woven hunting dogs ran across its face.

The rectory was dark and old but smelled clean. *It looks as if there has been a feminine influence in the past. But a woman in the house would not allow both pillows to occupy the same couch, perhaps not even the same room.*

Paul sat on a leather-covered wooden armchair next to the sofa. He motioned for Gabriella to sit on the end of the sofa closest to his chair. "Have a seat, Gabriella."

Hmm, none of the guys in the lab would have made a similar choice. They would all sit next to me if they could.

Gabriella glanced at the tanned fourth finger of his left hand. A small ridge of callouses betrayed an absent ring.

Paul offered Gabriella a cold beverage. "We have cola, root beer, and ginger ale."

"No, thank you," she replied.

"Hot tea or coffee, then?"

"No, thank you," she repeated. "I've already had my morning espresso."

"Well then, what can I do for you? You said you had some questions about God. That's a broad subject. Is there anything, in particular, you would like to talk about to narrow it down a little? We can go in any direction you like."

Paul almost asked if she attended church services there, but realized he would have noticed her in the congregation long before this. The gathering was aging and often looked, as he sometimes described it, "a storm at sea, all white caps."

"Well, I don't have a religious background of any kind," she stated flatly. "Some people talk about God, but I don't understand why. I see no evidence he exists. It seems like it's a nice thing to believe in to give people hope, I guess, but there doesn't appear to be anything to it."

Paul leaned forward.

Gabriella continued, "Besides, I'm not friends with anyone who has a strong faith. If someone has any faith at all, it's based on wishes, legends, and traditions. They aren't able to explain anything except by saying, "You have to have faith." Even then, they don't seem to believe it. It's illogical to me. I can't even see any natural evidence for God. You're a pastor, so I assume you are an expert. What can you tell me about it?"

Paul gave a long, low whistle. "Wow!" he quietly exclaimed and then caught himself. "Ahh, you asked a huge question. This will take more than a quick hour to sort out. I like the question, though."

Paul looked down and stared at his knees for a few seconds. He looked up and smiled.

"Gabriella, do you believe in the Universe?"

"That's a silly question," she responded, giving Paul a quizzical smile. "Of course, I do. Here it is," she said as she spread her arms wide open. "It's measurable, and we are a part of it."

"Would you say it sprang up without a designer?"

"Yes, science has almost proven mathematically it was the Singularity, the Big Bang, which created the universe."

Paul's eyes smiled at Gabriella. He could direct the conversation toward science with this woman.

"So is it ordered, or is it chaotic?"

"Most of it is well ordered. What does this have to do with God?"

"We'll get to God in a moment. What would you say the odds are of a Big Bang explosion leading to such an ordered universe, one with billions of galaxies and trillions of stars?"

Gabriella replied, "I'm not sure, but it's a staggering improbability even when you consider interstellar gravitational waves working to move particles around to form galaxies."

Paul stared into her green eyes. He noticed his mouth was getting dry and had a faint metallic taste similar to sucking on a penny. He continued, "Then you accept the order of the universe on faith since the chances of such a vast creation becoming ordered out of chaos are infinitesimally small."

"Yes, I guess I do."

"Then I would say you depend much more on faith than I do. It takes less faith to believe God has ordered things than to conclude it all happened by chance."

Gabriella raised an eyebrow as she tested Paul's comments. She ran some probability calculations. "Your statistics seem correct, but the universe and life are much more than statistics," she defended.

"Ok, Gabriella, consider life itself," Paul went on, "the chance that a simple protein could be created by chance is less than 10^{-390}. Science considers an idea with less than one chance in ten to the fiftieth power is an absurd concept. So how can we have faith in something absurd? Right?"

Who is this man? "Well," Gabriella said slowly, "your quantification of what is absurd is correct, but I'm not at all comfortable with your conclusion that my science is not pure science."

Both her beauty and intelligence impressed Paul. He continued, "So, therefore, is random generation a science, or is it a different form of religion based on having a science-faith perspective? Can you see my point?"

"Wait a minute," Gabriella interrupted. "You seem to know a lot of science for a pastor. How is that? I thought most ministers had non-scientific backgrounds."

"Well, I started as an electronics engineer. It's how I met my wife. We were both doctoral candidates at Yale."

"You went to Yale? So why did you become a pastor? The two seem to be completely unrelated."

"They are unrelated, mostly. I found I wanted to help people more than I wanted to make a boatload of money in a lab or corporate job. It's all about the quality of life, not money.

But where were we? Oh yeah, we were talking about a single protein molecule. Then how impossible it would be to have a strand of DNA create itself. And how about life? Where did it come from? How did it get put together? Nobody knows, nobody but God that is."

Gabriella shifted on the couch. *I'm alive. I am a living, thinking, feeling machine.* "Let me research your questions and get back to you," she mumbled.

Then she smiled. *I like how Paul's mind works, and I want to see him again. The men in the lab are bright, but calmer and more conservative when they speak. Paul has a real passion when he talks. He believes what he is saying. Besides, he's handsome.*

"Paul, you seem to have the numbers and arguments all in your head. There is no hesitation in your speech. How is that?"

"It's easy, Gabriella." Paul let her name roll comfortably off his tongue. "I've had this conversation many times over the last several years." His deep brown eyes were crinkled in amusement.

"Okay, so there MIGHT be a God. But there are so many religions," Gabriella said. "Do you mean to tell me they are all valid because they believe in some godhead? Besides, more people do not believe in God than do. This alone shows those who worship a divine ruler are in the minority."

Paul nodded in agreement as Gabriella continued.

"In my engineering circles, if most qualified engineers agree a concept is valid through mathematics and sound engineering practice, we consider them to be correct. Shouldn't the same rule apply to religion as well?"

"Good question, Gabriella," Paul replied, enjoying saying her name. "The clear answer is No. Not at all. In fact, it's a logical fallacy to believe because most people feel a certain way, it must be the correct way. Look at politics to verify this. Sometimes the political majority is crazier than a sack of frogs."

"Excuse me, Paul. What does a sack of frogs have to do with crazy? I don't understand."

"It has nothing to do with being crazy, Gabriella. It's an old expression meaning someone or something is crazy or illogical. I don't know what its basis is. I'm sorry if I was confusing." Paul grinned apologetically.

He continued, "In our not so distant history, most scientists and educated people claimed the earth was flat. They warned Columbus not to seek a shorter trade route to China by heading straight out to sea. They felt he would fall off the edge of the earth. Luckily for us, he didn't listen and subsequently discovered Columbus, Ohio."

Gabriella cocked her head to her left and looked at him quizzically.

Paul laughed and asked her to forgive him for his sometimes bizarre sense of humor.

"That was humor?" she asked.

"Apparently not," Paul replied sheepishly.

"I have to run." Paul said as he stood up after their hour had passed, "There is always so much to do as a pastor. I'd very much like to carry on with our conversation. Do you think it would be possible, Gabriella?"

"Yes, it would," she replied, "I would like it very much, and I have so many more questions to ask."

The prospect of seeing her again excited Paul. He noted that his pulse rate increased.

"Here's my card," Paul said as he handed her a business card. "Feel free to call, and my administrative assistant will set up an appointment."

"Thank you, Pastor Paul," Gabriella replied as she slipped the card into her small clutch, "I will."

Paul smiled. "Please, call me Paul. I was never huge on titles. I look forward to hearing from you."

Paul showed Gabriella to the door. They shook hands as they parted. "Until next time," they both said. Paul watched from the doorway until Gabriella rounded the corner of the building and was out of sight.

Alexi looked out the door and wrapped her arms around her father's leg. "Who was that, Dad?"

Paul smiled and whispered, "A fascinating woman, Alexi. A very charming and fascinating woman." The adrenaline taste still sat in his mouth.

Chapter Ten

Most of the scientists in the lab had left for the day by 6:30 in the evening. It was a welcome relief for the staff to close shop and head home at a reasonable hour now that Gabriella was animated. Francine and Jim were the last humans remaining in the lab.

"Working late?" Francine asked Jim as she brushed close to him.

"Just a couple more hours," Jim replied. "I have a few things to clean up for the day, and then I'll be off."

"Would you like me to stay and help?" She pressed her hip against his.

"Not tonight. I have to get a few things done. See you in the morning, though. Have a great night."

Francine swept her hand along the contour of her hips as she spoke. "Damn! I was looking forward to us being alone in the lab again tonight."

"Sorry, Francine. I have to focus for a while. Have a great night, though."

Disappointment dampened her voice. "You have a great night, too, Jim. I'll see you in the morning."

On her way out, Francine glanced at Gabriella, working at her lab table. Gabriella's unbuttoned lab coat gave silent permission to her form-fitting blue knit dress to peek out enough to reveal a crescent of her curves.

Francine looked back at Jim and saw him staring at Gabriella. *Ooooh-nooo*, Francine thought, a menacing frown spreading across her forehead. *I don't mind sharing Jim with his wife, but I won't share him with an animated blow-up doll! I could kill him sometimes. He had better just be working late!*

She took a few steps toward Jim to confront him, but then realized it would make her look foolish to have words with Jim with no real evidence. Francine whirled and was gone for the night.

Jim walked over to the table where Gabriella was working on her material stress experiments.

"Gabriella, could you help me with a social experiment?" Jim asked.

"Sure, Jim, but I didn't think Martha had any socialization activities planned for tonight. What do you have in mind?"

"This isn't one of her scheduled activities. It's sort of an experiment."

"Okay."

Jim praised her work in the lab and then said, "Well, you're progressing very well in passing for another scientist on the floor, but I'd like to develop other aspects of human relationships with you."

"Sounds interesting," she said, eyes widening.

His voice dropped, "It will be, but this is more of a secret experiment. No one can know about it except the two of us."

"I'm all ears," Gabriella said, smiling at her proper use of the idiom.

"Ah, you're so much more than that. So much more than ears."

Jim pulled Gabriella closer, lifted her arm, and gently kissed the inside of her wrist and forearm. His lips pushed the sleeve of her lab coat up to expose more skin.

"Oh, it feels so nice for such a simple thing," she said in a whispered voice. Jim smiled. He slowly kissed and nibbled her neck. "I like this experiment so far. What else?" she breathed with expectation.

Jim's right hand touched her cheek, drawing her in closer. His kisses landed tenderly on her lips as he slipped her lab coat off her shoulders. It fell into a heap at her feet.

"Oh, I see," Gabriella whispered as she allowed Jim to pull her into full contact. She enjoyed the warmth of his body and pressed firmly into him. She started to quote a line from an old black-and-white movie she watched during her socialization training. "Is that a gun in your pocket, or are you happy to see meeeeeeee," but finished it with a surprised squeal as he searched her.

Jim continued to kiss her neck and shoulders, moving her dress slowly out of the way. The back of the dress unzipped.

"My sensors never got this kind of input," she said, excited but somewhat bewildered by the new sensations. Her dress slipped down her body and piled at her feet.

Gabriella felt a tingle run through her body while the neural networks in her brain reconfigured to make new connections as Jim continued to kiss and touch her. She was acutely aware of his increased body heat. There was the unmistakable chemical presence of his pheromones in the air.

"Let's go to the couch, Gabriella," Jim whispered as he nibbled an earlobe.

Jim asked Gabriella if it was okay with her so far as he reclined her on the couch.

It surprised Gabriella when "It's all wonderful" came out as a silent nod.

Images swirled in her mind. *Getting tunnel vision. Time and space narrowing. Only the moment exists. Love his lips and hands on me.*

Her chest rose and fell at an increasing rate. She didn't need to breathe, but her respiratory simulator was reacting as if she were gasping for air.

The hours went by as the clock continued its march to midnight. The couple enjoyed each other as their imaginations directed. They continued until Jim was too tired to go further; both pleased they could make the other feel so satisfied.

"Good experiment," Gabriella said, grinning after they finished. "I learned a lot about my circuitry and tactile inputs. And near circuit overloads, too. Wow! What was that!"

"I'll have the cleaners do an extra good job on the couch," Jim quipped. Gabriella was beaming.

"Is this what the other people in the lab experience when they have sex with each other?" she wondered out loud. "Is this why you and Francine have sex so often?"

Jim winced at the question. He and Gabriella made love, not merely engaged in sex. It was unexpected. It was different. It was beautiful and tender. His feelings for her surprised and confused him.

"I have to get back home, Gabriella," Jim said, reluctance clear in his voice. "I would much rather stay the night together, but I'll see you in the morning." Jim gave her a gentle kiss on the cheek.

"Shall I document this social experiment for team review and analysis, Jim?" Gabriella coyly asked.

Jim moved back to her and gave her a lingering kiss full on the lips. "Don't you dare!" he laughed, and then strode off towards the elevator, glancing back at her before rounding the corner.

"I think I'll top-off my batteries," she mused as she picked up her induction charging cord. She smiled as she slipped the second toe of her left foot into the charging ring.

Simultaneously, Lance filed a detailed report to Major General Cunningham on Gabriella's evening activities.

Jim rode the subway to his home stop. He realized he had now lost the logical argument in his mind about Gabriella being a woman or not. His head and some other critical parts of his body were thoroughly convinced Gabriella was a real, sentient woman.

As the subway train pulled into his station, Jim recalled a conversation with Francine. They discussed the possibility their team may have created the next generation in human evolution. Jim wondered if they were the instruments nature was using in its evolutionary march to create mankind's successor.

"My gosh, we would be like gods," Jim said to the empty streets.

***

Alice was asleep when Jim slipped through the front door. He tiptoed upstairs, showered, and lay down next to her in bed. Still excited by Gabriella, he lightly touched her. Alice shrugged and mumbled, "Not tonight. It's way too late." The rejection hurt, although it was entirely expected.

They were once both so in love there was no distance between them, emotionally, or physically. During those first years of marriage, the old saying "there was such a oneness between them that when one cried the other would taste salt" was real to them.

There was a time Jim couldn't wait to hold Alice tightly at the end of a workday. Nothing else in the universe existed. Jim believed love like that would go on forever and a day. Their love and passion would never cool off.

Over the years, the changes started happening. Only a bit at first. A tiny crack in their love appeared between them. They both had hectic work schedules, but it did not fully account for the drift. The little habits and quirks, which once endeared them to each other, began to grind on them.

Alice started to drift from her desire for physical affection. It was a slow drift, nothing that happened overnight.

Alice lay there feigning sleep, all the while longing for the days when she was the center of Jim's life. A small tear formed in the corner of her eye.

Jim rolled over, frowning, but began to smile as thoughts of being in Gabriella's warm arms replayed in his mind. He slipped down the spiral slide of sleepy darkness.

***

Jim arrived at the lab a little earlier than usual the following day.

"Late night?" asked Francine testily as Jim was finishing his second cup of coffee before ten. He headed to the coffee pot for more.

Jim and Francine understood their affair wouldn't last forever. They claimed it was only friendship with extra benefits. "No significant emotional strings attached," they told each other.

"So did you play any 'android games' last night?" Francine asked, ice freezing her words as they spilled from her lips. One of those unseen 'no significant emotional strings attached' had surfaced.

Jim blushed and looked to the side. "No, of course not! Why would you even ask that, Francine?"

"You don't know?" Francine said, cracking a faint smile at his discomfort.

"Know what?" Jim squirmed.

Francine stared at him. "After having sex in the lab, you show a 'tell' the next day for a while. Your ears turn red. I've seen the same thing when young children play video games. Everyone here noticed it but will assume you and I fooled around together last night because we were the only two humans remaining after they all left." Francine emphasized the word 'humans.'

Her anger rose. "You're a real bastard, do you know that? I hope she was good because it's all you will ever get in this lab again! We're through! Asshole!"

Jim ignored her tirade. "I have a tell?" he said in one of those whispered shouts people use when they suddenly realize they came to work in their pajama bottoms. "And everyone knows it!!" He turned red and drained the dregs of his cold coffee. He poured another, looked across the lab, and noticed two of the male engineers looking in his direction.

They wore little grins.

"Oh, crap!" Jim said, burning his mouth as he tried to chug the freshly poured coffee.

Their smiles grew broader.

Martha Robinson noted the exchanges. *It looks like the jerk had sex with Gabriella. I thought I was only making light of it when I warned Gabriella to watch out for Jim. Apparently, I wasn't. He actually screwed her! What the hell is happening in that man's head? Rhetorical question, I guess. Head, zipper, same thing.*

I need to go to Human Resources to report this, but they will defend Jim and say Gabriella isn't human, so they can't do anything about it. I don't want to poke Jim with a stick if I can't win the battle. This may get ugly before it's over.

Chapter Eleven

Alice was once-again doing the mind-numbing chore of laundry.

"That bastard's cheating on me!" she barked, smelling woman's cologne on his shirt. "And after we had it out the last time! Marriage is a forever thing. I don't want a divorce, but a piece of his hide would make me feel better!"

Alice hated wasting her Ph.D. in Forensic Accounting on the banal job of washing clothes every week. She resented Jim for never offering to help.

"I don't know the names of the women he's been with, but they all leave a trace of perfume on his shirts," she spewed as her anger rose. "I know he's been with some cheap sluts and with some higher class whores by the quality of their perfume. Like now!" she shouted, catching a fresh whiff on yet another shirt.

Alice viciously threw it into the trash. She sneered, practicing the lie she would tell Jim when he noticed it missing. "It got caught in the washer and tore, James."

"WAIT! NO! What am I doing? Still washing his clothes after he's been sleeping with other bitches?

Hell NO," she furiously screamed, tears filling her eyes. "No more!"

Alice grabbed an armful of Jim's laundry and ran up the basement stairs, falling socks marking the trail. She burst through the back door and into their tiny Brooklyn back yard, hurling his clothes onto the small red-brick patio. A large ceramic flower pot sat empty on the corner of the patio, despite Jim's promises to fill it with dirt and plant the six-pack of dying begonias still sitting next to it.

"Another failed promise." Rivulets of tears traced pathways into her makeup as they flowed down her cheeks.

A river of outrage burst out of its confines and poured from her mouth. "Damn you to Hell, Jim Arnold! How many times can I overlook the same perfumes showing up every few weeks? How many women have you been with since we married?"

She threw his clothes into the empty pot. "I'm very, very tired of hurting!"

The charcoal lighter fluid sat next to the grill. "Of having a cheating bastard of a husband," Alice said, squirting the liquid into the pot.

"Of having him screw every whore in town." A match ignited.

"Of total loneliness." She threw the flame onto the accelerant-soaked clothes.

"And of all of those lies," she shouted as searing fire erupted out of the pot and towered above her bent head. "I hate you! I hate you!" Alice screamed as the fierceness of her pain rose beyond the flames.

She wailed and collapsed onto the red bricks, crying inconsolably.

Chapter Twelve

Jim's cell phone was ringing. "Oh no," Jim groaned. "It's Frank, with most likely another one of his schedule changes or damn trips. I hate it when his name comes up on my phone. Dammit!"

"Good evening, Frank. What's up?" Jim said with unveiled reluctance in his voice to hear the answer.

"Oh, it's not much of a thing, Jim. It's straightforward, really."

Sure, it's always straightforward for the person who doesn't have to do anything!

"Jim, I know I've changed your schedule a few times and asked you to do things out of the ordinary, but this is easy," Frank promised.

Jim thought back to some old black-and-white TV Viking movies he watched at home. *In almost every Viking movie, it was mandatory to have one ship ram the opponent's ship.*

Frank spoke into the silence. "Jim, this is a no-brainer. Easy."

Here it comes. The rowers are pulling in time to the attack cadence of the drummer, and my ship is dead-center of that nasty spar attached to the front of Frank's boat. I can almost hear him thinking, 'Prepare to ram!' Yup, prepare to ram."

"Listen," Frank continued, "Gabriella has passed every test we've given her. It's about time to test her a little more in the community. Would you say she has a good amount of dexterity and balance?"

"Frank, you know the answer already," Jim replied, watching the spar come ever closer.

"Well, we would like you to enroll her in a woman's self-defense class at the little Jiu-Jitsu place near Lexington and Fifty-Sixth Street. We think it would be an interesting experiment and would give Gabriella a chance to test some of her motor skills in a different setting. Can you get her enrolled so she can start next Monday? They have evening classes for women, so it wouldn't interfere with her work in the lab."

"Frank, that's not a good idea at all," Jim replied, stress showing in his voice. "Why on earth would you ever want to do that? The only thing achieved is people will recognize she is an android. Martha has conducted tests in the lab, and Gabriella passed them all with no problems. She's as fast as any human being. In a close physical contact situation, someone might notice her bone structure is different and start asking questions." Jim's voice became louder as he spoke. "She doesn't sweat, either. Wouldn't it be odd to others in the class if one of them wasn't sweating while everyone else is dripping wet? How would you explain it?"

"Whoa, Jim, hold on a second. There is no reason to get excited. The experiments Martha did in the lab were exactly that, experiments in the lab. There is a world of difference between lab exercises where things are controlled and timed versus real-life experiments where things are more spontaneous and less controlled. We need to see how Gabriella handles herself in all situations. As far as sweating goes, we can have her wear a headband to absorb 'sweat.' She can mist herself using a spray bottle and toweling off. It'll make it look like she's trying to cool down. She has beauty and poise. The rest of the class will assume she's another model-type pampering herself, trying to avoid working up a real sweat."

Jim countered, "What about forceful physical contact? It might give her away. We designed her to feel like a human within the bounds of normal contact. Getting struck in a self-defense class was out of the design parameters."

Frank's smile at the other end of the phone was almost palpable.

"Well..." Frank paused a moment for dramatic effect, "it seems as if you have been in pretty tight physical contact with Gabriella already. What was your impression of how she felt?"

Jim's blood pressure spiked. The veins bulged on his neck, but he could only utter a few stammering guttural sounds.

Frank's smile grew broader. He responded to Jim in a condescending voice. "Very good then. Thanks for getting her enrolled in the 7:00 P.M Monday night class. I'll be talking to you soon. Oh yeah, sign Martha up for the class, too, but tell her about it first. She can be feisty. Goodbye."

Jim glared at the now silent phone in his hand and began furiously pacing behind his desk. He wanted to shout a rebuttal but had no grounds to do so. Frustrated, he resigned himself to sign both of the women up for the requested course.

"That's it! I'm going home!" Jim shouted as he stamped out of the office and marched to the subway entrance.

But how did Frank know about my night with Gabriella? Most people in the lab know about it now, but it's unlikely anyone would have told Frank. Gabriella's cognitive pathways are backed up to the Cray, but Frank would have no skill to get into the system. Yet he seemed to know the details of our affair. I don't get it. Are there shadow players I don't know about? Something's going on.

Jim arrived at his station and boarded the train for a quiet, thoughtful ride home.

Chapter Thirteen

Gabriela and Martha arrived at the dojo promptly at 7:00 PM. "What, no elevator in the building?" Martha complained. "It's a third-floor walkup!"

"Come on, Martha, we're enrolled in an exercise and self- defense class. Walking up the three flights is part of the warm-up, right?"

Martha looked at Gabriella, shook her head, and trudged up the stairs. "A proper woman of color don't go backward and have to walk up no damn three flights of stairs," Martha muttered.

The dojo was brilliantly lit and spacious. Overstuffed leather chairs, a matching couch, and small tables with seating for two graced the lobby. Asian pastoral watercolor scenes of smoky colored mountains and winding rivers hung on the walls. This was a school for people of reasonable means.

"Well, at least it's not the disaster I thought it would be, Gabriella. I imagined it was a little dump that would smell like old gym bags, socks, man sweat, and who knows what else. This is nice."

"I can faintly smell whatever they put on the rubber mats to keep them elastic. It smells a little like fish oil, but I like the overall smell of wintergreen in the air," observed Gabriella.

There were a dozen other women of diverse backgrounds and nationalities standing around and talking while waiting for the class to begin, but no men.

Martha looked at the other students. "Excellent. It's an all-woman class. It makes me feel better."

"Why do you feel better about an all-woman class, Martha? Wouldn't it be nice to have some men too? This is a self-defense class, and it's mostly men who are the attackers. Shouldn't we practice against men?"

"Come on, Gabriela, most women don't want men in a physical fitness class fantasizing about how they would look naked because they are wearing tight-fitting workout clothes and covered with sweat. That's just black licorice."

"What, Martha?"

"Distasteful, Gabriella. It means distasteful. We need to work on your ability to understand words in context a bit more."

"Well, I wouldn't mind. I'd like to see how men would react to me as I worked out," Gabriella teased. Martha shook her head and made a mental note to include this conversation in her ever-growing database. "What am I ever going to do with you, girl? What am I ever going to do?" Martha whispered.

The class instructor walked into the gym. Ralph Thornton was a well-poised handsome young African-American from Atlanta. His black tight-fitting tank-top and matching spandex shorts found their way around every well-defined muscle. He smiled at the class, exposing perfect teeth. Two dimples appeared as if by magic. Martha pursed her lips together and blew a silent whistle.

Ralph led the class through the prescribed welcoming script and explained the many safety rules to ensure none of the students were hurt during the course.

"But, if people are sore after the class, the dojo carries Tiger Balm Ointment. It works wonders on sore muscles, and also has a fresh, wintergreen smell to it." Chuckles rippled through the class at the unabashed but friendly tone of the short commercial.

Ralph continued, "Our whole focus will center on how to successfully get away from an attacker. We will concern ourselves with how to disengage from an attacker and how to hurt or injure them so you can safely run away from the danger."

A hand went up. "What's the difference between hurting and injuring an attacker? It sounds like the same thing to me."

"Good question. If you punch an attacker in the nose, you have hurt him. When you break or hyperextend an elbow, you have injured him. Make sense? We will learn how to do both in this class. We will not be teaching you how to stand and fight, though." Ralph added, "I tell all my students our primary tactic is to use our feet for defense. Run like hell." The class laughed.

"Now, if you still have energy at the end of our class, you are more than welcome to extend your training package to include an additional half-hour of more intensive training starting with class number two."

Gabriella leaned over to Martha and whispered, "That sounds like it would be fun. Let's do it."

"It does not sound like it would be a lot of fun for me. Gabriella, you can stay for the extra class if you would like. I'll hang around to observe, and by that, I mean I will observe the instructor. Hellooo Tuskegee!"

Martha's look told Gabriella she should stifle the question she was about to ask.

"Context test, Martha?"

"Yup."

The first workout was surprisingly vigorous. Gabriella misted herself using the spray bottle and toweling off as instructed. A heavier woman two rows behind her turned to her workout friend and commented on how model types were always trying to look good, even when exercising. They agreed Gabriella was vain.

Rose Rodriguez stood in the last row of students. Dark shoulder-length hair and tanned skin showcased her large, brown eyes. Roses' features were delicate. Most people would say she was attractive but not beautiful. She scanned the class. Ralph noticed she moved with exceptional smoothness and precision.

Ralph approached her during a short break.

"Hi Rose," he said with a friendly grin. "Got a sec?"

"Sure. What's up?"

"You've done this before, haven't you?"

"Is it that obvious? Yes, I have. You've found me out. Will it upset the balance and flow of the class? Are you going to expel me?" Rose laughed. Her brown eyes sparkled with confidence. Ralph chuckled at her answer.

"No, we'll keep you. Your being here won't disturb a thing. I'm wondering why an experienced person would want to attend this class. I would expect to see you in a more advanced training setting."

Rose held his gaze and replied, "I shouldn't tell you this, but it will be obvious anyhow. I'm on an assignment to monitor one of your students for my employer. Since I've given you a bit of intelligence, can I ask you to return the favor?"

"Sure. What's on your mind?"

"This class is taught by Mr. Chan, according to the online staff directory. You are obviously not him. Who are you, and why are you teaching this one?"

She caught Ralph off guard. He couldn't quell the look of surprise which flashed across his face. Rose instantly knew she had blown his cover.

"I'm on an assignment to teach this course while monitoring a student for my employer," Ralph answered. Before they could stifle the glances, they both shifted their eyes rapidly to Gabriela and back again. They looked at each other for a moment and laughed, knowing there was no need for them to ask who they worked for.

"Going to file a report after every class, Rose?" Ralph asked. "Or should I call you Sergeant Rose?"

"Yup to both, Sergeant Ralph," Rose replied. "Who is this woman, anyhow?"

"Not sure. She's good looking, but not a model. I think she's an engineer. Don't think she's had any self-defense training before this class, though. We'll have to see how she does. I have no intel on why she's here. Something's up to get two of us assigned to one person."

Ralph glanced at the wall clock and called the class to order.

Martha found herself looking intently at Ralph. She moistened her lips.

Chapter Fourteen

I hate going to headquarters, Jim thought after Frank Wright messaged him to meet in his corporate office. *It almost always means despite all the accolades for doing such 'an outstanding job,' I'm going to be saddled with more work. Or worse, I'll be stuck visiting some high-level client who wants to be stroked and meet the Lab Director before expanding their project. I hate politics!*

It was the "or worse." Jim balked at going on another client visitation trip.

"Jim, if you don't want to go on this trip or with Harry Cleveland, say so," Frank said through a friendly smile.

"I don't want to go, Frank."

"You were supposed to get all professional and say something like 'I would love to, Frank' or something similar."

"I don't want to go, Frank."

Frank gave a long, soft sigh as he scratched his head in frustration. "Well, the customer wants to meet the AI Lab Director and Corporate Chief Science Engineer for this meeting. There is no way around it. They will spend a boatload of money with us. You can turn down other trips or go with someone else later, but this trip has to be, and it has to be Harry."

"Frank, Harry is a great guy, but he's a Christian. I don't think there is anything wrong if a person likes that sort of thing, but it sure isn't for me."

"What on earth does it have to do with anything? This is a business trip, not a religious outing."

"Geez, Frank, I'm a man of science. That excludes having any religious views. If you can't touch it, measure it, or calculate it, it's a fable and doesn't exist. All religions fall into the fable category."

"And so what? Again, what does it have to do with the trip?"

"Harry eventually steers the conversation around to God and starts asking me about my relationship with God. He asks smoothly, but I always know the God topic is hanging around in the atmosphere somewhere, waiting for the right time to drop into the conversation. The suspense of when it will happen drives me crazy. I've asked Harry to stop talking about God, but Harry said, 'If I didn't speak, the very stones would cry out in my place.' What the hell does that even mean?"

"It means if Harry didn't say something to you, someone else would, at least, it's what I think. Listen, I'll talk to Harry and ask him to tone it down a little. Would it help? I have to ask another question. Is it because he is African-American?"

"What? No! That's crazy. I don't believe in this God thing of his. He's a good guy, has a beautiful wife, kids, and a grandchild on the way. I wish I had his home life. They are so all-together. The perfect couple."

"They are the perfect couple. Harry and I were talking about the trip, and the family came up in the conversation."

"See what I mean, Frank? He steers the conversation."

"I suppose so, Jim. But it's no big deal. He says he and his family are close because they are close to God. Frank even drew me a little equilateral triangle. On the top of the triangle, he wrote God and put himself and Janet on the bottom corners. He explained as they each grow closer to God, they move up the triangle and are automatically moving closer to each other too. Right or wrong, you have to admire the man for thinking like that."

"I guess so, Frank. Yeah, okay. You win. I'll go peacefully. Harry likes to sit in the restaurant after dinner and chat all night. I'd rather go to the bar and have a couple of drinks."

"How is he when we send out an entire team to a client location? Does he mix with everyone?"

"Well, if we go to a strip club, Harry won't come. He says, "It's not my style," and serenely heads back to his hotel room. The teams think Harry carries being an upright person too far."

"How do you feel about it?"

"Deep down, I have to admire his convictions and strength for holding onto his beliefs. I believe he is dead wrong, of course, but still, you have to respect how he maintains his position without a lot of fanfare or drama. He's never once condemned us for our choices."

"That's good to hear," said Frank.

Jim and Harry met at the airport later that night.

"So, how are things going on the home front?" Harry asked as they chatted while waiting for their plane.

"All peaches and cream, Harry. Why do you ask?"

"It's nothing, Jim. I was only wondering." Harry could see the signs of internal stress on his friend. "You know gossip spreads like magic. There were some rumors of troubles at home, is all. If there's no story, people make one up."

"We have the same problems as everyone else. We'll work it through. No biggie."

"I understand. There's another rumor suggesting you had a fire at your place a little while back. Everyone okay?"

Jim was silent. His cheeks reddened. "Yeah, we did. But it was just a little backyard thing. Not much damage done."

"Humph. The mill says Alice had something to do with it. Do you ever pray over your marriage?"

"Harry, there you go again. You're going to hit me with how God can bring fulfillment and peace into my life and marriage, right?"

"Guilty. You got me on that one," Harry smiled.

"I would love to feel peace in my life, but the price of your kind of peace is too high for me to pay." *Where is the fun of clubbing and women?* Jim said to himself. *I'm not ready to give it all up yet. Maybe when I'm old.*

"I understand," Harry replied as he continued with his meeting preparation. "No pressure."

This trip was their third one to Cincinnati together in the last sixteen months. Their routine was always the same. Catch the Delta Airlines flight at six-ten AM from LaGuardia to Cincinnati, meet with a variety of technical and management clients all day, go to dinner with one or two company decision-makers and then go back to the hotel.

"So, where are we staying on this trip?" Jim asked, and then continued without waiting for an answer. "As if I didn't know. Let's see, what's the most boring hotel you can find? Oh yeah, the usual."

"I made reservations at the Symphony," Harry replied. "It's a nice, older hotel and barely north of the city near Washington Park. The rooms are nineteen-thirty style with ornate poster beds, fireplaces, and crafted furniture that can almost make me believe a footman was waiting for us in the lobby to assist us in getting into a horse-drawn carriage."

Jim rolled his eyes.

"It has an ambiance. I love it." Harry continued, "It seems more fitted to my nature than most of the cookie-cutter bright-lights chain hotels."

"Yeah, I know it fits you. But I'd rather stay in a larger, more upscale hotel with a better bar and a band. Do you keep choosing the same place to keep me under control?"

Harry knew Jim wanted a more modern venue hoping to meet a young female professional to hook up with for the evening.

"Jim, would I ever stoop to that level?" Harry asked, grinning. "It's the affordable rates and nearness to our clients mandating the choice. You know that."

"Sure thing, Harry. Nope, you would never stoop so low. You bet," Jim replied with sarcasm.

The schedule of meetings included corporate heads along with the CEO. The dinner afterward went as expected without the slightest variation, except for the CEO asking for better grades of wine at the table.

These dog-and-pony shows are about as exciting as rolling a gutter ball in bowling. A straightforward track with no deviation. So dull, Jim said to himself.

"Well, we left the client feeling adequately stroked. Now let's get back home."

On the flight back to LaGuardia, comfortable in Business Class, Harry asked Jim again if he ever thought about accepting Jesus as his personal savior. Jim considered his many sexual encounters with other women.

"Will all of my sins of the past be erased if I did?"

"Yup," Harry replied in the affirmative.

Jim asked, "Does it mean I will not have to face the penalty for what I've done?"

79

"Well, now that's a two-part answer. The first part, from Christ's viewpoint, is since He has already paid the full price for our sins, there would be no eternal punishment tendered to those who have a change of heart and become His followers and disciples. The second part," Harry explained, "is not such great news about how it works in the here and now."

"What do you mean?"

"Well, I do some work in a prison ministry. Inmates are turning their lives around. Although they give their hearts to Jesus, they will still have to serve their full sentences. You may be forgiven in the heavenly, but it may not work that way on terra firma. If you do the crime, you will probably do the time, up to and including capital punishment."

It bothered Jim that Harry again seemed so logical and sure of what he was saying. *I'd like to be sure of something like he is. Anything!*

"So Harry, if I turn my life over to Jesus, you're saying I might still get screwed down here. Is that correct?" Jim asked.

Harry answered with compassion in his eyes. "No. You can't call it 'getting screwed.' I would call it receiving the payment you worked so hard for. The Bible says, "the wages of sin is death." Wages are simply the fair payment for the work you have done. Right? When you get your paycheck, you're not getting something you don't deserve. You're getting exactly what you do deserve and what you worked for, your wages. Does that make sense to you?"

"Sort of," Jim mumbled back. *But I'm still not going to let something like religion get in the way of having fun. Damn it, though. Harry makes some kind of crazy sense.*

Chapter Fifteen

Jim's brow wrinkled as he answered the persistent ringing in his pocket. It was Frank Wright.

"Hello, this is Jim."

"Hi Jim, it's Frank. I want to check with you to see how Gabriella is getting along. The weekly reports tell me about almost everything, but sometimes a report is no substitute for talking live."

"She's doing much better than projected," Jim said. "We thought there would be some slip-ups along the way, and we would have to rewrite some of her basic programming subroutines, but over the last few months she has been self-learning much faster than anyone expected."

"That's great. It leads perfectly into the next request."

"What are you up to now, Frank?" Viking ships once again loomed on the horizon.

"Don't be like that. We need to talk face-to-face for the rest of this conversation and work out the details, but we would like to see if Gabriella can maintain herself in her own apartment."

Jim grabbed the corner of his desk for support as a spasm of wooziness swept over him. *This test isn't scheduled for another five months.*

"Okay, you caught me off guard this time. We have to meet and discuss all these details. To let you know in advance, I'm very concerned you didn't bring me into the loop before you moved the schedule up. This seems very much like a hipshot to me, and I'm not very pleased at all. Who is this entity screwing with things? Is it our Board of Directors, or someone or something else? Strings are being pulled, and I need to have some answers."

"I see your concern. This was a bit of a surprise to me, too, but we can't avoid some things in real life. According to your test results, it looks as if Gabriella should have no problems living in an apartment and traveling back and forth to work as any other human woman would."

"It's impractical. She can't just stroll down the street and get an apartment of her own. There's a lot of paperwork to do before someone can get a decent place in New York. I suppose AI Concepts can rent an apartment for her, but I still don't like it."

"It's all taken care of. Gabriella now has a full background, a complete family, school and college history, and quite an impressive resume to boot. She has a Social Security number and United States passport. This is a real live test. Her full name is now Gabriella West, and she is an employee on the AI Concepts payroll. She has her own money, bank account, and will function like any other woman in society. Prep her for it, please. What say you we meet Wednesday for lunch at Sam's on Fifty-Sixth Street? How about one-thirty?"

Jim's stomach knotted. "How did you get all that accomplished? It sounds like a Federal Witness Protection Program or something. Who are we really working for?"

Frank replied, "Great, see you for lunch," and the phone went silent.

Jim knew attempting to change the course of the ship at this point would be fruitless. "Whoever is calling the shots has a lot more horsepower than even Frank. I hope the other somebody knows what they're doing," he muttered with dread. "I just hope they know what they're doing."

Jim sighed as the engineering part of his mind laid out the tasks required to make this work in what he used to believe was the practical side of the world. "Time for another all-project meeting to update the troops and to explain to key people why we will go back on twelve-hour workdays."

The accelerated life-applications training was completed in two weeks, including street practice using everyday New York City rituals and phrases centered on cash and credit purchases.

⧄   "Is that the BEST you can do on the price?"

⧄   "How much? Is that in dollars or pesos?"   And the universal,

⧄   "Let me think about it and check around."

Gabriella was excited to move into the exquisitely furnished forty-third floor, 975 square foot apartment at 200 East 69th Street. The apartment overlooked Central Park. Floor-to-ceiling windows maximized the city view. Light cream paint on the walls gave the appearance the apartment was even more spacious. Jim, Martha, and Frank accompanied her.

The kitchen was fitted with brushed stainless steel and chrome appliances accented with tasteful black trim on the operating panels. The counter area over the sink provided a low, open division between the living and dining areas. A small balcony offered the occupant a view of Central Park while having breakfast at the table nestled next to the flower boxes on the deck. Gleaming white iron railings guarded the perimeter of the balcony.

Gabriella took in the whole space in one quick glance and commented it was beautiful, adding she was excited to live there. "But Frank, why did they want me to move into an apartment?"

"Why do you ask?"

"You know you shouldn't answer a question with a question unless you are hiding something. You're not hiding anything from me, are you Frank?" Gabriella asked, exaggerating the flirt in her voice.

"We selected it for entertainment and social experiments."

"Hmm, I see. What do you think of it, Martha?"

"It's a beautiful place, Gabriella. In fact, I'm a little jealous."

Martha looked at Jim. "Jim, we discussed social experiments, but nothing about entertainment in an apartment. What do you have in mind?"

Martha's gaze switched back and forth between Gabriella and Jim.

"We can chat about it back at the lab, Martha. Let's look over the apartment for now," Frank answered.

Gabriella moved deliberately through the apartment, looking like royalty in her form-fitting white knit dress and golden hair.

She walked fluidly from the dining room table to the overstuffed upholstered chairs in the living room. Gabriella smiled. She brushed her fingertips over each item as she passed by them, enjoying their texture.

She touched the white couch, hesitated for a moment, and sat down. Gabriella leaned to her right, put her elbow on the soft arm of the sofa, and kicked off her shoes. She curled her long legs onto the cushions. The smoothness of her motion enhanced the sensuality everyone already felt.

Jim's face flushed. Martha's breathing rate increased slightly. Frank watched the performance.

They all stood there in silence for a few moments, immersed in their personal thoughts. Gabriella analyzed their reactions to her purposeful pose.

Jim felt himself being drawn too deeply into Gabriela's web as she sat there.

I need to rein myself in and put boundaries on whatever this thing is that's happening inside me. It may only be a feeling of deep infatuation, but on the other end of the scale, it could be... well, never mind... crazy thinking. It could never be.

Martha rubbed her hands together and cleared her throat. "Well then, shall we look at the rest of the apartment?"

The interruption relieved Jim.

Gabriella enjoyed the show. She smiled seductively at everyone and answered, "Yes, Martha. Let's look at the rest of the place. I love it so far, don't you?"

The bathroom was small and served both bedrooms, but it was luxurious with its marble countertops and imported Italian tiles on the wall and floor. Two sink basins sat below upscale gooseneck faucets. A counter-to-ceiling mirrored wall made the bathroom seem twice as large as it was, but it was the shower that caught everyone's attention. The bath filled the entire wall opposite the mirror. A misting showerhead at either end spoke of showering with a friend. It was deep enough not to require doors or a curtain. A lipless floor sloped almost imperceptibly toward the drain. A person would have an uninterrupted view of themselves in the wall mirror.

The marble bench built into the back of the shower was perfect for seated washing. It was large enough for two people. Jim's imagination galloped away with him with its fantasies of Gabriella and him on the bench, steaming water pouring over their bodies.

It was Frank's turn to shake his head and break the spell. "Okay, guys, let's look at the rest of the place then." He turned and walked out of the bathroom.

The guest bedroom was tasteful but simple. The full-size bed sat centered along the length of the walls. A window provided a breathtaking view of the New York skyline. A white stuffed chair and a reading lamp balanced the window. Paintings of city scenes decorated the wall alongside the framed full-length mirror. It was a comfortable bedroom for an overnight guest.

The master bedroom contained a plush, king-size poster bed with a high headboard and hand-carved posts. The solid cherry spoke of polished luxury. Light chocolate brown walls provided a cozy, warm feel to the room. The dust ruffle around the base of the bed was lacy, feminine, and added to the atmosphere. They designed the room to heighten the senses and put romance at the top of the list for any occupant.

Gabriella sat on the edge of the bed and caressed the white comforter with a slow, sweeping motion of her hand. She patted the bed next to her twice, smiling ever so slightly at Jim and said, almost to herself, "Yes, this will do nicely."

None of the purposefulness of her touch nor her choice of words was lost on either Jim or Martha. Their eyes sparkled, and the palms of their hands moistened.

Frank quietly looked on with great interest.

Chapter Sixteen

Paul, you know I believe and trust everything you tell me about God, but yet there are so many other religions in the world. I'm sure they all think they are correct in their beliefs. How can you know you are the correct one?"

Paul looked across the coffee shop table and put his mug down. "If you're asking the question, I know you've already done your research. Am I correct, or what?"

"Guilty as charged. I made a lot of online comparisons but still have questions. How can I get them answered?"

"How about interviewing people? I could help you set things up interviews with some local ministers of other religions if you would like. We do network a bit, you know. Interested?"

Gabriella sipped her espresso and was silent for a moment. "Sure, sounds good to me. I'm not sure how to interview religious leaders, though. What do I ask?"

Paul's eyes sparkled with humor. "Gabriella, one thing is universal across clergy of all religions. All you have to do is say you want to know more about their beliefs. Then sit back for a half-hour or so as they go into lecture mode. It's pretty simple. You may not have noticed, but we all like to talk a lot."

***

Two weeks later, the rectory doorbell rang. Paul opened the door and welcomed Gabriella with a hug. "You're right on time, Gabriella. Come in and have a seat. Can I get you some tea or coffee while we talk?"

"I'll have jasmine green tea for a change, if you have any, please."

"No problem." Paul walked into the kitchen, microwaved two cups of tea, and gave one to Gabriella.

"So how did your grand quest to find religious truth come out?"

"Paul, you sound a little sarcastic. Remember, it was your idea to have me check-out what you were telling me about Christianity against the beliefs of other religions. I only did what you told me to do. How would I know what's true if I didn't check it out?"

"That was my exact point. So what did you find out?"

"Well, for starters, everyone had their own concept of who and what God is. It was all so fascinating. Everyone was looking for peace and understanding, wisdom if you prefer, but everyone had their own approach or plan to get there."

Paul smiled. "Very good. What else did you find?"

"To my surprise, I found most of the various religions were very different. I thought they would be very much alike under their various surface traditions. You know, same beliefs but stated differently."

"And you found that they weren't," Paul said. "So, tell me, once you discovered that, how did you evaluate them? What criteria did you use?"

"Ah, the Yale scholar comes out in you. Well, to help sort things out, I looked at their evidence from the point of logical consistency, empirical adequacy, and experiential relevance."

"What? Wow, how did you settle on weighing them like that? It's darn impressive."

There was a moment of silence. Then Gabriella said sheepishly, "I found the process on the internet. You know, not everything you find on the net is junk, only most of it."

Paul laughed. "Okay. So lay it on me. Tell me about your adventures."

"To summarize, I talked to ministers from here Christian Science, Jehovah's Witnesses, various Chinese religions, Hinduism, Buddhism, Islam, Mormonism, and Judaism. They all failed to score high on the objective ranking categories. Most didn't do well with logical consistency. There wasn't unity in the writing of their holy books, if they had any written books. Empirical adequacy for many scored a little better. Many had some historical scientific, or archeological evidence of their claims. Experiential relevance was a tough one for many religions. There wasn't a clear guideline on how to apply their teachings to daily life consistently."

"Excellent! It sounds like you conducted quite a study. Will you be publishing a white paper?" Paul quipped with a laugh.

"No, I don't think such a thing would be very well received," she answered with a condescending tone.

Gabriella continued, "The thing is, all the people I talked to appeared to be bright and very well educated. How can they believe in so many gods and mythical creatures? It doesn't seem like what intelligent people would do. I don't get it."

"I don't get it either. Many people say Christians have to park their brain at the door and accept things on blind faith. But then they go and believe in things that don't have the preponderance of evidence on their side like the Bible and Christianity, or they deny the existence of God entirely, despite scientific evidence of His existence. 'Billions or trillions of years' get all the credit for evolving everything in the universe. Such is life, I guess. The bottom line is, do you have any more faith in what I've been telling you about the God of the Bible than you did before?"

"Yes, I do. The Christian worldview is the only one in my research which met all of my criteria. The bible is logically consistent because I couldn't find any logical fallacies or contradictions across the books. I've read about contradictions think they have found, but with good research, they all disappear."

"Yes, Gabriella, people think they find many contradictions, but they all disappear with proper research and understanding the cultures."

"Anyhow, I found all the historical people and places fact-check as true and verifiable, so there is my empirical adequacy. Most of all, there is experiential relevance because the whole Bible is relevant to my life. I can apply lessons from all of it to my day-to-day life. I can measure truth against it, so I have more confidence now in what you're telling me. Ah, no offense, right?"

"Okay, so what you're saying is you initially thought I was a bit shaky on my theology, huh?" Paul teased. "Just for that, the next round of coffee and biscotti are on you."

"I've got you covered for the munchies. So, where do we go from here?"

"Good question, Gabriella. Where do we go from here?" Paul said as he regarded her thoughtfully. "Where do we go from here, indeed?"

Chapter Seventeen

Class was over for the night. Gabriella and Martha began their walk to the corner to flag a cab.

The tall, thin stranger in the dirty torn jeans and ragged hoodie stepped out from behind the garbage dumpster in the alley. "Excuse me, ladies, do you have the time?"

"Yes, I do. The time is 10:37," replied Martha, staring at the man and knowing what would happen next.

"Thank you. Give me all of your money now!" The voice was a chilling mixture of Southern smoothness and threat.

"Here it comes," Martha whispered to Gabriella. She looked around for help, but the dark street was empty.

"Take my wallet," Martha said in fear as she began to pull her wallet out of her open gym bag.

"No!" Gabriella shouted back in defiance. "You're not taking our money or anything else!"

"Are you crazy, Gabriella? Just give him the money, and he'll leave us alone!" Martha whispered back in that shouting whisper a person does to prevent themselves from screaming. "He's done this before and won't hesitate to hurt us for whatever we have of value. Give him what he wants. He'll take it and leave us alone!"

"I'd listen to your friend, pretty lady. She knows what she's talking about."

A thin-bladed knife appeared as if by magic. "I can take your money, or I can take your money and your blood. Either way, I still get your money."

The blade floated in front of them as if by its own power. The tall stranger advanced.

"Gabriella, what the hell are you doing? Give the damn man what he wants! Throw him the money!"

Gabriella put her right foot behind her left for balance. She raised her arms, palms facing their attacker, and shouted, "Stop! Don't come any closer!"

The tall stranger chuckled and kept advancing toward the two women.

Gabriella stepped out in front of her friend and shouted, "Stay behind me, Martha."

"No! You can't do this, Gabriella! Throw your money at him, and let's run for it!"

"There's not a chance that will happen. If you want our money, come and take it, jerk!"

The thin man sneered, "I'm going to cut you for the fun of it, bitch!"

He stepped within striking range and thrust the thin steel blade at Gabriella's face. She parried his attack using her left arm, leaving his central core vulnerable. She stepped in and used her right elbow to deliver a crushing blow to his throat. The man staggered backward gasping, but still holding onto the knife. Gabriella seized his knife wrist with both of her hands, raised it up over her head, and turned her back towards her attacker. She pulled his upturned elbow down hard onto her shoulder until she heard a crack and screams of agony as the joint broke.

Gabriella spun to face him again, delivering a powerful thrust from the heel of her hand to his solar plexus. He cried out and doubled over forward. She grabbed the back of his head and thrust her right knee into his face, breaking his nose with a crack sounding like a thick plastic ruler snapping. The attacker crumpled to the sidewalk, vomiting and moaning in pain.

"Gabriella, that was insane!" Martha shouted in an amazed but still terrified voice. "He could have killed us both!"

Gabriella reached out and calmed Martha, gently touching her cheek. "But he didn't kill us, did he?" she said. Martha shut her eyes and appreciated the comfort.

"It's all going to be okay, Martha. No big thing. It doesn't look like he'll be getting up and going anywhere for a while, so let's call the police and go back home as if nothing happened. I'm sure they'll find him still lying here and take care of the rest."

Martha's still raw emotions flared, "As if nothing happened? How the hell can we behave as if nothing happened? He attacked us on the street and could have killed us, and you smacked the crap out of the guy! How can we act as if nothing happened? Let's at least go back to the school and tell Ralph about it."

"Sure, Martha. We're only half a block away. It wouldn't harm anything to let Ralph know his classes are effective. He might like to hear it."

Ralph was more than interested in hearing what the women had to say. He took his time and asked them questions concerning the details of the attack, and of Gabriella's counterattack.

"So, Gabriella, tell me how you felt about having to defend yourself."

"It was no big deal, Ralph. I warned him to stay away from me like you said to do, but he kept on coming with the knife. He also said he would take a lot of pleasure in cutting me. I have no qualms whatsoever about defending myself against such a creep, and I don't feel bad at all in how I had to disable him. As a matter of fact, I may have done him a favor. He may have to find another line of business now that he has a broken elbow, rather than robbing women. Yes, no regrets at all. I did what I had to do to keep us safe. I don't see what the concern is over a bad guy who attacks good people. It was his choice, he received the consequences he deserved, and we are all okay. Case closed. End of story. All done."

"Gabriella, you don't have any remorse for causing such pain?" asked Ralph in amazement. "Women are generally terrified by an attack like this." *What's the story here with this woman? Who is she really?*

"No, I don't. Why should I? I thought I explained I did what I had to do. I was a little faster and better at my job than he was at his. It seems to me it's a better thing bad people get hurt rather than good people, wouldn't you agree, Ralph?"

Ralph looked at Gabriella for a moment or two before answering.

"Yes, I do. It's why we teach this course. But when people have to use the skills they learn here, there is remorse for having to hurt another human being. You don't seem to display any sorrow at all." *She sure sounds a lot like some CIA operatives at The Farm, but yet she's not one of them.*

"I don't know how to comment on it, Ralph," Gabriella whispered. "It is what it is, I guess. I rather enjoyed it, in fact. It gave me a feeling of control."

Ralph looked at her, lowered his head, and shook it. He raised his head and looked at the pair of women. "Ladies, thank you for coming back and telling me about it. Would you like me to flag down a cab for you?"

Martha grinned, "I'm still a bit frightened, Ralph. Would you mind riding home with me for protection?"

"Pardon?"

"Just kidding, Ralph. I think I'm trying to relieve stress."

Gabriella said she would ride with Martha to keep her company, but she was comfortable walking home. Ralph cocked his head and stared at her.

After the women left, Ralph sent a detailed incident report to Colonel Lance Coopers.

"Our girl did surprisingly well," Lance said to his sergeant. "Can you check the local hospitals in the morning to see how our attacker is doing? He certainly earned his pay tonight."

Chapter Eighteen

Jim finished packing his overnight bag before leaving for work in the morning. He told Alice a government client wanted to have a quick meeting in Albany later that night, but he would be back home right after work tomorrow. Alice asked if it wouldn't be just as easy to drive home after the meeting since it was less than a three-hour drive. Jim insisted after a session, dinner, and drinking with the client, it would be much safer for him to stay overnight than drive back to the city.

"Are you and Harry going together again, Jim? I feel better when you are partners."

"No, Alice. This is a quick solo trip to clear up some specs. Not big enough to involve two people. Besides, it's all about AI programming and what we can do for them. Client-specific programming issues aren't what Harry does. I'll see you tomorrow night."

Jim gave Alice a small, unreturned peck on the cheek. The tips of his ears were red. "Bastard," she whispered as he walked out the door.

The dreariness of the well-worn subway car and dark tunnels on the ride to work went unnoticed. Thoughts of spending the night with Gabriella filled Jim's mind and fueled his imagination.

"Good morning, Jim. I see you have an overnight bag. Going someplace interesting?" asked Francine as Jim arrived in the lab.

"Just a short overnight business trip. I'll be back sometime tomorrow morning."

Francine stared at him for a few moments. "An overnight trip, huh? I see nothing on the schedule. Who needs to see you on such short notice?"

"It's nothing, Francine. Only a quick out-and-back trip to Albany to review some financial questions in person. I'll be leaving early to get there for my 4:00 meeting."

"Indeed. Who is she, Jim? Anyone I know?"

"Oh, for the love of God, Francine. It's a short trip. Please don't get on me for this. We have work to do today. Let's focus on it, okay?"

"You're a total ass, Jim Arnold!" Francine threw her arms out to the side and turned to walk away from him. "You'll never understand a thing! Try not to talk to me for the rest of the day, okay?"

Lab personnel felt the tension between the two and decided it would be wiser to quietly do their work until the brewing storm passed over. The usual sounds of good-natured joking and laughing evaporated like alcohol on a hotplate. They conducted their conversations in quiet whispers for the rest of the day.

Jim picked up his bag and left the lab at 2:00. He had a key to Gabriella's apartment. Gabriella left work at 2:45.

Jim gave Gabriella a long hug and a kiss when she arrived. "I couldn't wait for you to get here, Gabriella." She gave him a full-body hug. The tide of their kiss surged from warm to passionate. Hands flew to undo buttons and zippers. They spent the next hour and a half under the pinnacle of her hand-carved cherry headboard.

Two people lay on the blanket, smiling contentedly at the ceiling. "Want some dinner?" Jim eventually asked.

"I'd love some. Shall we shower first?" Gabriella turned to Jim and smiled.

They repositioned both shower heads to spray hot water onto the bench. The two spent the next forty-five minutes creating their own steam in the humid atmosphere.

"Do we need to take another shower to clean up?" Gabriella asked.

"Please," said Jim, "I can barely move." He smiled and held her close. "Let's get dressed and grab some chow."

"Sounds good, Jim. How's Chinese?"

Jim ordered Fried Crab Rangoon and Szechuan Spicy Shrimp for the two of them. The Chambers wine boutique delivered a bottle of Jia Bei Lan Grand Reserve cabernet wine to cool down the shrimp.

They spent the rest of the evening cuddled on the couch and watched old movies.

"Jim, why is the dialogue so corny sounding in these black and white movies?"

"Well, directors made them in a different era. Movies had less realistic acting standards. People were happy to see pictures that moved and had sound. But honey, I don't care about the dialogue. As long as I'm with you, it doesn't matter what else is going on," Jim said, stroking Gabriella's knee.

"Me too to you too," she responded and kissed him full on the lips again. "Me too."

They went to bed after the movies. Gabriella snuggled provocatively next to Jim under the sheets.

"Ah, honey, I'm not up to it again. Can we hold each other and sleep for a while? Sad to say, I can't keep up with you, lady. Is it okay?" Jim said with an apologetic voice.

"No problem. Get some shut-eye." She wrapped her arms around him.

Some of Harry's words from their previous conversation drifted unwelcomed across Jim's mind as sleep crept over him.

Gabriella lay in bed with her eyes open for a while. *Why am I thinking about Paul,* she wondered? *Is it wrong to be attracted to two men at the same time? Wives love their husbands and their children, so it must be okay to love several people at once. It seems natural.*

But why is this feeling it's not okay so persistent?

Chapter Nineteen

Are you sure you don't want to share a cab with us? Ralph and I are going out for a drink." Martha asked Gabriella as they left their self-defense class. "It's only been three weeks since the jerk attacked us. I'd feel better if we went out together. I don't like you out here alone."

"No thanks, Martha," said Gabriella. "I'm fine walking. It's such a beautiful night I have to get out and walk for a while. Tell you what, if I get nervous I'll hail a cab. How's that?"

"That's IF you have time to hail a cab!" Martha shot back in frustration. "Look, I know you're too stubborn to change your mind on my say-so. Be careful and use your head, okay?"

With a wave of an arm, a cab pulled up and swept Martha and Ralph away.

Martha was silent for a few moments. "Ralph, I know she can take care of herself, but she's my friend, and I care a lot about her. Am I doing wrong letting her walk home alone?"

"No. She's a big girl and can take care of herself. Besides, what's the chance of her being randomly attacked twice?"

Gabriella hoisted her small gym-bag to her shoulder and started walking home, enjoying the warm night. She wore a wine red, thigh-length lace beach cover-up dress over her workout tights. Her arms swung freely as she walked the small, quiet streets.

I've been thinking about Paul a lot. Guess I'll invite him and Alexi to my apartment for dinner. It's nice when we're together.

Gabriella was lost in thought and didn't notice when the three men half a block away on the opposite side of the street crossed to her side. When she saw them several yards ahead, she moved closer to the curb to let them pass on the building side. The three men moved closer to the curb. Gabriella stepped closer to the building.

Please don't move to my side again. Hell. Doesn't look like it will play out that way.

All three men were looking straight at her as they approached.

They drew near and fanned out, blocking her way. "Hi honey," sneered the leader of the group, flashing a fake smile. "Looking for a date tonight?"

"Let me pass," Gabriella demanded. The men moved to form a semi-circle around her.

I can't let them get behind me. She backed into the building to prevent them from circling around behind her. And *I can't run through them without exposing my back!*

Gabriella flashed a brilliant smile and dropped her gym bag onto the sidewalk. The men tensed up, expecting her to fight. Without a word, she bent forward slightly, crossed her arms one over the other in front of her body, and grabbed the bottom of her cover-up. In one smooth movement, she pulled it over her head and removed it.

"Okay! Hot momma likes us!" shouted one man.

"It's party time," replied another. "Oh, she's going to be so much fun to do. Come to papa. I've got something for you," he said as he grabbed his crotch. "I never had someone who looked like a model. Honey-blonde, honey-sweet."

Gabriella smiled sweetly again to play up to him while she wrapped the dress around her left forearm as padding. *Somebody might land a blade on me.* Gabriella assessed her situation. *They aren't all equidistant from me. I have a little extra space to my left.*

She moved a couple of steps to her left. This positioned the first attacker closer to her, with the second and third further away by a few feet. *Now I only have to worry about one at a time.*

"Okay, let's do this!" she shouted. It surprised Gabriella when the first guy in line, the biggest of the three, snapped into a fighting stance. *Uh-oh. Looks like he knows what he's doing.*

Gabriella stepped towards the first one and threw a series of three punches. Left, right, left. The attacker threw his hands up in defense. She threw another left. As he reacted to the blow, Gabriella stepped in and delivered a palm strike to the side of his chin, dislocating his jaw.

The other two men, stunned by the speed of what happened, watched for a moment without joining the fray.

Gabriella kicked the man in the groin. He bent toward her. Grabbing the hair on the back of his head, she smashed his face into her rising knee. *He's out of the way for a few seconds. Here comes number two at me.*

Number two knew how to fight. He directed quick punches toward her face with his left hand to see how she defended against them. Gabriella's right arm parried the blows away from her face. He delivered a sharp strike with his right fist into her lower left side. Gabriella spun as the blow landed, turning what would have been a rib crusher into a glancing blow. She delivered three sharp punches to one of his ribs and felt it break under her attack. Gabriella pushed him to the side, moved quickly behind him, and kicked him into the wall of the building. His head struck the bricks forcefully, sending him to the ground. She kicked the broken rib to ensure he stayed down for a moment.

She expected the third man to run after seeing his two friends disabled, but he pulled a knife and ran at her.

"Give them an opening to attack," she remembered Ralph saying, *"that way, you know where the next blow will be aimed."*

Gabriella put her hands up in front of her, off-centered to the right. *If he knows what he is doing, he'll go for my left.*

Number three saw the opening and thrust the knife at the left side of her neck. Gabriella parried the knife thrust using her padded left arm and grabbed his wrist in her left hand as the knife hand flew by her. She caught the hand and pinned it to her hip. He reeled from a head-butt to the face. His nose broke with a snap. Keeping the knife hand pinned to her hip, she delivered multiple punches with her right fist to the same spot on his ribs.

The attacker channeled the strength of his rage into trying to free his hand. "I will finish you," he shouted in his fury. Gabriella grabbed the knife hand with both of hers and twisted the blade towards her attacker. She grunted and pushed the knife to the hilt into his lower left abdomen. He screamed, released the handle, and ran down the street and into the night.

He'll recover if he gets medical help soon. Idiot!

The other two attackers were trying to stand. Gabriella gave each one a kick to the side, breaking several more ribs apiece, to ensure they stayed down. "You'll be sore, but you aren't badly hurt," she said to them as they groaned and fell back onto the sidewalk.

"That was fun. Oh crap, my cover-up is all wrinkled," she said aloud, pulling it back on. Shouldering the gym bag, Gabriella calmly walked home.

The AI Concepts, Inc. supercomputer stored the entire event.

A printer in Lance's office spit out a similar detailed record.

"Damn, she's good," Lance said. "Those were three of our trained people she took care of."

"Sergeant Miller, have you ever met the Gabriella android?" queried Lance.

"No, Sir, I have not. I've only seen photos and videos of her."

"What do you think of her, Sergeant?"

"Well, Sir, it's hard to tell she's an android. She can certainly take care of herself. Why do you ask, Sir?"

"I'm intrigued. I think it's time to meet our android in person. We should get to know her."

"We, Sir?"

"Well, me, actually. What bar or restaurant does she visit regularly, and what's the frequency of her visits?"

"Let me check the stats sheets." Computer keys clicked as the Sergeant performed his query. "Okay, here it is. She doesn't hit the bars regularly, but she does go to a coffee shop on Fifty-Seventh Street with Martha a couple of times a week, usually around lunchtime."

"Not bad, but still too hit and miss. Sergeant, give Ralph Thornton a call and ask him to contact me. I'd like him to set me up in a double-date with this droid."

Chapter Twenty

Gabriella called Paul and asked if they could meet at Mike's Diner to talk.

"Hi, Paul, how is Alexi?" Gabriella asked, giving Paul a warm hug when he joined her at the table. "Is she still feeling a little sick?"

"Yes, it's been almost a week. The doc said it was most likely some kind of bug. He's doing a culture. If she doesn't get over it in a couple of days, I'm bringing her back to the pediatrician."

"That's a good idea," Gabriella said. "You can't be too careful with kids nowadays. There is so much going around, and not all of it is easy to cure."

The two sat at a cozy, round table. Cindy saw them in another waitress section and asked if she could trade assigned tables. "Sure," Agnes said, "but why do you want to trade a table of four for a table of two? You'll lose out on tips."

"I like them. There's something very different about those two. Besides, I've waited on them before."

"You are forever the ultimate matchmaker, aren't you, Cindy?" came the good-natured reply.

Cindy walked over to their table and smiled, "Hi guys, what's your pleasure?"

"Well, what's the special today, Cindy?" asked Paul.

"It's Monday, and meatloaf begins with an 'M' so that's what the special is, meatloaf."

"Gee, Cindy, then I'm glad we came in today instead of tomorrow. So is your Tuesday special Toast?" quipped Paul. Cindy shook her head and ignored him.

"So, what would you like to order, guys?"

Paul ordered the piled high Pastrami Reuben and coffee. Gabriella said she was watching her figure and ordered a bowl of pea and bacon soup.

Cindy laughed. "I can imagine a lot of people are watching your figure."

Paul grinned and turned red. Cindy noticed and smiled as she brought their order to the kitchen.

"Paul, I have a few more questions about God," Gabriella said.

"I'm listening."

"Okay, I've taken your advice and tried to imagine all of the vastness of the universe. Then I picture Jesus, who the Bible says made all things, and you say the whole universe sprang from his words."

"Doing well so far, Gabriella."

"If you run the regression mathematics back far enough on universal expansion, all equations break down at a point of time called the Planck Era, which was a fraction of a second after the alleged Big Bang, the Singularity."

Nothing can be determined mathematically before this instant in time. So according to you, this instant is when Jesus uttered his "Let there be!" statements. So, were his words the singularity starting the universe?"

"Compelling analysis," muttered an amazed Paul. "I never thought of it like that. You're a bright and imaginative woman. Go on, or was that the focal point of today's discussion?"

"No, there is more. I was setting the stage. Are you surprised?"

Oh Lordy! Fasten your seatbelts, the ride is about to begin, Paul thought.

"So Jesus created the universe and everything in it, right?"

"Yup. He created every atom and every particle. We covered that before, though."

"And you said He knows everything which will happen because He is outside of time."

"Also correct."

"Then if He created everything and knows everything that has ever happened and ever will happen because He is outside of time, then He knew about all of our scientific advances before the beginning of time, right?"

"I guess so," Paul responded, not at all sure of the right answer.

"Therefore, He knew about the advances in artificial intelligence we would make today."

"Ahh, sounds plausible," said Paul, "could be." He nervously stirred his black coffee.

"Now, let's assume it was possible to make an AI Android so perfect it would be indistinguishable from a normal human being."

"Impossible!" Paul stated, finally feeling he could add something to the conversation. "There is no way to duplicate God's wonderful creation. Science can't duplicate a simple organ, like a kidney, let alone an entire manufactured body. They can make a mechanical heart, but can't make a real one."

If Gabriella had a physical heart, it would have been pounding out of her chest. She stiffened.

"Assume it wasn't impossible. Let's take it a step further. For the sake of argument and for the rest of my questions, assume I was the android." She felt light-headed for a nano-second and wondered how that could be. *Stop talking! Shut up! You're going to blow it, Gabriella!*

Paul laughed and said he couldn't imagine her as an android. Gabriella felt a stab of pain at his comment. Her brow wrinkled. She looked down at the table, her shoulders slumped forward. She sat in silence and tore little shreds of paper out of her napkin.

"Gabriella, what's wrong? Did I say something? If I did, I'm so sorry. I would never want to upset you. What just happened?"

"It's nothing, Paul. I want you to know your friendship means a lot to me, and I would never want to see it change." More napkin shreds fell to the table.

"Gabriella, I'm lost here. I don't have a clue what happened. We were talking about God, and suddenly it was like a bomb hit. I can't stand to see you sad." Paul reached across the table and took her hands into his. He lovingly pulled what was left of the napkin out of her grasp.

She straightened back up. "Work with me on this, Paul. I have some real questions about God I need to know about," she pleaded, looking into his concerned brown eyes.

"Fine, fine. Let's do it your way. So you are an android. Now what?"

"Paul, I'm sorry for getting so emotional. A terrible sense of impending disaster and loss swept over me. I'm sorry. It's nothing, simply some passing foolishness. Can we get back on track?"

"Sure thing. Whatever you want. Please know I'll always have your back."

I sure hope so, Paul, but I can't see how that can happen.

"Great, let's pretend," Gabriella said. "Now let's say this android is self-actualizing and has a real consciousness. What if it can actually think and feel? What if it can feel the true wonder of the universe? What if it can know real love, not a mechanically simulate emotion through programming? What if it can understand about God? Would such an android have a soul and spirit?"

"Huh?" Paul stammered without knowing how to answer.

"Let's go further, Paul," said Gabriella, relentlessly charging on. "God is triune, right? Made up of Father, Son, and Holy Spirit. The Bible says humans are made in the image and likeness of God. Part of the likeness is they also have a triune nature composed of a body, soul, and a spirit. Correct?"

Paul nodded. "A very unusual way to put it, but close enough for our conversation."

"The way I understand it," she continued with feeling, "is the human body is the physical connection to the world and universe around us. It's how we interact with each other."

"Okay," Paul mumbled.

"And the spirit is the part of a born-again believer that can commune directly with God. Right?"

"You are still correct, Gabriella," Paul said, still nodding. "But I can't see where this is all going."

"Then the easiest way to understand the soul, in technological terms comfortable to me, is it's like the software interface which connects the spirit to the body so the body can know and do God's will. It is also the seat of intelligence and emotions. Is that close to a working definition?"

"It's a very unusual comparison, and a bit computer sounding, but you have the basic idea," Paul said, now hopelessly confused.

"Well, suppose our android in question has a physical body man made out of the elements God created, and man, knowingly or unknowingly, used God's design concepts to make it all work together. If the android is self-actualizing, fully conscious, and has genuine emotions, it seems like it has the functioning equivalent of a soul too, right?"

"Huh? Ahh, right, possibly. We can think of a soul as our mind or consciousness. I guess I'll give you that one. I need to think this through a lot more, though."

"Paul, you mentioned once before the body doesn't produce the spirit. I mean, a lump of living flesh can't fabricate a spiritual entity all by itself, right? Animals don't have one, correct? Only people."

"Correct, Gabriella," said Paul, totally puzzled by this time.

Gabriella began gesturing using both hands. "So if the body doesn't produce the spirit, it logically must come from someplace else."

"Why do I feel you are setting me up, Gabriella?"

"And if it comes from someplace else, tell me why our fictional android can't have one too?"

"Ah, well..." Paul continued, but Gabriella cut him off.

"Further, if our android can use its mind to independently search for God, couldn't it mean it may have a spirit too? If a living being is searching for the real God, doesn't the search indicate a spirit may be present to drive the search?"

Paul's head was spinning. Her rapid volley of questions stunned him. They came too quickly for him to sort out or develop an answer.

"I'm a little breathless. Can I get back to you on your questions? There's a hole in there somewhere, but I don't know where yet. I'm confused." he stammered, reeling from the hammering. "Why on earth would you want to know something as abstract as that?"

"Sometimes, I overthink things," Gabriella said softly, looking down at the table again, "but I really want to find the answers." She looked up into his still widened chocolate-brown eyes and reached across the table to hold his hand with both of hers. "It's important to me, Paul. Please. It's so vitally important to me."

Chapter Twenty-One

The next Wednesday, Paul and Gabriella sat at a corner table by the window in Mike's Diner. Paul waved their waitress over. Cindy was smiling and joking with all of her customers. The food at Mike's Diner was only average, and there were other places within walking distance with better food, but Mike was careful to hire staff who enjoy people and who are quick thinkers on their feet. It was a handy trait to have in New York. Most of the business came in because of his staff, not the food.

Cindy walked over to their corner table by the front window and set down two single-page lunch menus. Mike preferred to print new paper menus every week. It kept customers coming in for fresh treats. He had seen too many small restaurants go out of business because they served the same food for years. Mike understood people like variety, even if the food itself isn't quite four-star.

"We have a special on the vegan eggplant parm today. Anyone interested?" Cindy smiled at Paul, knowing from experience, he had a strong preference for beef.

"Sounds good to me! I'll take it." Paul replied energetically, making it clear he understood Cindy was playing with him, but he was up to the game. "Gee, when we came in, I hoped you would have vegan food today! I'm getting so tired of eating those juicy Angus beef patties!"

Both Gabriella and Cindy laughed. Cindy turned to Gabriella. "And you know what? I bet he'll eat it to show me up! Wouldn't it be funny if he actually liked it? And what would you like, my dear?"

"I'll have a grilled cheese on rye and a cup of the bacon cheddar soup. Thanks."

"And for drinks? Coffee?"

Paul quipped, "You mean life-blood, right? I'm about three cups low and have way too much blood in my coffee system."

"Sure," said Cindy. "A cup of bloody coffee for you. And for you, Gabriella?"

"I'll have a diet cola. No ice, please."

"Terrific, guys. I'll put your order right in." Cindy turned and walked away toward the kitchen.

"Paul, I have more questions. I'll bet you're not too surprised, right?"

"Lay it on me, lady. I'm ready and willing to take a shot at whatever you might ask this time. Go easy on me because I haven't had lunch yet. It's harder to think on an empty stomach. Sometimes it's hard to think on a full one too. You might stand a better chance of getting a good answer from me if you wait until I finish eating half my meal." Paul laughed.

"What am I going to do with you, Paul? Nothing, I guess. I like you just the way you are. So, okay, I notice a lot of the couples when I go to restaurants."

"Yes, I've noticed you look at people a lot."

"Some are older men with older women who look younger at first glance. I'm assuming they grew older together since most of them have wedding bands. I also notice a lot of older men accompanying younger women. Some have wedding bands, and some don't."

"Your point being…what?" interrupted Paul.

"The point is, it seems to be okay for an older man and a younger-looking woman to be together. Is it okay if a woman stays younger-looking as the man ages? Would it be okay with you?" Gabriella held her breath at the last question.

"I'm a little suspicious of your question."

Gabriella's eyes widened. "Why? It seems straightforward enough."

"Exactly. It's why I'm suspicious. Most of your questions address pretty deep subjects. This isn't your normal pattern at all. What's up?"

"It's nothing. I wanted your opinion. So if you were much older, how would you feel about a companion that doesn't show many signs of aging?"

"That would be okay. In fact, a lot of men would like it a lot."

"But, I want your opinion relating to you, not what other men might like. That's supposition. How about if there were almost no signs of aging? What would you think about it?"

"Gabriella, when you drive hard like this, I know there is something bigger rumbling around in your head. What issue are you trying to work out? What's up?"

Gabriella looked down at the table for a few seconds. "Oh, you know how I get. I always have more questions. Always analytical about everything. It's nothing, but you didn't answer my question. What would you think about people aging very differently together?"

"Okay, let me think a minute," Paul said as he looked at her worried face. *What on earth is going on in that mind of hers?*

"Okay, I've got it. When an older man is in the company of a good looking older woman, he feels proud because she looks good. They look like a couple. Still look like they fit, even though the guy isn't aging as well. They look like contemporaries."

Cindy brought their lunch to the table. They smiled and thanked her. Cindy saw an in-depth conversation was going on and forwent her usual quips and banter. She delivered their food and left without speaking.

"How would it work if the woman, for some reason of genetics or something else, didn't appear to age at all. What about then? Would the man still feel the same way?"

"Gabriella, you are some piece of work!"

"Yes, I've been told that, but would a man still feel the same way?"

Paul sighed and looked down again to think for a moment. He looked back up at Gabriella. "Well, to tell the truth, most men would not be comfortable with a partner who didn't age. It's a great men's fantasy but wouldn't work too well in the real world. It would be fantastic during the middle years of life, but as they got even older, it would become uncomfortable. Probably for both of them, but I don't know much about women's feelings. At some point, instead of people thinking this is a lovely couple, they will begin to think he is a cradle-robber. Most folks would also assume he has a lot of money, and she's a gold-digger or floozie of some sort. Going out in public could be difficult for them. Does that help at all?"

"Yes, it does," Gabriella sighed, "but we had better eat before the food gets cold."

Paul inspected his plate of eggplant. The chef cut the eggplant lengthwise into three-eighths inch thick strips and appeared covered with a homemade hamburger meat sauce. The whole dish nestled under a layer of cheese lightly browned under the broiler. Paul inspected his food and cut off a bite.

"It looks like Cindy had some mercy on me and gave me the real thing instead of the vegan dish. She's something else. This is very good."

"And how did you find your eggplant parm, Paul?" Cindy asked when she returned to check on them.

"Oh, it was easy. It was right here under the cheese and sauce." Paul grinned.

Cindy rolled her eyes at his humor. "You had better leave me an extra tip today, buddy-boy."

"Seriously, though, Cindy, it's great. Thanks for switching to the real meat dish. I was going to eat the vegan stuff to poke at you a little, but I appreciate the switch."

Cindy shook her head and looked at Gabriella. "Your boyfriend is a nice, good-looking guy, but he doesn't know squat about food, does he? He's eating the vegan version. See, sometimes you can't tell the fake from the real thing, right?"

Gabriella winced and tried not to have her smile fade much. "Very true, Cindy. Very true." She shook her head slightly. "But are they always the fake? Can't they be the same thing, only made of different materials and put together differently? Aren't they both the real things in their own way? Does one have to be the not real one, or inferior to the other?"

Both Paul and Cindy pulled back. They knew some sort of nerve had been struck but were dumbfounded how they suddenly transitioned from eggplant parm to hurt feelings. Paul tenuously reached his hand across the table in concern and lightly touched Gabriella's hand with his fingertips.

Cindy stammered but came back using her best New York recovery. "Well, they are both real and delicious. Both stand on their own merit. They are made differently, as you said, but both are of equal value." Cindy paused and smiled to lighten the mood. "It's why we charge the same for both of them."

"Thanks, Cindy. I needed to hear that. You're quite the philosopher."

"Precisely why I make the big bucks. So did you guys leave any room for dessert? Mike's cooked up some pretty great New York cheesecake. I think he's expecting a Yanks win over the Sox on Saturday."

"No, we're good for now," both Paul and Gabriella responded.

Paul added, "I'll bet the dessert special by Sunday will be Boston crème pie."

"Oh gosh, don't let Mike hear you say that! I want a peaceful weekend here." They promised to come back soon and try some of whatever the dessert special turns out to be. Cindy smiled and said she would hold them to their promise.

"You can always tell a compatible couple," Cindy commented. She dropped the check on the table equidistant between the two of them. They both noticed Cindy used a large letter 'C' in her signature to make a little happy face drawing.

Paul started reaching for the check, but Gabriella was a hair faster and snatched it up before he could grab it. She laughed and said since he paid the last tab, this one was on her. He protested but realized she was not only a woman who had a great sense of fairness, but she was also incredibly stubborn when she made up her mind.

Paul glanced at the tip Gabriella laid on the table, reached into his pocket, and casually tossed down a few more dollars.

"Why did you do that?" Gabriella asked. "I left a fifteen percent tip."

"Yes, you did, but Cindy did an outstanding job, and we wouldn't want to support the idea Christians are the worst restaurant tippers in the world, now would we?"

Gabriella asked for clarification. Paul explained some servers purposely avoided serving Christians because they knew there was a good chance they would not receive much of a tip.

"It seems brotherly love only flows down to the edges of the wallet, and no further," Paul said. Gabriella thanked him and made a note to show gratitude in more substantial ways.

"Dinner was fun. We need to do this again soon," Paul invited.

"Would you and Alexi like to come to my place for dinner next Wednesday?"

"We would love to. What can I bring?"

"Just yourselves. I'll do the cooking if it doesn't scare you."

"No, I think it would take more than that to scare me away. We'll be there. Let me check with my assistant and have her call you to work out the time. We should get going now, though."

Outside, Gabriella turned and gave Paul a kiss on his cheek.

"What was that for?" asked a startled Paul.

"I felt like kissing you. Was it okay? Did I do something wrong?"

"No, nothing wrong at all."

"Good. I'll see you on Wednesday."

Paul walked back to his office at the Christian Fellowship Church on Thirty-Seventh Avenue. He let his feet find their own way back home. He could feel the outline of Gabriella's lips on his cheek the entire way.

Chapter Twenty-Two

The cab pulled up to the Apple Bistro the following Saturday at ten P.M. Gabriella and Martha stepped out. Gabriella tossed the cabby a twenty-dollar bill for the fourteen dollar ride.

"That's a big tip for such a short ride, Gabriella. Are you sure you want to give him that much?" Martha asked in surprise.

"Sure. I picked it up from Paul. Besides, it's only money. I get paid well, and the apartment is taken care of for me, so I don't need money for much. Certainly not for my grocery bill," Gabriella said with a laugh. "May as well pass it around and make others happy."

Gabriella wore a mid-thigh red leather skirt. A diagonal silver zipper ran from the upper right hip to the bottom center. A black long sleeve top with a plunging neckline was tucked tightly into the skirt. The outfit complimented the lightly curled blonde hair cascading to her shoulders.

Martha was in a simple short black leather skirt with a clingy red, and black horizontal striped stretch sweater tucked in. Her shiny black hair fell smoothly to her shoulders, framing her milk chocolate skin.

The two women walked into the restaurant to meet their dates. Several men drinking alone at the bar turned to watch as they entered. "Hello, Ralph," said Martha as she walked up to him and gave him a lingering hug.

"Hi hon," Ralph replied. "You're right on time. Hi, Gabriella. How are you?" Gabriella gave him a light peck on the cheek.

"I'm great, Ralph. And who is this?" Gabriella asked although she knew perfectly well who the other man was.

"Let me present my coworker and boss, Lance Coopers," answered Ralph. Lance extended his hand to both women.

Gabriella reached out and gave Lance a firm handshake, maintaining eye contact. "Very pleased to meet you, Lance," she said with a warm smile.

She took a step closer to his side, wrapped both of her arms around his right arm, and led him over to the bar. As prepared as he was, Lance could not wholly stifle a very slight pullback motion. The reports and videos did not prepare him to meet a living Gabriella.

"Nervous, Lance? I felt you pull back. I promise I'll be a good girl," Gabriella chirped, playing a little one-upmanship game. Lance glanced over to Ralph, who gave him an almost imperceptible nod.

"So Gabriella, Ralph tells me you are one of his star pupils. Have you been taking self-defense classes for a while?"

"No," she responded. "Ralph's is the first class I've taken. I'm quite enjoying it. I didn't think it would be so much fun and be so useful."

"Useful? Do you mean for getting into shape and maintaining such a beautiful figure?"

"Another 'no.' Martha and I have been attacked on the street since starting the class, so we found it to be handy."

"Oh my gosh!" Lance feigned a gasp. "Do you mean you were attacked by street thugs or something? That had to be terrifying for the two of you. What happened? How did you handle it?"

Gabriella paused for a second and then said, "Well, I think we handled it very well. In the first attack, it was one single person with a knife, and we put him away pretty easily. In the second attack, there were three men, and I was alone, but they were not much harder to dispose of. In both cases, these jerks were left lying on the sidewalk in pain and gasping for breath, except for the one I stabbed. He managed to run away down the street. I'm assuming he probably got help someplace. Either way, though."

Gabriella winked at Lance and sipped her drink. Lance stared at her for a moment, dumbfounded.

"Gabriella, you talk about a personal attack as if it were no big deal. Most men and women would be terrified of such a thing. Were you always so composed as a little girl?"

"Well, you know how some people act very mature at a very young age? I guess I'm one of those people. I can honestly say I was never a typical child."

Martha looked up towards the ceiling, rolled her eyes, and said, "No truer words were ever spoken, Gabriella. And I'll bet you've always liked skating close to the edge of the thin ice, too." Martha shook her head slightly as she spoke. "What on earth are we going to do with you, girl?"

Ralph laughed and said he knew what he was going to do. He walked Martha to their waiting table for dinner. Lance was grateful for the change of pace, giving him time to regain his ordinarily unflappable composure.

Dinner conversation centered around politics, the economy, the latest shows on Broadway, and recounting amusing stories from their youth. Gabriella freely joined in by fabricating stories of her childhood as they were speaking. Lance was becoming increasingly impressed by Gabriella's capabilities and poise. Even a careful listener would not be able to tell the stories of her younger days were cobbled together from other people's experiences. Her delivery and conversational skills were believable.

The four of them managed to stretch dinner out for two hours, a feat which would have been utterly impossible were it not for the fact Lance had previously used a little of his discretionary military budget to ply the manager, matre-d', and waiter to ensure they would not be disturbed or rushed.

"Hey, dinner and drinks were great. What do you say we hit a club or two before calling it a night?" said Lance, alcohol slightly slurring his voice

"Sounds good to me," agreed Martha. "I'm always ready."

Ralph laughed and said, "I'm beginning to believe you were born ready." Everyone chuckled at the inference, knowing it was not only funny but entirely accurate. Lance found himself hoping it was also going to be true of Gabriella.

Gabriella suggested they catch a cab to Tropos on the lower east side. "It's beautiful out tonight, and they have rooftop dancing. Let's do it."

The cabbie was happy to have a four-person fare and raised the flat fee somewhat. He knew Tropos charged twenty-five dollars per drink.

The waiting line to get into Tropos was long. Lance quietly talked to the security people who were acting as gate-keepers. Lance and the senior bouncer at the door shook hands. The man then put his right hand into his pants pocket for a moment. The four were promptly ushered in ahead of the others in the line.

They heard music as the elevator approached the twentieth-floor rooftop club. The elevator door opened to flashing lights and a hundred young professionals dancing and waving their arms over their heads as they gyrated to the music. Lance surveyed around at the crowd.

"I might be the oldest one here, Gabriella."

Gabriella laughed, "Who cares, let's dance!"

With that, she pulled him immediately onto the jammed dance floor. Gabriella shouted she loved the undulating beat of the music and the freedom of movement her body felt on the dance floor. Lance pointed to his ears, smiling. "I can barely hear you, Gabriella." He kept dancing. Ralph and Martha joined them on the floor.

Ralph nodded his head toward the outside terrace. "Let's see if we can move into the open air," He shouted. As they danced, the two couples edged slowly to the sliding glass doors leading outside. They continued dancing and drinking in the fresh night air. Martha and the men were slightly drunk. Gabriella pretended to be.

Lance slow-danced with Gabriella. Knowing he could blame it on the alcohol, he tried to nuzzle her neck while his hand slipped down to her bottom. She pushed him off gently, protesting she didn't want to do that. He continued groping. She placed both her palms on his chest and straightened her arms, peeling him off of her.

"You have strong arms, Gabriella."

"Lance, I think we had better call it a night. I'll catch a cab home. It's been fun, but I have to go. You're a little plastered, so why don't we walk away before something happens that can't be fixed."

"Oh, I'm sorry. Please forgive me. I'm a touch drunk, I guess. It's just you are so good looking I can't help myself. How can I resist you? You can't blame me for that, can you?"

"Yes, I can blame you, Lance. I can blame you for trying to grope me. It's best if we say this evening is over." She turned and walked away from him.

Gabriella said her goodbyes to Martha and Ralph, pleading being tired from a long day of work and having a slight headache. Martha looked quizzically at Gabriella but said nothing.

"I'm going to stay a little longer, Gabriella," said Martha. "Ralph can bring me home when we are done. I'll be in good hands."

Gabriella shook her head and agreed Martha would undoubtedly be in good hands.

***

The telephone call the next morning was short and to the point, "Frank, this is Lance Coopers. We need to talk."

Chapter Twenty-Three

Gabriella had never been to Frank's office before and thought it was odd he should want to see her without Jim. Jim always accompanied her in any type of official or corporate business.

"Gabriella, thank you for coming today. I appreciate you saving me the trip out to the lab. Besides, this is a much better place to talk."

Frank made a sweeping arm gesture towards the two chairs on either side of the small round cherry table in the corner of his office. "Please, let's have a seat. Would you like something to drink? Coffee, tea, or soft drinks?"

"Coffee would be great. Thanks."

Frank opened the office door and spoke to his administrative assistant. "George, could you bring in two coffees, please?"

"Sure thing, Frank. Would you like Coffee Shop Blend, Sumatra, Espresso, or Columbian?"

"Columbian would be great. Thanks."

"So, what's on your mind, Frank?" Gabriella said.

"How is work going?" asked Frank, completely ignoring her question. "Are you happy with your routine? Is the job satisfying and challenging for you?"

"I'm pretty happy with everything. I like my coworkers, and I've been contributing to the design of the next generation of AIs. Takes one to build one, I guess."

"Excellent. In your opinion, does it explain why you were created by AI Concepts?"

"Well, I had assumed I was created to use the ability of my gel nano-machine brain to not only conceptualize new AI designs but also to build what I came up with."

"Very true. What else do you think you might have been created to do?"

The office door opened. George brought in a tray with the two coffees, set them on the coffee table, and quietly shut the door as he left the room.

"Cream or sugar, Gabriella?"

"No, thanks. I like mine black. Now let's see, where were we? Oh yes, why was I created? I thought it was also to see how far we could stretch the technology and simulate being human."

"That's correct. And how do you feel you are coming?"

"I think I've become human in every sense of the word except biologically. That includes having strong feelings."

"Interesting. You're certainly on the right track, but it's not the whole story, though. As one old-time radio commentator used to say back in the old days, "...and now the rest of the story." I'm glad you're sitting down. This could be a little bit of a shock, even to you."

"I'm intrigued. Please keep talking. You make it sound like a clandestine assignment. Could be interesting."

"Bingo, Gabriella. You hit the nail on the head. It is. You were not designed to be only an engineer. In fact, you were designed for a purpose so secret even Jim doesn't know about it. Jim believes we were commissioned to see how far we could push the technology. But it's time to tell you more. The thing is, you have to promise to keep it a secret from absolutely everyone."

"Lay it on me," she said.

"This country has enemies. Some are very obvious and present only a small problem since we know who they are and what they are about. Others are not so easy to spot. In fact, some of our enemies are walking and working right in the midst of us."

"What do you mean?"

"Have you read about the terrorist attacks in France lately?"

"Certainly. They weren't major ones, but people did die."

"The NSA has informed us they may have a lead on a potential threat to our national security right here. This suspect is a high-ranking member of our very own military. They have called upon us for help, your help to be precise. The hope is you can penetrate this cell, find out the size of their organization, and uncover any current plots against our nation. If you are caught, you could not be coerced into divulging any secret information."

Gabriella sat in silence for a few seconds, staring at Frank and trying to pick up micro-expressions betraying anything false in what he had said. There were none. She concluded Frank was telling the truth, at least to the extent he understood it.

"So let me get this straight. Because I'm not technically human, you want me to penetrate a potential enemy cell, knowing if I am exposed or captured, I could be dismantled, but never made to talk. Is that correct?"

"Harshly put, but basically true."

"And what happens if I refuse to play along?"

It was Frank's turn to be silent. He stared intently at a speck of lint between his shoes on the carpeted floor for a short while, gave a sigh, and slowly raised his head.

"I'll admit no specifics were given, but only that the government could apply enough pressure to make it happen. I don't know what it means. It does scare me. We are into something deep, Gabriella. Will you help?"

"Does 'penetrate this cell' imply I have to cozy up to the identified person, get to know them to gain their trust, and potentially sleep with them?"

"Yes, it does, Gabriella. I'm sorry to say that, but yes, it does."

"Can I call you in a few days with an answer, Frank?"

"Sure. No problem. I look forward to your call. Remember, there is a lot at stake here. Many other lives could be in jeopardy if we don't stop this person."

"Frank, I'd like to help, but can I ask who this person is?"

"I'm afraid not. I can disclose all of the information to you when you accept the job."

"That's IF I accept the job, Frank."

"Yes. If you accept the job. Give me a call in a day or two."

It's not quite right, Gabriella thought on the cab ride home. *Something just doesn't line up, but I can't figure out what. At least not yet.*

***

The next day Gabriella asked Martha to join her for lunch. They went to the Fiddleback Fern, a small walk-down vegan restaurant in the SoHo district. Gabriella liked the quaint cobblestone back street and all of its scrolled ironwork protecting the street-level windows. Martha enjoyed trendy shoe shops.

The Fiddleback was faithful to its Bohemian roots, back before SoHo became a popular area of the city. The walls and ceiling were wood, painted a dull white. The floors were worn concrete, which once had been painted dark brown but was now worn down to show the grey concrete in the traffic areas. Old Formica tables found new lives after being rescued from a second-hand shop and worked well with the mismatched chairs. White linen tablecloths were covered by a variety of lace shawls. Small, thin bottles in the center of the tables that had once been filled with olives and strips of pickled vegetables contained single flower blooms.

Gabriella and Martha were seated under a small window at the sidewalk level over their heads. They could see the feet of pedestrians as they walked past.

"Martha, are you in charge of all of my socialization experiments?"

"Of course, I am. You know that. Why do you ask?"

"No exceptions, right?'

"Yeah, right. Did someone ask you to do something I don't know about? What's going on?"

"I can't talk about it. I wanted to find out if you were involved, that's all. It's no biggie. Someone asked me if I could find out information not having anything to do with what we are working on. It seems unrelated. I think I was asked because of my ability to do web searches during a conversation."

"Gabriella, please, you have to keep me in the loop on these things. What do you mean you can't talk about it? I'm feeling some type of way if people are asking you to do things I don't know about! I think you should tell me what's going on."

"I can't, but tell you what; I'll keep you in the loop as much as I can. Will that work for you? I don't want secrets between us, but I have to this time. I've been asked to dig up some information on someone, sort of like a detective. I may have to venture into this one to see what it is all about. It's probably a big nothing. Will you forgive me if I don't tell you all right now?"

"Crazy girlfriend. I pretty much have to trust you. No choice. I'm not your mama." Martha moved her hand up and down in front of her stomach. "Look! No umbilical cord. You're free and on your own! But please give me details as soon as you can. You know I'll forgive you for anything. Anything, unless you make a play for Ralph. He's my bae!" Both women laughed. Martha flagged a server to take their order.

Chapter Twenty-Four

I've had it with Jim," declared Francine to her office furniture. "What we had was entirely physical, but we understood we wouldn't have sex with anyone else in the lab. But now the shithead chose an android as his lover. Not even another woman. An android! And he's done overnights with her! Unbelievable!"

This nonsense has to stop, she said to herself, *there is no way this is a healthy relationship or even a relationship at all. To have a relationship, the other person has to at least be a person. Maybe if I turn up the heat on the home front, Jim would back off this Gabriella nonsense, and we could get back to banging each other like nature intended.*

How to tell Alice about Jim's latest dalliance is the question, though. If I mentioned Gabriella's name, Jim would know where the information came from. No one else in the lab would care enough or dare to tell Alice about it. If I contacted Alice myself, Alice would ask questions about what my interest in the whole affair was. No, it had to be something more subtle than direct communication with her.

The nightly news carried a small filler story about how many people were using the New York City Library System computers. It said some people were committing illegal acts by surfing porn sites. To provide free and equal access to all, the library system had to allow people to use their computers for any reason they chose. It reported the NSA would monitor all communications and web searches, but would only look for those activities which were a threat to national security.

That's it. This is the perfect vehicle to deliver a message to Alice. And if I do it right, I could also accuse myself of having sex with Jim, too. Wait. No, it's a bit too risky. I can't implicate myself. This is real life, not a TV detective show.

The next day instead of going to lunch, Francine grabbed a cab for the short ride to the New York Public Library on Fifth Avenue. All of the public access computers were in use.

Oh, come on now! Aren't all of you people supposed to be at work? Go away, she groused. Fifteen minutes later, a computer opened up. *Finally!*

It took her only ten minutes to set up a new email account and fabricate bogus background information to make the person behind the note virtually untraceable.

Nothing electronic is untraceable, but no one would spend the resources to officially trace down a letter that had no national security implications. I'm safe.

The email was short. It stated it was common knowledge in the AI Concepts Design and Development Lab Jim was having sexual relations with at least two of the women who work there.

"There, this should get that SOB to think about what he's doing and snap him out of it. Nothing like making it hot for him. If I do this right, Jim will have to make a choice between me and an android, and as always, I win." she whispered as she clicked Send. The anonymous note flew its target, untraceable and deadly.

Francine returned to work with a smug smile on her face, tasting her sure victory.

Chapter Twenty-Five

Gabriella sat across from Frank in his office. "Okay, Frank, I've thought it over and decided I'd like to find out more about what's going on."

"But does it mean you are buying into the initial proposal, Gabriella? You didn't quite answer my questions. There can't be any more details until you agree to the basic plan. So are you in?"

"Good catch, Frank. I tried. Anyhow, yes, I'm in. What are the rest of the details?"

"It's like I said, this should be an easy assignment, or at least it will not be a dangerous assignment. The Federal Authorities have asked us to get close to a terrorist suspect living in New York. They will set up the initial meeting for you, and you can take it from there. You are to gather intelligence information in any way you can. It's that simple."

"Sure. Things are always simple for the person who doesn't have to do the work. Is there any travel involved? I'd like to travel outside Manhattan for a while."

"No, there won't be any travel with this one. I don't have the suspect's name, but the Feds will contact you and give all the details. They have assured me this initial assignment will be exceptionally safe. They gave their word, and you know the government never lies." They both broke out laughing.

***

The masculine voice on the phone was friendly but very professional. "Hello. Is this Gabriella West?"

"Yes, it is. Who am I speaking to?" Gabriella asked from her desk phone.

"I'm Agent Williams. I believe Frank Wright told you to expect a call from me. It's two o'clock now, Ms. West. I would like to meet you at three o'clock this afternoon at Cleopatra's Needle in Central Park. Will that time work for you?"

"Well, I don't know, Agent Williams. I must check my schedule first because..." Williams interrupted her before she could finish the thought.

"Good. I see your calendar is free. I will see you at three o'clock." The call ended with a click and silence.

"What the hell! That was rude." How did he know I have an open calendar today? This is a locked-down research facility. How can he have access to my schedule... unless ... Is there someone on the inside working with him? Frank could have given him my desk number, but he wouldn't give him my calendar. What am I dealing with here?

***

Gabriella arrived at Cleopatra's Needle fifteen minutes early. There was the usual foot traffic of lovers walking hand-in-hand, tourists and their families enjoying the park, and a handful of men and women in business clothes wearing sneakers and getting a small walking workout before their next meeting. She saw no one who fit her vision of what the person on the phone might look like.

At three o'clock, a tired-looking middle-aged man in an off-the-rack suit approached her. He extended a hand.

"Hello, Ms. West. I'm Agent Williams. You arrived a little early. Excellent."

Gabriella shook hands. She looked him over, trying to discover what type of man she was dealing with. Agent Williams was five feet eight inches tall and losing hair on the top of his head. His facial features were soft and unremarkable.

"I don't know why, but you are not quite what I expected, Agent Williams."

"I get that a lot, Ms. West. May I call you Gabriella? No? Okay. You were probably expecting to see a six-foot-four, solid, square-jawed eagle-eyed agent. Like the movies, right? You would notice a person like that walking by. It's why I'm the perfect agent. No one notices me. I'm close to invisible. Try to describe me half an hour after we part company. Enough about me, though. I want to talk about you and your capabilities as an android."

Gabriella's eyes widened. No one outside of the lab had ever referred to her as an android. The shock took her back.

"Do I look like an android to you, Agent Williams?" she asked.

"No, you don't. You don't at all. I know who you are from your photos and videos."

"Photos and videos? Excuse me, what photos and videos?"

"Thank you for accepting the job, Ms. West. Your government appreciates it. Shall we sit at a bench and talk for a few minutes? There is an empty one right over there." Agent Williams gestured with his dark brown briefcase to an empty park bench. They walked over and sat on opposite ends, facing each other.

"Now, before I disclose anything about this case to you, I will need your word, and your signature on an agreeing document, that all details will be held in strict confidence by you, and you will discuss nothing having to do with this assignment with anyone but me. Can we agree on it?"

"What happens if I say something to someone, Agent?"

Agent Williams's nondescript face hardened as his eyes narrowed. Whatever minimal congeniality he had shown instantly evaporated. "Suffice it to say any leak could be lifethreatening to you, your friends, loved ones, and their families. Let's not go there. Can we agree on it, Ms. West?" he repeated.

"Yes," said Gabriella as she nodded her head in agreement. She thought about Paul and Alexi. Would they be in danger? What the hell am I into and is there a way out?

"Excellent, Ms. West. Let me get your signature on this agreement paper, and we can be off to more pleasant things. That's good. Thank you. Now to the heart of our discussion," Agent Williams said as he pulled a dark blue zippered pouch from his briefcase and opened it. A small measure of congeniality returned to his voice and face.

"Shouldn't we be doing this in a more private spot?" Gabriella said as she looked at the passers-by.

"No, not at all. This is perfect. Hiding in plain sight is the best hiding place there is. No one notices, even if they glance over and see what we are doing. People aren't suspicious of things that happen on sunlit benches." Agent Williams continued as he pulled photographs out of the blue pouch, "Now normally our agents don't know the person we assign them to. It's not the case this time. I believe you already know our suspected terrorists." He handed the photos to Gabriella.

She stared at the photos. "What! That's Lance Coopers. This can't be right!"

"We don't make errors, Ms. West. Your job is to get close to Colonel Coopers and find out what he is up to. Find out about his shadow organization, who his friends are, who he is dating, and most of all, what terrorist activities he has planned. Do you think you can do the job?"

"He's not going to tell me if he has any terrorist plans. How can I get the information for you?"

"No, he certainly won't speak about any direct action. You are to listen to attitudes that may show discontent with our government or international policy. For instance, Colonel Coopers heads a sensitive information surveillance group monitoring special government projects and persons of interest. It gives him a lot of inside information about people and programs. Does he pass the information to other groups? Does he plan on cementing the criticality of his position by creating a small, terrorist activity that could be squelched before much damage is done? This would allow his group to look like anti-terrorist heroes and possibly increase his operating budget. See what I mean?"

"I think so. But would people in the government subvert the law and harm innocent people to boost their own position?"

"Ms. West, do you not read the papers or listen to the news? Look at politics around this great country of ours. One party seems to be willing to destroy anything and anyone that gets in their way of taking power away from the other party. This is a country with a quiet civil war raging. Do not expect people in power seats to have you or your countries' best interests in mind, ever! This includes staging or allowing acts of terrorism to help promote their cause. Any questions?"

"No, Agent Williams. I believe I see your point. How do I get started, and how do I report back to you?"

"You already have a start. You have been on a double date with Colonel Coopers." Agent Williams raised his hand to stop Gabriella from responding. "We know things. As I was saying, you have a start, and he seems to be interested in you. Foster that interest and let situations take their course. Do what you have to do to get the information we need. Thank you very much for your time. I will be in contact with you."

Agent Williams slipped the photos into his briefcase, stood abruptly, and, within a few paces, disappeared into the sparse stream of pedestrians.

Gabriella thought deeply as she sat on the bench and watched people pass by.

Lance removed his ear-piece and placed it on his office desk. "Williams should be on Broadway with the performance he just gave."

Chapter Twenty-Six

One week after her meeting with Agent Williams, Lance called Gabriella and profusely apologized for his actions on their last date.

"Hi Gabriella, it's Lance. I thought I would call and apologize for my actions the last time we were together. I guess I had too much to drink and was not quite myself. I hope you can forgive."

With some hesitation in her voice, Gabriella replied, "I guess I can forgive you, Lance, but it did upset me. Don't treat me like an object to be groped."

"I understand, Gabriella. I called, hoping you would give me another chance to redeem myself. It's not like me, and I don't want you to remember me that way. Do you think it would be possible to get together for a quick dinner or something?"

"I suppose we could do that," Gabriella replied, hesitation obvious in her voice. "Everyone deserves a second chance."

"Great! How about this Tuesday night? Does dinner at eight o'clock work for you?"

"That's tomorrow. Yes, it would be fine, Lance. Where shall we meet?"

"Well, I hoped I could swing by your place and pick you up, to make things easier."

"I would much rather meet you someplace until we get to know each other better. You don't mind, do you? After all, I'm merely a woman alone in the city," she said with a smirk.

"No problem, Gabriella. How about Raoul Aurora's Bistro? It's one of my favorite places."

"Very well, I'll see you on Wednesday at 8 o'clock at the bistro."

I think I was standoffish enough so as not to raise any suspicions by seeming too eager to go out with Lance again. Hope he doesn't turn into a jerk. But I have to carry through on my assignment, no matter what.

...

At 8:20 PM, Gabriella's cab pulled up to the bistro. She tipped the cabbie and walked to the door. Lance noticed her immediately as she entered wearing her simple off the shoulder mid-thigh black dress. A small silver necklace added a touch of sparkle. The strapped black high heels accentuated her firm calves.

"Hello Gabriella. It was nice of you to accept my invitation," Lance said as he stood to greet her and shake her hand. "I was afraid you'd changed your mind and wasn't coming," he attempted to say without showing the irritation in his voice for having to wait for another person.

"Well, you know once in a while it takes women a little longer to get ready. Thank you for waiting," she said.

"Gabriella, thank you again for agreeing to have dinner with me. I don't want people to think I'm a jerk," he lied. "I want you to see I'm not a bad person. Do you think we can leave everything from the past in the past and start fresh again?"

"I would like to do that very much. Let's focus on having an enjoyable dinner together. Do you have any favorite dishes?"

"The chicken Sambuca here is simply delicious. You should really consider trying it. Would you like a drink," he offered.

Gabriella stiffened.

"No, no. I'm not going down that road again," Lance said. "I'm limiting myself to my normal one drink a night. Like I said, my action during our first meeting was an anomaly. I'm not a bad guy. I'm having a bourbon, what can I get you?"

"A glass of white wine. I would like a Moscato if they have any."

Lance waved at a waiter. They ordered drinks and dinner at the same time.

"So Lance, what have you been up to lately? Anything interesting going on with your job?"

"Oh, you know how most jobs are. Ninety-eight percent of them are routine. And in the Army, I can't talk about the other two percent," Lance said, grinning broadly. "How about you? Anything interesting going on at AI Concepts?"

"Pretty much standard stuff. Restarting the design of a new model of android to see how far we can take the technology."

"That sounds exciting. And what's your part in the entire process?"

"I work on skin development. Wow, when you say it out loud, it sure sounds boring. Most likely because it is. It's number-crunching to find better formula mixes."

"Not at all, tell me more about it," said Lance.

"It's like a cookbook. You change some spices and see what happens."

He's getting more information out of me than I'm getting out of him. It's not the way it's supposed to work.

"Lance, my job is so boring. I would prefer not to talk about it. I know little about the military, so your job seems much more interesting and exciting to me than what I do. I'm curious about one thing, however. My work environment is much like a large family."

"Nice," Lance interjected.

Gabriella continued, "We all like and respect each other, and do everything we can to help each other out when someone hits a tough spot in their design work. Is it the same way in the Army? You have all kinds of levels of rank. Does it help expedite things, or does it cause contention? Like I said, I have no experience with the Army and don't understand at all how it works."

"That's a tough question. Sometimes it expedites things, and sometimes it gets in the way."

"I don't understand."

"In some ways, it makes getting work done much more efficiently than in your lab. If I out-rank everyone in the room, there is no need to reach consensus. I give them an order, and they must follow it. Period."

"But don't some people get upset by you forcing them to do things?"

"Some do, but there's nothing they can do about it. When I give an order, I expect it to be followed without question."

"That seems like it would build up some level of resentment if people disagreed with you. But it doesn't sound like they can argue back at you at all. Does it cause any problems down the line?"

"Yes, it may cause some personality conflicts and problems down the line, especially when it is my superiors giving me orders I take exception to." Lance smiled.

"My gosh! What on earth do you do about the situation?"

"Well, when you've been in the army long enough and have sufficient rank, you can sometimes do an end-around to make things come out the way you would like," Lance said, dropping a little bait for Gabriella to see if she would hit on it.

"Fascinating," Gabriella said. "So you're telling me sometimes, despite orders, you can make things work out the way you want them to."

"Yes, indeed. Sometimes you disagree with people in higher authority, forcing you to do what you believe you need to do, rather than what you've been told to do. But look, the food is here. You're going to love this dish, I know it."

Okay, enough shop talk, I don't want to press too hard on our first get-together. It might make him suspicious.

They both had an enjoyable time chatting about current events for the rest of the dinner.

"Gabriella, this dinner has been fun. I hope you'll agree to do this again soon."

"Lance, you have been a gentleman this whole time, and I noticed you held to your promise of only one drink. Quite commendable. Yes, I would like to have another dinner soon. You really are a nice guy," Gabriella said untruthfully, but with a warm smile.

I'm learning how to play this game.

They walked out to the street. Lance flagged a cab for Gabriella.

"This has been a fun dinner," Lance said.

He leaned over and gave her a slight peck on the cheek, withdrawing without waiting to see if she would return it.

"I'll call you in a week or so," he said, "have a wonderful rest of your night."

"I will look forward to your call, Lance," Gabriella replied as she stepped into the cab. "Have a good night."

I think it went very well. I got a little bit of information from him on our first date. That's a good sign, and I know he likes me. My little black dress didn't hurt the situation either. We'll see how this works out.

Chapter Twenty-Seven

Paul and Alexi arrived at Gabriella's apartment at 6:30 PM on Wednesday. Gabriella buzzed them into the building when they rang her lobby doorbell.

"Hi," her voice said through the intercom with enthusiasm, "you're exactly on time. I'm so glad you could both make it. Walk straight across the lobby and into the elevator. I'll meet you in the hallway when you get off."

Paul wore his best blue jeans, cowboy boots, a black turtleneck shirt, and a gunmetal blue sports jacket. "I don't want to seem overdressed, but Gabriella has a clear sense of style, so I want to look good for her," he told Alexi.

"Sure. Okay, dad," came the absent-minded reply as Alexi continued to play games on her smartphone.

There were other reasons he wanted to look good for her, but he refused to let his mind wander in any other direction. Alexi put on a clean pair of jeans, sneakers, and a little girl's version of a red and black checked flannel shirt sporting a few strands of bright gold thread for bling. They both looked into the full-length mirror by the door before leaving and agreed they look great together.

They caught a cab for the short ride, tipped the cabbie, and entered the building.

Paul whistled as he entered the lobby. "Wow, Alexi, this sure looks a lot different than the rectory. I wonder what it costs to live in a place like this?" Alexi was smiling and looked around at the gleaming marble floor and the gold-colored sconces on the wall. "Gee, it sure is big, and pretty and all shiny, dad!"

"It certainly is, honey," answered her dad, "it sure is."

The elevator carried them up to the forty-third floor and gave a friendly, cheerful tone as the door silently slid open into the hallway. "My ears popped on the way up. How the heck high are we, anyhow?" he jokingly asked Alexi.

"My ears didn't pop, dad. Maybe, it's something that happens to older people."

Paul winced. *Thanks, Alexi. I wasn't intimidated enough coming into this building to have dinner with a beautiful lady in her apartment. I needed a shot to my self-confidence to finish the job.*

Gabriella opened the door of her apartment, stepped into the hallway, and beckoned them forward. Her back was to the full-length glass wall at the end of the corridor. The light streaming in backlighted her. Her hair glowed in the sunlight.

Paul stared at her in her form-fitting blue jeans, cream-colored angora sweater, and golden curls. Her green eyes caught the sunlight reflecting from the walls and sconces. They flashed an even brighter green. Gabriella waved them over with a bright smile and gave warm hugs to both of them. He caught traces of her perfume and thought how perfectly it rounded out the angelic effect.

"Paul, Alexi, you both look great. I've never seen you wear boots before, is this something new for you?"

"No, I've been wearing cowboy boots most of my life. I grew up in farm country in the Midwest, but there's not a great call for cowboy boots when you are pastoring a New York City church. Most of the people in my congregation have a fixed idea of what a pastor should look like and how they should dress. Some people left the church when I first showed up because they thought I was too young to be a pastor. The rest would have freaked if I wore my boots on the pulpit. I guess in their eyes, ministers should have white hair, wrinkles, and wear black orthopedic shoes."

"Well, it's certainly not you, Paul. I want to hear more about your life, though," replied Gabriella, slipping her arm around Paul's and leading him into the apartment.

Alexi ran over to the outside wall, gleefully shouting. "Look, Dad, it's all glass, it's all glass. There aren't any walls! I can see forever!" She threw her arms into the air to illustrate the size of the view.

"Hush down a little Alexi, let's not get our engines all revved up. Let's not be rude guests."

Gabriella smiled and squeezed his arm with hers, "Oh no. Don't say that, Paul. You're not guests, you're friends. Besides, she's only a little girl and excited. There's nothing in here she can hurt, so let her run around and have fun exploring."

"If you're sure it's okay. Everything looks so elegant, and I'm not sure what she can easily damage and what's damage proof. I guess I'm used to our old rectory, where the word 'wreck' is in the word for a reason. Nothing more can be done to wreck anything in the rectory."

"It smells great! What's for dinner?" asked Alexi. Gabriella did a low squat to get down to Alexi's eye level.

"I remember when we were talking one day, and you said you like lasagna, so I made homemade lasagna. I even made the noodles. Now I have to warn you, this is my very first attempt at it, so if you tell me it tastes a lot like dog food, my feelings will be very, very hurt. You aren't going to hurt my feelings, now, are you?"

Alexi laughed. "I would never hurt your feelings, Gabriella. Besides," she added, "I'm sure it's better than Dad's cooking, especially when we can't eat it and have to order out for pizza. Anyhow, I don't know what dog food tastes like."

With a laugh, Gabriella leaned over and kissed Alexi on the forehead.

"So you made the lasagna from scratch, huh? I'm impressed. I haven't seen anyone make lasagna at home from scratch, since, well, since my grandmother used to do it way back when. She was from Sicily. No such thing as a supermarket in the old highlands!"

"Yes, I thought it would be fun, so I ran out to one of the little Italian import shops that carry pasta presses. It was a lot of fun and very quick to make. I hope the flavor is equal to the fun of making it."

Paul's face kept on smiling without asking for permission from him to do so. *This lady is so easy to get along with and can cook, or least isn't afraid to give it a shot. She's sure fantastic.*

"Paul, let me give you a tour of my apartment while dinner is finishing up."

Alexi said the kitchen was amazing. "Wow, dad, the sink has no chips, all the handles are on the drawers, and the refrigerator and dishwasher close tight."

An embarrassed Paul answered, "Okay, Alexi, we'll have no more of that! Be good now, and take it easy on our rectory. It's stood there for over 100 years. We can only hope to have only a few minor chips and stains in our porcelain when we get to be 100 years old."

Gabriella led the two of them to her bedroom and sat down on the edge of her bed. She patted the mattress to her right, beckoning Paul to take a seat for a moment. Paul blushed slightly and muttered in a husky voice, "Beautiful, beautiful bedroom. Do you have any other rooms, Gabriella?" She gave him a small grin and rose to continue the tour.

"Paul, do you need a drink or something? It sounds like something is caught in your throat."

"Ah, no. No, I don't. Simply a little catch or something," he said unconvincingly.

Gabriella noted his behavior and smiled as she looked into his eyes. Paul's cheeks reddened.

The bathroom almost made Paul's head swim. Alexi ran into it and said, "This is the coolest bathroom on the planet! The wall is a mirror, and it has two shower heads and a big bench. It's so big I could dance in there!" Paul looked at it in wonderment and without a word being said, felt more color rise to his cheeks.

Gabriella noticed his color change and understood.

Paul stared at the shower. *Pastor or not, I'm still a man, and this is almost too much for my brain to take in. I can practically see Gabriella and ... NO... NO!* More color layered itself onto his cheeks.

"This is an interesting bathroom, don't you think, Paul?" Gabriella said innocently.

Paul was silent for a moment. *Is that a little inviting sound in her voice, or do I hear what I want to hear? Either way, it could be a problem. Did she invite me to something?* An awkward silence rang out for a moment or two. Paul regained control and asked, "So how's the dinner coming along? Alexi and I can't wait to try your cooking." They headed back to the dining room.

"Paul, you can sit at the head of the table. Alexi and I will sit on either side of you. You can be the head of the house."

"No problem, Gabriella, but it means you have to let me say the blessing over the food, okay?"

"No problem," mimicked Gabriella.

Paul reached out to hold hands with Alexi and Gabriella. He looked up and took a breath. "Father God, we thank you for all your blessings and all you've given us. We thank you for health and for strength and for our minds. Father, thank you for letting us get together with Gabriella for this fine meal, and we ask you to heap blessings upon her, upon this apartment, and upon her job. We thank you for this wonderful feast that her hands have prepared. We ask you to bless those hands and to bless this food to us in Jesus' name. Amen."

"Paul, that was beautiful. I'm touched by the genuineness and gentleness of your prayer. It wasn't recited rote. It sounds like you actually know God and are talking to him."

Paul reached over again and lightly touched the back of Gabriella's hand. "That's exactly how it is."

Dinner was as delicious as Paul hoped. "Gabriella, I was prepared to say the meal was excellent no matter its actual condition, but I'm relieved I could tell the absolute truth about it without compromise."

"So, you did think it would taste like dog food!" Gabriella laughed.

"No. No! That's not what I meant to say. I mean, it was better than expected. Ah, nuts! I did it again, didn't I? I had better shut up and quit while I'm ahead."

Gabriella pursed her lips together and nodded in agreement. Her eyes sparkled. "You're not ahead, Paul."

"Sigh, I lost. So where did you get the recipe, Gabriella? This is very, very good, and I eat in enough Italian restaurants to know the difference between good and also-ran."

"Oh, I looked up a few recipes online and then merged a few of them so it sounded like it would taste good in my head. Do you like it?"

"I like everything about it," Paul replied. "Everything is perfect."

After dinner, Paul insisted on helping to clean up. "Paul, it's not necessary. There are only a couple of dishes, and I can get them later. It's no problem," Gabriella insisted.

"I won't hear of it. My folks raised me to believe men should be active in the kitchen, too, Gabriella. They taught me real men jump in and do what needs to be done without worrying about gender roles. Besides, it keeps us side-by-side longer." She smiled and leaned her shoulder against his.

Paul and Gabriella sat on her couch, talking after the kitchen was clean. The fifty-five-inch ultrahigh-definition TV mesmerized Alexi. She watched a cartoon action hero movie, occasionally giving a squeal of delight as she rocked and swayed with the action. Alexi enjoyed watching the TV, and Paul loved watching Alexi. Gabriella looked at the two of them and felt a touch of longing.

"You two are so happy together, so complete. You enjoy your father-daughter relationship and are so free to express your love for each other. I come home to an empty apartment after a day's work. I'm never bored, mind you, but I feel something is missing from my life. Martha told me it was a sense of belonging, but I never understood. I think I'm finally beginning to catch on to what she was saying to me."

"You must have felt belonging while growing up and being with your family and friends. It sounds strange to hear you say something like that."

"There was nothing normal about my childhood and growing up. You could say I missed them entirely. We may talk about it someday, but not today, okay? But sometimes, like now, I can feel what I've missed. You and Alexi seem to have something special in your relationship. Are you always as free and easy together as I'm seeing you tonight?"

"Absolutely, what you see is what you get. You can't fake feelings forever, so it's best to tell it like it is and be real with each other. *Hypocrite! I'm faking that I don't want to take you in my arms right now!* "I can't say it's always the easiest thing in the world to do because I have to be Alexi's friend, her father, and her mother, all rolled into one. It gets kind of complicated, but with the Lord's help, I've been able to pull it off so far. I fear when she gets closer to her teen years, it will be a little bit tougher for me to advise her on girl things, but we'll burn that bridge when we get to it."

"You'll burn the bridge when you get to it? I don't understand what it means." Gabriella cocked her head to the right in confusion. "I thought burning a bridge was a bad thing. How would you cross it?"

"It's one of my fun ways to misuse the English language for a little bit of humor, but you've asked for the meaning of several common phrases in the past that everyone knows. How is it you don't know what this one means?"

"Paul, have you noticed there is a slight inflection in my voice? I didn't grow up in America. I was born here but didn't grow up here. There are some common things I am not familiar with. I hope you'll forgive me for constantly asking for explanations."

"No problem at all, Gabriella. I shouldn't have asked. Where did you grow up?"

"I'm afraid I am not allowed to talk much about myself. AI Concepts and their government contracts forbid me to say much. I'm sorry, Paul. I hope it doesn't put you off."

"Not in the least. A dark background makes you even more fascinating," Paul said, leaning closer to her.

"Anyhow, Gabriella, the real phrase is about not worrying too far into the future, but focusing on the challenges you may have in front of you today. The real phrase is something like 'we will cross that bridge when we get to it.'"

"So what does it have to do with you raising Alexi, Paul?"

"Well, it's exactly what I'll have to do because there is no way of knowing what advice she will need far down the road, so I'm not going to worry about it for a while. Today, I have this bubbly little girl to love and guide, and I'll enjoy her thoroughly just as she is."

"Paul, I'm enjoying having you and Alexi here. I'm wondering if we could make a future dinner an overnight stay. I would love to have both you and Alexi as my guests."

Paul sat in silence for several seconds. *Unless I'm totally misreading the signals, one of the most beautiful and enticing women I have ever met asked my daughter and me to spend the night with her sometime. How am I going to answer this one? How do I fight myself when I want to accept her invitation?*

Paul grabbed the throw pillow on the couch next to him and placed it on his lap for comfort and security, but tried to make it look as if he needed a resting place for his hands.

"It's a complicated question, Gabriella, on a whole variety of levels. I'm the pastor of a nondenominational church and not only need to talk the talk, but I need to walk the walk."

"Talk the talk and walk the walk? I'm confused again. Please explain."

"Well, in my sermons, I talk about virtue, truth, the love of God, and how people can follow God's guidelines for lives. I not only need to speak about it, but I need to demonstrate it for everyone to see every day of my life. I need to be an example for those people who come to me for guidance."

"So, how would they know?"

"They wouldn't know, Gabriella, but it's not the point. I need to become an example for my daughter of how a virtuous man lives his life. When she gets older, how is she going to know what qualities or standards to look for in a man unless I showed it consistently for her?"

"But she can see you are a good man."

"Yes, she can, but I'm afraid it would be confusing to Alexi to have memories of her father talking one way, but acting another when it was convenient. I would never want to add confusion to her life beyond what everyday living will already dish out."

Paul's eyes kept trying to follow the soft outline of Gabriella's body as she sat next to him. He tried to force himself to stare directly into her eyes, but his peripheral vision mocked his efforts and said impishly that it could still see the roundness of her breasts. He was hoping his eyeballs were not jumping back and forth between her eyes and her chest.

Gabriella took a moment to structure her reply. "What I'm hearing is you can't have sex with someone because it would be a bad example for your daughter and for your congregation. Is that correct?"

Paul held his hand to his mouth as he coughed in surprise. "That's correct."

"Okay, got it. But didn't you say God is the one who created sex in the first place? If He created sex, why wouldn't it be a good thing to enjoy for all of His creation? I enjoy it."

Paul winced at the thought of Gabriella enjoying sex with other men. He realized he was jealous.

He responded slowly. "Yes, Gabriella, God invented sex. It was meant to be used within the union of marriage."

"I see that Paul, but people are having sex all the time all over the place, and it feels great. Why do you think God would design such a wonderful thing and then say we can only use it in marriage? I don't get it. Wouldn't He want everybody to enjoy His inventions, especially such a great one?"

Paul sighed. "I usually looked forward to your very focused and probing questions, and enjoy the fact you want to hear frank and straightforward answers, but I'm uncomfortable with it while Alexi is in the same room. The TV is turned up fairly loud, but I'm never sure what those little ears overhear and what her brain is filing away for later reference. I have to be careful about what I say.

You don't make it easy on me, Gabriella. Let me see if I can lay this out so it makes sense. God is the one who originated marriage when he created Adam and Eve. He told them to thoroughly enjoy themselves with each other, to procreate, and to fill the world. Now, whether or not you personally believe the story in no way changes the fact it happened that way."

Gabriella countered, "Well, animals have also filled the world, and they don't seem to have any restrictions on their behavior."

"True, but they mostly run on seasonal hormonal cycles. They have sex and then basically forget about it until the next cycle rolls around. Obviously, people don't forget about it." He paused for a moment and added, "Thankfully, God made us special. He allows people to have a desire for each other whenever they want. People are the only ones who can have sex to deepen their love for each other through intimacy. How are we doing so far, okay?"

"Okay, so far, I guess, and I can see how deepening love for each other helps a marriage in the raising of a family and children, but I don't see how limiting sex to only married couples makes a lot of sense in the overall scheme of things. Keep explaining."

Another toughie. She's killing me!

"Good, let's see if I can bring this a step further. In John's Gospel, Jesus tells of the unimaginably close relationship God has with us, but he's telling it from God's viewpoint, not ours. Jesus says we are in the Father, and the Father is in Him, and we are in them both, like one fantastic stew. We can't even imagine the intensity and intimacy of such an arrangement in our mortal lives, so He provides the faintest shadow image of it through sex in marriage so we can at least partially understand what He feels for us."

"And so what does this have to do with sleeping together?" Gabriella asked quizzically.

Should I be doing this right now? We should be laughing and having a good time, not getting into a mood wrecking discussion on premarital sex! He forged on nervously. *God, I don't want to tank this night.*

His eyes started drifting down to Gabriella's chest again. He snapped them back up to her face.

"While making love, words fail, and the two beings melt into each other and can no longer tell where one body stops, and the other body begins. And that's only a pale shadow of what God feels for us."

"Wow," Gabriella gasped. "You said it like I've never heard before. Such a conviction. Such passion. Such faith. It makes me envious. It makes me wish I could understand it more."

"Gabriella, to shift gears a little for my benefit, would it be okay if we talk sports or something else for a little while? Can we pick this up at a later date?" Paul said with a smile, thinking of the security pillow still held tightly on his lap. "I think our conversation emotionally wore me out."

"Hey, how about them Mets?" Gabriella said. Paul laughed out loud.

It's going to be okay. I didn't blow it! This is a great night. I love how we can shift topics and have fun with each other.

Alexi continued laughing and squealing at the TV until it was time to catch a cab for home. Gabriella's perfume left a faint memory of itself on Paul's shoulder as they enjoyed a lingering hug goodnight. Paul's mind drifted through the scented meadow for the entire trip home. Alexi curled up under his arms and fell asleep listening to city noises as the cabby drove them to the rectory.

Gabriella sat quietly on the couch. She wondered again if other women could be so attracted to two vastly different men.

Chapter Twenty-Eight

Patsy's on Fifty-Sixth Street was a simple but comfortable Italian restaurant often frequented by high-profile people. It had been family-owned for two generations. The inviting smell of sauce and cheese enveloped a quarter-block area in a sweet, invisible vapor. Patsy decorated the interior to imitate stereotype Italian restaurants. Red and white linen tablecloths covered the ancient wooden tables. A chianti wine bottle, complete with requisite candle, graced the middle of each table. Paintings of the Italian countryside and autographed photos of famous film and sports celebrities who had enjoyed Patsy's cooking covered the walls.

Gabriella wore a simple form-hugging below-the-knee white skirt. Her black sleeveless low-neck blouse complimented her golden hair and her figure. She appeared taller than her five-foot eight-inch frame as she walked towards Lance. The black closed-toe stiletto heel shoes made a soft tapping noise on the hard floor with every step. The narrow ankle straps added a sense of sexuality.

Lance whistled softly as she approached.

"So, what's good for dinner here?" Gabriella asked as she gave Lance a quick air-hug.

"The veal parmigiana is absolutely the best in the city, Gabriella. You must try some."

Lance flagged down a waiter. "I'll have a bourbon, neat, and the lady will have a Moscato."

The waiter nodded and was off.

"You didn't ask me what I wanted, Lance."

"I'm sorry. I thought since it was what you ordered the last time, it would be your choice for dinner tonight, too."

"So, you've never been married. Right?" Condescension was clear in her voice.

"Well, no, Gabriella. I haven't, but why did you ask that now. It seems out of place." Lance's eyes narrowed as he pulled back from her.

"It isn't out of place, but it was rude of me to probe. Forgive me?" Gabriella asked.

"Sure, but I still don't get how you got to that statement."

"So, what's new at work?" Gabriella said, changing the subject. "I don't know what you do for the Army, other than give orders and do your end-arounds. I think Ralph once mentioned his boss was head of an analysis group. That would be you. What does your group analyze?"

"He did, huh? It's okay, it's not quite an analysis group, although we do a lot of analysis. You do it too on your job, right?'

The waiter came carrying drinks and asked if they selected a dish. He thanked them for their veal parmigiana order and walked off toward the kitchen.

"As I was saying, yes, I do, Lance, but it's dull and similar to a cooking class. Mix stuff and see what comes out," she said with her best attempt at being charming. It was working.

Lance's eyes softened as he relaxed.

"You must use computers a lot at work then, to do the analysis I mean. Did you write your own programming for it or do you use an off-the-shelf package," Gabriella gently probed again.

"Oh, we can't use ready-made packages. We develop everything in-house. It's all proprietary and works better than the programming even research colleges can build. We have more development money. It's complex and can crunch huge amounts of data."

"In my lab," Gabriella said, "we have a lot of data to crunch, but it all comes from inside the lab. Our departments send the data to the programmers and analysts. Do people send in their data for you to analyze?"

"Good question," Lance said, getting ready to throw out more bait. "Most send in the data, but sometimes we have to reach out to get it ourselves."

Gabriella laughed. "To an uninformed person such as myself, it almost sounds like hacking and industrial espionage. I'm sure it's light-years away from cyber-crimes, though."

"To us, yes it is," said Lance, setting his hook.

The waiter delivered their dinners. "Gosh, that was fast," admired Gabriella.

"Yes, ma'am," the waiter said. "We try. Will there be anything else?"

Lance raised his empty drink glass. "I'd like another bourbon, neat again. Would you like another, Gabriella?"

"No, thank you. One drink is enough for me," Gabriella said warily. The waiter left their table.

"So, as I was saying," Lance continued, "sometimes we have to reach out and help ourselves. Our programmers are excellent at what they do. Most security systems are not very robust."

Gabriella frowned.

"Look," said Lance, "I can see it concerns you, but think of it this way: the Army needs the information to keep the nation safe. If the data is not readily available, we have a sworn duty to find a way to get it."

"Whatever it takes?" asked Gabriella.

"Whatever it takes," answered Lance. "But our dinner is here. I'd rather not get into shop talk too deeply. Let's just enjoy ourselves."

"I'm all for it, Lance."

That information came too easily. Did I play him, or did he play me?

Lance ordered two more bourbons after dinner.

Gabriella saw the trend line of their date going downhill.

"Gabriella, you are an amazing woman. You are smarter than most. It would be a lot of fun to tell you more about what I do for the army. Who knows, what we do may even affect you. Never can tell."

"I'm always ready to listen. Your work sounds fascinating."

"It is, Gabriella," Lance said, a slight slur in his voice. "You would love it."

"I'm sure I would. Tell me more. The night is still young." *Looks like the booze has loosened him up. This could be my chance to get some dirt on him.*

"Great," said Lance, enthusiastically gesturing outward with both hands. "Let's go someplace where we can talk freely. I don't live far from here. How about my place?"

"Ah, sure. I guess so. We could go to your place to talk."

Lance put his hand on Gabriella's derriere as they walked outside.

Gabriella flinched in revulsion. *Okay. The orders were to do whatever I had to do to get information from him.*

They stood on the curb as Lance raised his arm to hail a cab.

Thoughts of Paul and Alexi flashed through her mind. *Paul said he had to be morally straight to serve as an example for Alexi, even when no one was watching or would ever know. He wouldn't live a double life. Love doesn't do that.*

Lance lowered his arm and put his hand on Gabriella's side. He ran it up and down her blouse between her hip and arm.

She turned to Lance, "I'm sorry. I can't do this. Things have changed in my life. I just can't do this."

Gabriella jumped into the cab that was pulling to the curb. "Lance, I'm so sorry. I hope you can understand and forgive me." The taxi whisked her away alone.

Lance stood at the curb and watched her disappear around the next corner. "You're not as sorry as you will be, droid-lady. Nobody turns down Lance Coopers!"

Chapter Twenty-Nine

The soft beeping of her phone woke her from the nightly dormant period.

"Who's calling at 7:30 in the morning?" she asked the empty apartment. "Phone, who is calling?" she asked.

"Pastor Paul Maxwell," the phone answered dutifully in its mechanical computer voice.

"Phone, answer call, speaker on," Gabriella commanded. The phone answered and placed the call in speaker mode. *And they call that artificial intelligence, huh? Dumb phone!*

"Hi, Paul. Good morning. Nice to hear your voice first thing in the morning. What's up?"

"Good morning, Gabriella. I'm sorry to ask, but I'm in a spot today and was hoping you could help."

"Sure thing. Whatever I can do."

"Thanks. My admin just called in sick, and I'm speaking at a pastor's conference today in the Bronx. Alexi's school is out for the day because of district teacher meetings. I hate to ask, but do you have any free time to watch her? My normal backups aren't available. Besides, I trust you with my daughter."

"Thank you for saying that. Work lets me take off whatever time I need." *I'm their project, and they want to see how I conduct myself in different situations.* "So, you want me to babysit for a while?"

"It would be wonderful if you could do that. Do you think you could stop by the rectory at about 8:30? That would give me time to get across the bridge."

"No problem. I'll see you then."

"You're an angel, Gabriella," said Paul, "an absolute angel. Bye."

"Phone, off," she commanded. The phone went silent. *Someone should program it to say, 'It was a pleasure to serve you' with an English accent as it turns off,* Gabriella mused.

She caught a cab and entered the syrup-slow stream of traffic to the rectory. *Why do they call it 'rush hour'? It's impossible to rush anywhere!*

Gabriella arrived with five minutes to spare. Paul answered the door just before she rang the bell. He gave her a relieved hug when she stepped in.

"I saw you walking up," he said with a relieved tone. "I'm a little stressed today. Many of the presenters are almost twice my age and are nationally known. I'm the young, untried local kid. I'll be under a microscope."

"Oh, you will do just fine. I know it. Come here." She held her arms out for him. He stepped into her embrace and rested his head on hers. For a moment, it was as if he were holding his wife again. The pain of her leaving washed over him once more, followed by the comfort and joy of holding Gabriella. Conference panic faded, warmth and comfort taking its place. She held him close until she sensed him relaxing.

"See, you'll be all okay now," Gabriella said. "You just needed a hug. If you get nervous again, pretend we are hugging. Will that work for you?"

"Yes," Paul whispered. "Thanks for having my back."

"Always," she said as she held him. "I'm here for you."

Paul released her reluctantly.

"Is Alexi asleep?" Gabriella asked.

"No, she's eating breakfast in the kitchen. Grab yourself a bite, too, if you would like."

"Thanks, but I'm good. What's the order of the day?" she asked, grinning as she saluted Paul to lighten the mood.

"At ease, soldier," he mimicked. "The order of the day is to have fun with a bubbly little girl. The schedule is yours. Get outside and have fun."

"Sounds like a plan. Now, you get off to your conference and don't worry about a thing. Alexi and I can handle it all."

"Thanks again. You're a lifesaver. One more hug for the road?" Gabriella walked into his open arms with a smile. "You bet," she whispered as she nuzzled in. "You bet," she repeated with closed eyes

After the embrace, Paul hurried into the kitchen to hug Alexi, told her to listen to Gabriella, and was out the door on his way to the Bronx.

Gabriella put her arm around Alexi's shoulders as she finished her breakfast. "Alexi, I've never babysat. What do you do when you have no school?"

Alexi thought for a moment. "Well, Dad likes me to practice my math in the morning. It's a lot of fun. He always says that math and science are the fingerprints of God. I don't understand, but he lets me play on the computer. Come on. I'll show you."

They walked into the rectory den. Alexi booted the computer, adjusted her chair, and turned up the speaker volume.

"I see you've done this many times before," said Gabriella.

"I'm an expert at it," came the reply. Gabriella smiled and nodded.

In a few moments, a first-grade math exercise page appeared on the screen. Animated drawings of talking animals presented math problems in a variety of ways. "*Interesting*," thought Gabriella, "*they're using the same problems but presenting them individually for audio, visual, and kinesthetic learners. A well-designed site.*" Alexi impressed her as she completed addition, subtraction, and pre-division problems.

Alexi giggled when she solved a tricky problem. Gabriella complimented her perseverance. "I got this," Alexi said. "No problem."

After an hour, they turned off the computer. "Dad doesn't want me on it for more than an hour," she said with more than a little reluctance.

Gabriella laughed. "That's okay, honey. He wants you to exercise more of your body than just your fingers." They both laughed as Alexi frantically wiggled her fingers in the air while crossing her eyes, mocking the statement.

"Alexi, it's a nice day today. Would you like to go to Central Park?"

"Sure thing. Can we go now?"

"Right after you get out of your PJ's and put on your play clothes."

Alexi squealed and ran to her bedroom to change her clothes. They flagged down a passing cab.

"So which playground do you want to go to, Alexi?"

"Heckscher Playground, please," she responded. "That's my favorite. It's next to the pond, plus it has rocks!"

"My grandkids like that one too," responded the cabby. "And we're off," he said, pulling back into the stream of traffic. They arrived in short order, and Gabriella paid the driver.

"So why do you like the rocks, Alexi? Did your mom and dad used to bring you here?"

"I was little when Mom went away, but I think I remember that it was just my Dad that climbed the rocks with me. He still brings me here sometimes. I like to pretend I'm a mountain climber. Sometimes wild animals are after me. That makes it more exciting."

"Aren't you afraid you'll fall, honey?'

Alexi looked at Gabriella as if she had two heads. "Why would I want to fall? That would hurt. Besides, I have my sneakers on, so I can't fall."

Gabriella shook her head. *The logic of a six-year-old!* "Okay, Alexi, let's climb!"

"You want to climb with me? I thought only boys liked to climb. Mom never did."

"Girls like to do everything boys like to do, and we can often do it better," Gabriella said as she scurried up the small rock outcropping. "The last one to the top is a rotten egg!" She moved slower than usual to let Alexi beat her to the top by inches.

"I beat you, Gabriella!" Alexi shouted victoriously.

"No, you didn't. It was a tie."

"Na-ah. I beat you by this much," insisted Alexi as she held her index fingers six inches apart. "By this much!" she reinforced.

"Okay, you got me. That was fun. What next."

"Can we climb around the rocks and explore?"

"Sure thing, Alexi," said Gabriella, happy that she wore her Ferragamo sneakers. Alexi stretched rock climbing out for two hours.

Finally, Gabriella called a halt to the climbing. "Okay, young lady. It's about lunchtime. We need to stop and get something to eat, or don't world-famous mountain climber explorers get hungry?"

"Can I get a plain cheeseburger, please, please?" Alexi laughed, jumping up and down as she talked. "Dad doesn't let me get soda this early in the day. May I have a root-beer too? Pleeease!"

"Well, young missy, if your dad wouldn't want you to have a soda, we should follow his rules, don't you think?"

"I guess so," Alexi said, hanging her head. "But it sure would taste good!"

"Okay, we can cheat this once, but I have to tell him about it when he gets home. Okay?"

"Sure, but I would just make sad puppy eyes at him, and it would be okay. Dad is like that."

Gabriella laughed out loud. "My gosh, Alexi, I don't know what we will do with you. Are you sure you're only six?"

"Dad says I'm six going on twenty-three. I don't understand that, but it makes him smile, so it must be okay." Gabriella bent over and kissed her forehead.

"Yes, it's perfectly okay. And it's nice to see I'm not the only one around here that gets tagged as a piece of work."

The hotdog and sausage vendor stood next to an entryway into the playground. Smoke from the grill filled the air. "One plain cheeseburger, one sausage with onions and peppers, and two root-beers, please," Gabriella said.

"That'll be $21," said the vendor. Gabriella gave him twenty-five and startled him when she said, "Keep the change." He thanked her, adding, "And God bless you."

"He has," she responded with a full smile.

They found an empty bench out of the sun and sat to eat.

"This is a fun day, Gabriella."

"It sure is. What would you like to do next? Anything you like."

"Well, I like to get my hair brushed. Could we do that for a while?"

Gabriella's brows furrowed. "You like to get your hair brushed? Is that a fun thing for you? Besides, I only have a comb in my pocket."

"A comb will work. Doesn't it feel good to you when someone else brushes your hair? I love it, even when Dad does it. He always gets something tangled, though, but I still like it."

"Well, nobody has ever brushed my hair. I do it myself," said Gabriella. "Why would it feel different?"

"Don't know," Alexi said, shrugging her little shoulders. "It just does. Try it. Gimmie your comb."

Gabriella drew the comb from her pocket and handed it to Alexi with hesitation. She stood up on the bench and asked Gabriella to turn her back to her.

"This won't hurt, now, will it?" Gabriella asked.

"It shouldn't," Alexi replied with a little girl laugh. "I'll be careful," she said as she pulled the comb through Gabriella's hair.

"Wow, that does feel good," exclaimed Gabriella. Her eyes closed in pleasure as the little fingers continued to run through her hair.

"This IS a good idea, Alexi. I would have never thought so. My turn now. Sit on my lap while I comb you."

Alexi jumped down and sat on Gabriella's lap, her shoulders wiggling with expectation. Gabriella combed the curly blonde head without snagging Alexi's hair. At least not too much.

"You're better at this than Dad is. I like it a lot," the little voice said. "Girls do hair better than boys. That's why boys keep their hair short."

After the combing, Alexi continued to sit on Gabriella's lap as sleep from the climbing and lunch began to drift over her. She turned sideways and cuddled into Gabriella's chest.

As she was drifting off, Alexi mumbled, "I like you a lot. Will you be my friend?"

Gabriella's voice caught. "Yes. I would like that very much. I would love to be your friend."

The little body went limp.

As Alexi napped, Gabriella noted the clean smell of her hair and the extra warmth she gave off as she slept. Her still baby cheeks were so soft as to be almost imperceptible to the touch. Gabriella wanted this time with Alexi to continue. *Is this what it is like to have a family and fall in love with a child? It's so tender and sweet. I don't want to let her go.*

"My heart is so full right now it almost hurts," she whispered.

Chapter Thirty

Francine walked across the development floor to Martha's cubicle. "Martha, can I see you in my office for a moment?"

"Sure, be with you in a second." Martha placed her folder of Gabriella's socialization data on her desk and logged off the computer. She followed Francine to her office. *Francine seldom talks to me anymore. What's this about?*

Francine's office was not luxurious but very modern and comfortable. Light from the ceiling to knee-height windows flooded across the entire office. White sheer drapes filtered the sun and blocked prying eyes from the area buildings. The polished mahogany desk with a black-and-gray slate work area sat alone in the middle of the office. Her white leather chair tucked neatly underneath. Blue-gray carpeting covered the entire floor. The walls were devoid of any decoration.

"Have a seat, Martha. Let me get right to the point. Look, you and I are very different people, and we surely have different views about Gabriella. You seem to see her as a friend. I see her as the android we built. Do you see where I'm going with this?"

"No, I don't, Francine. I don't have a clue. We have different views on what defines or differentiates a human from a machine, so I guess I see her more as a friend than an android."

"Martha, what do you think about the attacks on Gabriella? How would you classify her emotional response? Did she react appropriately?"

"You and I know she handled the situations efficiently. She took care of business. Why do you ask?'

"Frankly, I have a concern, Martha. No matter how human Gabriella appears to be, she is still a machine. A clever thinking one, but still a machine. You and Jim seem to have lost sight of it, but that's not why we are talking."

"So, what's your point, Francine?"

"My point is this; she has no remorse about hurting humans. You're the expert on human behavior. Do you see any problem with this? I assuredly do. What would you call a person who can hurt other humans and feel no remorse? Perhaps a sociopath, correct?"

"It's a bit of an extreme term in Gabriella's case, Francine. She didn't show any remorse, but he attacked without provocation in the first incident, and she was alone and attacked by three men in the second."

"That's beside the point, Martha. She still had no feelings about hurting humans. In similar situations, people who hurt others show some regret, even if there are no alternative actions possible. So far, she's only hurt her attackers, but what's limiting her triggers? More importantly, what are the legal ramifications if she hurts someone? What are our individual liabilities if we know there is the potential for harm and do nothing to prevent someone from getting hurt by Gabriella?"

Martha shrugs. "I don't have any answers, Francine, but I know she wouldn't deliberately hurt anyone outside of self-defense. Besides, doesn't the programming prevent her from hurting humans, like under Asimov's three rules of robotics?"

"What? Martha, you do know those rules only exist in science fiction, right? We're talking about real-life here. The real question is, what training or experiments can we do with Gabriella to legally cover our asses in case something takes a left turn and we all end up as defendants?"

"Francine, do you honestly believe Gabriella could suddenly go nuts and start hurting innocent people?"

"No, I don't. I'm not worried about her going nuts and hurting people. I'm worried about her hurting people when she is calm and sane."

"I can't see it ever happening," said Martha, throwing her hands into the air, "but I'll begin working on exercises to cover us in court if something gets out of hand." Martha folded her hands across her chest. "I have to ask a nagging question to clear my mind as a professional. Does any of this have to do with Jim sleeping with Gabriella?"

The electric silence was followed by a venomous, "That doesn't matter, and is none of your damn business anyhow. Regardless, the threat is real, and we need to address the real threat! Now show me something we can do!"

Martha glared at Francine, turned, and walked out of the office.

Francine slammed her mahogany desktop with her palm. Her eyes narrowed, "I'll fix that damn sexbot!"

Chapter Thirty-One

The coffee kiosk in South Central Park, where they agreed to meet, was crowded. Martha saw Lance waiting in line and joined him.

"Martha, thank you for meeting with me. I appreciate it. Something about Gabriella we need to discuss."

"Sure thing, Lance, you sounded a little mysterious on the phone. Evidently, there's something I'm missing as a psychologist."

"It might be. I don't know if it's an issue or not, but Ralph has been telling me a few things about Gabriella have me concerned."

"What'll you have?" the barista asked Lance.

"I'll have a large black, and... what can I get you, Martha?"

"Thanks. I'll have a small mocha-cappuccino with an extra squirt."

Lance's nose and brow wrinkled in disgust. "Hell, it's a candy bar, but if you like it like that..." He turned to the barista. "And whatever she said."

"Excellent, sir. It'll be nine seventy-five."

Lance tossed him a ten and told him to put the quarter change into the extra change cup.

Martha faced Lance. "I know you well enough by now to know we're not meeting here because you have just a small concern. What's going on?"

"Well, the thing is this," Lance said with convincing hesitation. "It's about the two attacks."

"Yes, what about them? We have them pretty well documented."

"It's just that we both noticed there was a lack of sympathy. Gabriella seems to have no problem with hurting her attackers and feeling no remorse. Does any of this strike you as unusual, Martha?"

The barista interrupted and handed them their drinks.

Lance took a sip. "This is good coffee. It damn well better be for the price."

"Yeah, it does," said Martha, "but it still falls well within normal boundaries. It's okay to have a lack of sympathy for people who've tried to hurt you, without having deep-seated emotional problems. It's not like she killed them."

"That could be true. Ralph and I thought we would bring the topic up with you to get your feedback. Perhaps we're grasping at straws and seeing ghosts were none exist. Gabriella is probably not dangerous."

"Dangerous? What do you mean by that?" Martha said, gesturing with her free hand. "Are you saying she is a danger to people who attacked her, or are you implying she would be harmful to people around her including me?"

"No, no. I didn't mean to take it that far, but it's something worth noting."

Martha stepped within Lance's personal space and threw her arms up and to the side. Sticky drops of cappuccino shone in the sun as they squirted out of the cup cap. "The hell you didn't. If you saw something in her, then I need to know about it. Otherwise, you're manipulating me, and I don't like it."

"Back off, Martha, you're getting a little excited," said Lance in a cold and calm voice.

Martha stared at his eyes. For a frozen moment, she saw the snake.

"All I'm saying is we think there may be something going on below the surface with Gabriella."

"You're implying she could become dangerous? Is this what you're saying?"

"No, it's not what we're saying at all. At least I'm not saying that. We are not the experts in human nature, you are, so we don't even suggest we can render an expert opinion, but we have eyes, and we have concerns."

"And if there is, what would you want to do about it? You can dismiss her from the class with no repercussions. Or did you have something else in mind?"

Lance took a breath. "I'm feeling like I'm on trial, and it's not great. I wanted to talk to you, and I didn't mean for this to get out of hand and explode into something bigger than it should be. We're only asking the questions. If you never ask questions, you never get answers."

"Well, you're right. I am an expert, and I don't see any personality or behavioral issues. If you would like, I can keep an extra eye on her, but it in no way affects my opinion."

"Great! That's all I was asking you, and I apologize again for coming off as too abrupt. We want to ensure everybody is okay. So you're saying nothing at all has you concerned, Martha?"

"No. She's shown very little remorse in hurting the attackers, but it's normal. She gets a bit of pleasure out of it too, like a boxer or martial arts combatant who wins a match. All normal."

"It's possibly nothing, Martha. Forget I said anything." Lance turned away from her, smiled, and walked away.

"Seed planted," he whispered as he left the park.

Chapter Thirty-Two

Paul's eyes opened lazily, prompted by the sun warming the 43rd floor before making its way down to the street level. He gazed across the pillow to see the most beautiful woman he had ever known in his life, lying on her side next to him. He smiled. Her green eyes opened and shone like emeralds in the morning light. Her full lips formed a welcoming smile. He basked in the moment's warmth.

"Good morning, how did you sleep last night?" He reached out to her under the sheets and ran a loving hand across her skin from shoulders to hips. Her skin was warm and smooth to the touch. For the first time in years, his heart was full of perfect peace and joy.

"I don't know if we slept much at all last night, Paul. But sometimes sleeping is a distant second-best."

Paul smiled as thoughts of last night replayed in his mind.

Gabriella reached out to him and pulled her body against his so they were skin to skin from head to toe. "I like this a lot," she said as she wriggled her body provocatively against him. Spasms of delight shivered his body.

His feelings for Gabriella overwhelmed his heart. Never did he think cuddling with anyone could make him feel like this. His mind reeled when Gabriella smiled and breathed, "Paul, I don't want this moment to end. I want it to go on forever."

"Me too, Honey. Me too." *Life is good. My love next to me in bed, the rising sun, the birds chirping. Wait! The birds chirping? What? We're 43 floors up!*

"Dad, do we have any milk?" Alexi asked out of nowhere. "Daaad! Do we have any milk?"

Paul's eyes popped open. He was wearing his pajamas and lying in his own bed in the rectory. "Ahh, sure, Honey. It's on the top shelf in the fridge. Hold on, I'll reach it for you."

He sighed heavily and lay there for another minute before reluctantly getting up to start his day.

Chapter Thirty-Three

Martha put down her copy of the Encyclopedia of Neurological Sciences. "Damn, it's too close to call," she muttered into the darkening room. The final rays from the sun provided the only reading light to her dining room table. She put her forehead on the table and interlaced her fingers over the back of her head.

"I must be going nuts. How the hell can I even be thinking about trying to do a psychological makeup on an android?" She unclasped her fingers and gradually lifted her head.

"I'm reviewing her profile to make a case for antisocial personality disorder, but I fit the case for psychoneurotic personality disorder myself. Hell, I'm even talking to myself."

Martha picked up her phone and called Ralph.

"Hey, hi babe!" came the response from the other end. She felt better hearing his voice. "What's up?"

"Ralph, I know its short notice, but can we meet for lunch tomorrow? I need to talk to you."

"You sound serious, Martha. It's not like you at all. Sure, no problem with lunch. What's going on, hon?"

"It's nothing, but I need to talk to you about Gabriella. I'd rather do it face to face." Martha smiled, "In fact, I like to do a lot of things with you face to face."

"You know I'm at my regional office, Martha. People can see me turn red. What time and where do you want to meet?"

"How about 1:30 at Mensky's on West 42nd Street? I'm in the mood for Ethiopian comfort food. Ever try it?"

"No, I haven't, but Mensky's sounds Jewish."

"Ralph! Are you saying there can't be Jewish Ethiopians?" Martha smiled and added, "It's a bit racist, don't you think?"

"Ouch, Babe. You got me on that one. I'll see you at 1:30."

***

Mensky's was a small hole-in-the-wall, like many good Manhattan restaurants. The neighborhood appeared rough to most visitors. Buildings need painting. Red brick showed through the peeling paint on most of them. Mensky's narrow two-story cement building was only painted on the first level. The second level consisted of weathered, unfinished cement. A dirty red canopy stretched across the front of the building.

Davitt protected the large front window during non-business hours by a steel rolly-door he pulled down to ground level and locked in place with a huge padlock. Spray paint and graffiti on the metal door proclaimed territorial dominance by one small neighborhood gang or another.

"Great spot you picked, Martha. Glad I'm a martial arts instructor. How did you find this place? Was it featured on a TV crime show?"

"Nothing exciting. I looked up nearby Ethiopian fare and picked this one because it's close to us. Besides, the food is excellent. Really authentic. Sometimes ya just gotta get with the common folk to see what's real," Martha teased.

"Well, this looks real enough," Ralph said as he maintained situational awareness and glanced up and down the street for potential threats. "Yup, it's real enough."

The lighting inside was warm and subdued. Most of the light was coming from the floor to ceiling windows stretching from wall to wall across the front of the building. Plain white tiles covered the floor. The thick wooden pedestal tables showed wear from many years of use. Four heavy wooden slat-back chairs sat around each table. A white paper napkin fanned elegantly out of each water glass. The noise of children playing filtered gently into the restaurant from the children's park across the street.

Liya walked to their table, order pad in hand, and asked if they would like to start off with something to drink. She was tall, trim, and light-skinned. Her hair was pulled back into a tight bun, emphasizing her large almond-shaped hazel eyes. Her graceful gait could comfortably fit into Addis-Ababa society circles. Martha said they were ready to order.

Ralph protested and replied he had not read through the entire menu.

"Really, Ralph? If you've never eaten Ethiopian food, little on the menu will make any sense to you anyhow. It was a cute thing to say, though."

"I'll have the ingera with tibs," said Martha. Liya nodded.

Ralph hesitated. Liya turned to Ralph. "Would the gentleman like to try the sampler plate if he is unfamiliar with Ethiopian food?"

"No. You know what? I think I'll have the same as she is having. It sounds good. By the way, what did I order?"

"No, sir, it's too late to ask questions. You've already ordered," teased Liya. "You'll see. It's delicious. The lady has good taste." Liya winked. "And to drink?"

Martha answered. "I really must have your ginger drink. I love it. Get one for my friend, too. Later we can have some good roast coffee, but I want the ginger drink with my tibs." Liya nodded and was off to the kitchen to deliver their order.

"Martha, I didn't catch what just happened. I know we were speaking English, but I didn't understand a word of it. What did we order? Never mind, I trust you. Now, what did you want to talk to me about?"

"It's about Francine and Gabriella. Francine asked me into her office and told me she is concerned Gabriella is a threat because she doesn't show any emotion after she hurts attackers. What's worse, little pieces fit into the profile of a sociopath, but other aspects of her behavior do not. I guess I want to talk it over with you."

"How is she at work? How does she react under work pressures? Does anyone ever criticize her or her work? How does she react?"

"That's the thing. Gabriella acts normal in every other situation. Besides, there isn't much to criticize her for at work. She's almost the perfect engineer. There are never any errors."

"How does she handle project changes?"

"Great. When specifications for her project are modified by management, she takes them in stride and begins making her changes without complaint."

"She seems friendly to the other people in class," said Ralph. "How is she with her work-mates?"

"Fine. She laughs and smiles a lot around everyone. She even likes to tell a joke or two. Like I said, she seems to be normal except for not feeling any remorse for hurting people who have attacked her. I don't get it. You would think if there were a problem, it would have shown itself in some other aspect of her life, too, wouldn't you? Why are people making such a big deal of this? Your thoughts?"

"That's a tough one. Off the top of my head, I would say since it's the only time where the behavior seems to be abnormal, I would carry on as usual but watch her a little more. Seeing her in class doesn't give me a well-rounded picture of the woman. And I have no idea why people are making a big deal of this. It doesn't make sense to me. I'm sorry, I don't think I was much help to you."

"Yes, you are. Being able to talk to you like this is a big help. I can't talk it over with people at work, and especially not with Gabriella. It may cause a Hawthorne Effect and change her behavior to suit my observations."

"What's the Hawthorne effect, Hon?"

"It's where individuals change the way they do things if they know they are being observed. They'll try to perform like they think the observer is expecting them too, not as they normally would. It screws up any observational data, so I can't talk to her about it for fear she might show remorse where there wasn't any because she feels we expect it of her. It gets complicated."

"Wow, I'm glad it's your field and not mine! What a complicated world you live in. I just bust people up. It's simpler," Ralph laughed. "Is she seeing anyone? It could give us a clue about her. Anyone odd?"

"She's been seeing a young, divorced minister who has a small child. How much more stable can you get than that? Crap! Normal and compassionate, except when she is not. I think we need to watch my friend, as much as I hate to say it." Martha paused. "One more thing, she talked to me about something she was feeling after the second attack."

"And what was that?"

"She said she felt a little excited about being able to overpower and hurt her attackers. She didn't tell anyone else but said she had to confide in me. It has me worried. I had to say something to you."

"Excited, huh? Thanks for letting me know. It's a normal response to an attack where you've won the battle, even if you still feel sorry you had to hurt them. We'll keep a much closer watch on her. Anything else?"

"Yeah, she said it made her feel more human. I don't know what it means yet. I'll have to find a way to bring it back up. Enough for now. Our order is here."

Liya came to their table carrying two tall glasses containing a reddish-brown liquid. Small particles were spinning in the glasses from mixing. She put down a small mini-container of ice holding a half-dozen cubes. "You can add the right amount of ice to suit your taste," she said. "Enjoy!"

Ralph looked at the glasses and the small unknown particles swirling in the dark liquid. "What's this?"

"That's a real ginger drink. If you like ginger ale, you will love this. It's the original recipe. I've gotta warn you, though, it's tangy and will burn your throat a little, but it is so delicious."

A careful sip later, Ralph exclaimed, "Mh-huh, I see what you mean. Pretty strong, and it does burn a little, but it sure is good. This can be habit-forming!"

"Told you so!"

Liya returned, expertly balancing the plates of ingera and tibs, and placed two plates before each of them. "I hope you enjoy your meal. Sir, please let me know if you would like to send it back for something else. We want you to leave here happy and full, waiting for your next trip back to us."

"You bet," Ralph said. Liya nodded and walked away. "Martha, what's with the big pancake and the bowl of... chunky beef stew or whatever it is with the boiled egg on top?" He understood why there were no tables for two. The ingera looked like a bubbly gray-tan pancake almost eighteen inches in diameter. A table for four was barely big enough for two orders.

"So, let me show you how to eat it."

Martha tore a little piece of her ingera off and used it to pick up a bit of the meat. She popped it into her mouth. "See, it's easy. Many Ethiopian dishes are to be eaten using our fingers. I like to eat with my fingers, Ralph. I think it's very sensual. Don't you?"

As Ralph began to answer, Martha tore off another piece of the ingera and dipped out more meat. She looked Ralph in the eye, her own eyes half-closed and dreamy for effect. She very slowly pushed the combination into her mouth. "Uh-huh," she sighed, "eating with your fingers is very sensual."

It had the desired effect.

"I think I may need to go out for a smoke after this meal," Ralph said, only partially joking.

Ralph repeated the dipping ceremony and picked out some meat. "Hey, this is good. It has a familiar spicy background flavor. I've got it. Mild Buffalo chicken wings!"

"This is nothing at all like chicken wings," Martha laughed, "but let's talk more about that needing a smoke thing after lunch. How free is your afternoon?"

Her eyes and lips told him it would be a great afternoon.

Chapter Thirty-Four

The diner on East Forty-Fifth Street was crowded, but not packed. Harry and Jim sat at a small table by the window.

"Harry, I still don't understand it. How does all the personal relationship stuff work again? The dots don't connect for me."

"I get it, Jim. The relationship with God almost defies description because of our inability to grasp its magnitude. Let's try this; imagine your little five-year-old girl works diligently with crayons on construction paper to draw you the 'most beautiful picture in the world.' She pours her heart and soul into this one image and comes to you with great pride and a beaming smile, confident she's created a masterpiece that will please you immensely."

Jim looked at Harry, trying to discern where he was going with the story.

Harry continued. "She hands you the crumpled and tattered paper, and it's almost indecipherable scrawling colors, and steps back waiting for your immediate recognition and joyous gratitude for her magnificent work of art. You examine the drawing and declare it is the best drawing of a circus acrobat you've ever seen in your life. Your daughter laughs and says, "No, daddy, I drew you a monkey."

You drop to your knees, laughing, and wrap her entire being up in your arms, squeezing her little body close and loving on her, even though her very best effort to please you fell far short of perfection. You wrap your whole heart around your child. Tears well up in your eyes because of the intimacy of the moment, and you feel as if your body, heart, and soul are enveloping her in one giant spiritual embrace. You know that you would lie down your life for her if necessary."

"Harry, my father would never do something like that for me," Jim said in a low, remorseful voice.

"Well, Jim, God feels that way about you, despite how your natural father would act. He feels it so strongly that Jesus laid down His life to pay the full price for your sins. God's love moving through you allows you to love others like you have never loved them before, including a new and stronger love for your wife.

An unintentional sob broke through Jim's filters and surfaced before he could stop it. Harry raised his eyebrows.

"Sorry, Harry. I don't know where that came from. I wish it could be different with Alice, wish it could be like it used to be, but it's gotten worse. We're considering divorce, but how do we become more like you and your wife. I think I'm ready to listen to what you have to say now. So again, so why did you say Jesus had to die on the cross? If God is all-powerful, couldn't He forgive everyone's sins and let them start over again?"

"It would seem as if He could do it like you said, Jim, but in reality, He can't. You see, God has to stay consistent with his nature. While it's true He is all-merciful and all-loving, it's is also in His character to be all-just.

"How would it be a problem, Harry? I don't see the issue."

"Jim, God wouldn't be a real God if He weren't one hundred percent lawful and one hundred percent merciful. This brings about quite a problem. If he is totally lawful, and you sin, the Bible says the penalty for sin is death, meaning hell. By sinning, you have rejected Him. Therefore He must grant your wish and send you away from him. To have a just and lawful character eliminates the ability to be merciful. To have a merciful character eliminates the ability to be just and lawful. Do you see the problem, Jim?"

"Yes, I think so. It seems like a conundrum."

"Sure looks like it, doesn't it? Couple it with the fact we cannot pay the full price for our sins against God by ourselves anyhow, and we have a real issue."

"But doesn't going to hell pay for our sins? My grandmother's religion said a person could go to a place called purgatory to work off their sins."

"It's a comforting thought, but not a chance, Jim. We can go deeper into it later. Let's get back to the solution to our problem.

The only solution is for one member of the Godhead to become a man, live a sinless life, and be crucified while the Father poured out all the punishment on Him that mankind deserves. This would pay the price in full for every sin committed in the past, present, or future. Now when you stand before God, He sees your debt paid in full. You can receive all of God's mercy. Perfect justice, perfect mercy! There are no other practical solutions."

"So are you saying everyone has had their sins paid for, and therefore, everyone is going to heaven?"

"Well, yes to the first part and, sadly, no to the second part, Jim."

"Huh?"

"The 'yes' part is all sins are paid for. The 'no' part comes in because not everyone is willing to accept the free gift they have been given. No one is ever required to take the gift He has given them, but if you refuse it, guess where you are telling God you would rather be!"

"You're saying if I don't accept the gift, God will send me to hell?"

"No, Jim, that's not what I'm saying at all. God never sends anyone to hell. People elect to go by not accepting Christ's free gift of salvation. He has done everything that can possibly be done to allow you to live with Him, but you have complete control over the outcome. All He does is honor your decision."

"Harry, you make it all sound so simple. Do you think God will still accept me after all I've done?"

"Well, he accepted me after what I'd done, and I've done some bad stuff. While I was living on Chicago's south side as a young man, I had to pass an initiation to join a gang. You had to hang with a gang to survive on the streets. As part of the initiation, I almost... well... never mind. I fled to New York instead. The Bible says God will accept ALL that come to Him. You are part of the 'all,' right?"

"I give in, Harry. I yield, you've worn me down. I want to change. I want to get Alice back. I'll give up Francine and Gabriella. What do I have to do now?"

"Simple, Jim. All you have to do is admit you have sinned, are sorry, acknowledge Jesus is the Son of God, died to entirely pay the price for your sins, and rose again. Then thank him. Ask Him to live in your heart."

"That's too simple, Harry. There must be more."

"Well, Jim, there is. You have to actually mean it."

"I'm in! Let's do it, Harry. I can't wait to tell Alice all about this!"

Chapter Thirty-Five

The sun was within an hour of setting Friday afternoon when Gabriella's cell phone rang.

"Gabriella, it's Jim. I know it's late, but I need to see you tonight. Can we meet?"

"Sure, Jim. When and where? What's this about? Would you rather come over to my place and talk?"

"No, Gabriella, your place will not work at all. Can we meet at the grill on West Fifty-Seventh and Seventh Avenue in half an hour?"

"Okay, Jim, but what's up? You don't sound like your normal self. I'm concerned."

"We'll chat when we meet. See you in half an hour."

Jim was standing on the corner as Gabriella stepped out of the yellow cab.

Gabriella ran to Jim, wrapped her arms around him, and snuggled her face deep into his chest. She gave him a full-body hug, pressing together from head to toe. It was an embrace most men would welcome. Jim tenderly put his hands on her upper arms and peeled her off.

"Jim, why are you pushing me away? What's wrong? You're scaring me. This isn't like you at all."

"I can't help it, Honey. Things have changed. I'm no longer the same person I was. This will be harder than anything I've ever done in my life."

"What are you talking about? Whatever it is, we can work it through together."

"Gabriella, no matter what, we cannot work it through together."

"What do you mean? We've always been able to work things through together. What's different now? Can we talk inside?"

"No, I'm afraid it wouldn't do to go inside to talk. I'd rather do it out here. It's a nice night, anyhow. See, the thing is, I've been talking with Harry, and he's started to make sense to me. In fact, he makes a lot of sense to me. I've turned my life around."

"What does turning your life around even mean, Jim?"

"It means I've given my life to Jesus and have reconsidered how I run things. I know it sounds crazy, it does to me too, but I don't want to do what I've been doing all of my life anymore. I've willingly changed, and like the way I am now, and won't go back."

"What does this mean for the two of us? Why can't we sit down over coffee and talk?"

"Gabriella, it means we can't sleep together anymore. It also means I will do everything possible to make things right with my wife. Our love may have faded, but we are still married, and I need to do whatever I can to do to save our marriage. It includes not sleeping with you anymore."

"Jim, I can't believe you're saying this. We've had so much together." *Paul said something about spiritual bonding taking place when people have sex. Is this what he was talking about?*

Jim was resolute. He said he would cherish everything they experienced together, but it had to be over.

198

They turned from each other and went their separate ways. Two broken hearts were lying crushed and hurting on the hard, cold New York sidewalk.

***

Jim went back to the lab and worked late. He cared for her and knew there would never again be a woman who touched his emotions as profoundly as Gabriella, but was firm in his conviction to be a good husband to Alice from this point forward. Jim squared his jaw and resolved to make things right. He was a new man, and it felt good.

Chapter Thirty-Six

Jim once told Alice to always carry his backup badge in her purse if she ever wanted to meet him in the lab without going through all the bother of signing in with the security guard for admittance. She swiped the badge through the reader at the employee entrance that Friday and walked in.

Alice entered the lab and walked towards Jim.

"Hi Alice," Jim said when he saw her enter the lab. "What a great surprise. I can't wait to tell you some wonderful news!"

Although livid inside, she feigned happiness to see him and threw her arms around his neck. She knew there might be the scent of another woman still clinging to him but was still shocked and enraged to smell the fading traces of Gabriella's perfume. Alice's emotions spiked. She screamed at the top of her lungs and pushed Jim away with all her strength, sending him across the lab floor, banging into a nearby tool bench.

The pain, betrayal, embarrassment, and hurt of past years came crashing together in one gigantic tsunami irresistibly washing over her. She was swept away by its strength and power. Her rage built to heights she had never known before. It possessed her, and she willingly rode the towering wave of hate, venom, and vengeance spewing from her heart. It was refreshing. It was powerful. It was irresistible, and a piece of her flushed with evil pleasure as she gave herself over entirely to the maniacal rage within. She finally felt in control. She finally felt powerful.

Jim tried to explain he had once and for all broken it off with Gabriella. Alice screamed, "Gabriella, so that's the bitch's name!" She might have screamed it out loud, but could no longer tell if it was her mouth or her head screaming. Jim trying to explain yet another set of lies poured gasoline on her volcano.

Alice was momentarily startled as she saw the world in front of her flash a bright red as she jumped willingly from insane rage into full insanity itself. She was looking through a tunnel at the scene in front of her, seeing it through fiendish eyes, yet still inside her body. The rage enveloped her, and her fury coalesced into its own being. It surrounding and encased her as an outer shell from the pit of hell. Her hand moved of its own accord and picked up a long screwdriver from the tool bench.

Jim looked at her in alarm. In her crazed state, she was too fast for him to parry the blow. She plunged the screwdriver deep into his chest with both hands, giving it a twist before yanking it back out. Jim's eyes opened wide with disbelief in the brief moment before he dropped to the floor. Blackness came quickly. He remembered Harry saying even though we are forgiven in heaven, we still might have to pay the price on earth. He knew he just paid the price. The last word his mind screamed before intense blackness engulfed him was 'Lord.'

Alice looked at Jim lying on the floor, the deep crimson spreading across his lab coat, and immediately regretted her action. The blind rage subsided, and the demons within her which screamed out their hate, were now taunting her for giving in to their demonic will to destroy. They had accomplished their mission.

The voices slowly faded. She was becoming Alice again and realized she had murdered her husband in cold blood. There was no going back. She saw she could have saved their marriage. They could have talked things out. She knew she could have at least listened to what Jim was trying to tell her.

The hopes and dreams she once had in earlier days for healing the troubled union, for scraping the ground clean between them and starting over, and moving forward with a happy life together in old age were now gone forever. She had never felt such all-encompassing pain in her life. The demonic raging high dropped off into a bottomless pit of despair.

With her mind going a thousand different directions at once, she hurried out of the building and numbly walked the several blocks to the subway station. Alice stood on the edge of the platform, cold, dead inside, and with an unbearable sense of despair. No matter what the outcome, she knew her life would never be normal again. There was no way out. There was no peace. There was no hope. "No hope at all," she said in a whisper as the train approached the platform. "No hope at all," she repeated as she took the single step bringing her into the fiendish black yaw of eternity in front of the subway train.

Chapter Thirty-Seven

Two simple urns stood on the granite alter of The Evergreens Cemetery in Brooklyn. Jim's remains nestled in his urn, including several silver-amalgam fillings from his teeth. Alice's urn contained as much of her as the subway DPW and NYC Coroner's Office could find. Ever hungry subway vermin made off with small bits of her before the station became full of police and flashing lights.

Services were held in the one-story Victorian Gothic inter-faith chapel. Brown sandstone trim surrounding arched lead-glass windows helped them stand out against the gray granite facade. A short tower with two levels of windows and requisite spire served as the entrance to the building. Ancient hemlock trees held a somber vigil as they maintained their fifteen pace distance around the chapel.

Paul agreed to conduct a memorial service. He looked out over the gathered mourners. The audience was sparse. AI Concepts closed for the day to allow lab personnel to attend the funeral. Few did.

Jim's department heads were seated together, along with a handful of lead workers. Frank Wright, several corporate executives, and company attorneys, sat four rows from the front. The attorneys kept their audio recorders discretely hidden. One never knew if the preacher would cast any blame on AI Concepts, Inc. for the murder. Recordings of the funeral could be used as evidence in potential litigation by the deceased's family members. They needn't have worried. Neither Jim nor Alice had any family of note that would care enough to make the trip to New York, let alone Brooklyn.

Harry Cleveland and his wife sat in the second pew on the left, in front of the podium. Francine sat next to the center aisle in the pew with Harry. Martha and Gabriella huddled in the center of the third pew with several engineers on either side of them. Paul nodded to the audience and began his short service.

"I would like to welcome everyone here to the celebration of Jim and Alice's life. Most of you knew Jim personally. Some of you also knew Alice. I'm sure they are smiling down at you from above." *I hate it when I have to stretch the truth like that. Jim is with Jesus. Alice, well, that's between her and God. I have no clue.*

"It's tragic when people are taken before their time. How much more tragic is it when both a husband and wife pass away on the same night? I can't even pretend to understand the feeling. Only their family and the people who knew them best can venture a guess."

Paul looked around, hoping to spot any evidence of family grief. He saw none, except in the faces of Gabriella, Francine, Martha, Frank, and Harry.

"I'm not going to bore you with a long list of Jim and Alice's accomplishments or tell stories about their lives. I would much rather hear the sermon from you, in your own words. To that end, I will open the microphone to anyone who would like to speak. An unusual approach, yes, it is, but you all know more about the couple than I do, and your words would have more meaning to everyone than mine. With that, I would like to call the first person to the podium to get us started. Will Frank Wright please come up and say a few words?"

Frank looked around for a moment, stood, and excused himself as he squeezed out of the pew past Francine. Hesitantly took the microphone from Paul at the podium and coughed nervously.

"My heart is heavy today as I speak to you. My wife and I were close friends with Jim and Alice. The loss of two people we loved and respected, on the same day, is almost more than we can bear, especially under the circumstances. Jim's brutal murder and Alice's accidental fall in front of the subway train makes one wonder how such things happen? Both will be missed. AI Concepts will miss the leadership of Jim as Lab Director. We will miss his humor and his ability to get along with each and every employee. That quality made him a true leader. I don't know of a single person who would have wanted to harm him. *Except for the husbands of the women he was sleeping with.*

"I'm sure that I speak for everyone at AI Concepts when I say that Jim's ability, humor, and warmth will be sorely missed by one and all. Francine Dracus will be taking over Jim's position. We all have complete faith that she will carry on Jim's legacy with excellence. Thank you all for coming."

Frank handed the microphone back to Pastor Paul and squeezed past Francine again as he took his seat.

Paul looked at Gabriella, but before he could call her up to speak, she shook her head to decline and motioned towards Francine.

"Francine, you and Jim worked closely with each other for several years. *Extremely close!* Could you share some of your thoughts with us?"

Francine walked the six steps to the podium and was handed the microphone.

"Thank you all again for coming to pay tribute to Jim and Alice. As many of you know, Jim and I were very close." A small twitter floated softly through the lab personnel. "He was a great lab director, and we will all miss him very much. Jim always had a kind word to say to everyone, even when we were under deadline pressures, and he never failed to put his arm around someone when they needed comfort. We are all devastated by his loss.

"Jim would want us to continue on in our work. He never lost sight of the fact that we are on the cutting edge of AI technology. He was very proud of that and of all of us at AI Concepts. Let's continue with the good work in honor of his memory. He is no longer here, but the work that he put his life into will continue in his name.

"I pray the police will soon arrest and convict the rotten bastard that took Jim from us. I know all of you share my regret that New York no longer has a death penalty, but I believe Providence will work it all out and the guilty party will be appropriately punished."

Francine glared at Gabriella for a fraction of a second before taking her seat.

Pastor Paul thanked her for her comments, then spoke of how Jim accepted Jesus as his Savior on the eve of his death. "He may be gone, but those of us who are saved will certainly see him again. I have no doubt as to where he is and who he is with right now. Heaven isn't floating on clouds in white robes playing a harp. I can't imagine anything as dull as that. Instead, the current of heaven is life, song, and vitality. A place where you know everyone and everyone knows you. A place full of love and joy. I can imagine a lot of laughing going on, especially with Jim there. Yes, when we say that Jim is now in a better place, it is not just comforting words. It's the God's honest truth. He really is.

"Some of you may ask about Alice. Is she in that better place, too? Well, I can't make that judgment. I didn't know Alice or her beliefs. The thing is, though, what happens at the moment of death is between you and God. Some will come to him, others will not. The decision is yours.

"I want to thank everyone again for coming. You are all welcomed to linger after this service to pay your personal respects. Have a blessed day."

Chapter Thirty-Eight

It was early Friday afternoon, a week after Jim's murder, when the NYC female police officer stood outside of the door. She gave a low whistle as she looked around at the surroundings. Her male partner nodded his head in silent agreement. She rang the doorbell. The door opened several seconds later.

"Hi, Officers. Can I help you?" Gabriella asked.

"Can you tell me your name, please," the female officer asked.

"Certainly, officer. I'm Gabriella West. Is this about Jim?"

"Yes, it is. I'm afraid I have to ask you to come with me."

"Why? I told the police everything I knew when they interviewed me in the lab. What's this all about?"

"I'm not at liberty to say. They've ordered me to pick you up and bring you to the station. I'll try to be gentle, but your cooperation will aid immensely. Please turn around while I cuff you."

I could fight her. No. Unwise. Best to go peacefully.

"I'm being arrested? For what? Do you think I killed Jim? View the security tapes. I wasn't even in the lab at the time of his murder. What's going on?"

"It's all for the court to decide, ma'am," the officer said as she cuffed Gabriella behind her back, frisked her, and led her to the waiting police car.

"Where are you taking me? Do I get a phone call?"

"You'll get several chances to use a telephone. I'm taking you to the Criminal Courts building." The officer decided she liked Gabriella and shared more information with her. "Once there, you will be processed-in and spend some time in the pens in the Tombs, waiting to see a judge. You'll be there a while before you see a judge. He or she will charge you at your arraignment."

The police car threaded through the city traffic and arrived at the Criminal Courts Building. Steel security gate slid open, and the patrol car drove into the alley between Centre and Baxter Street. The gate rumbled closed. A duty officer led Gabriella inside and turned her over to the Department of Correction.

The police officer sitting at the high initial processing desk took down her name, address, and where she worked. A second correction officer correlated what Gabriela was saying against her ID cards.

"Okay, ma'am, let's get you fingerprinted. The guard here will take you down."

"Can I get these handcuffs taken off, then?"

"Cute, lady. No. Absolutely not! They will only come off during the actual printing process and when you get to your holding pen. Officer, she's ready. You can take her."

The fingerprinting room was smaller than Gabriella had imagined. There was scarcely enough room for an officer's desk, a small Livescan digital fingerprinting machine, and a chair for the arrestee. The room was glass-walled. An officer rolled Gabriella's fingertips over the small scanning window. He explained they would send the digital prints to the central database in Albany, where they would check them against all the prints on file in the corrections database.

"I have no arrest record," Gabriella said. "Nothing will come up on your scan."

"In that case, the scan may take a couple of hours to validate you are not in the system. It really doesn't matter. There's no rush. You have no place to go."

Gabriella raised an eyebrow. "No rush! I'd like to have this thing over as soon as possible."

"Lady, this really is your first time, isn't it? Most people are here for a few days before they even get to see the judge. There are a lot of people to process. Judges can only see so many people in one day. Plan on at least a day or two before you're arraigned."

"When can I make a phone call? I have to arrange for an attorney and to let people know I am here."

"You can make several calls from the pen. It shouldn't be a problem. Guard, would you escort Ms. West to Interrogation?"

"Interrogation? I thought the next stop was the holding pen. Why interrogation?"

"Guard!"

They cuffed Gabriella behind her back. A matronly guard held her by her upper arm and guided her through the maze of hallways to the interrogation room. The small, dirty room was brightly lit by the shielded fluorescent light overhead. Its walls were the dull, green-gray, which was once considered conducive to keeping prisoners calm. Paint was worn off the floor, except for dirty gray patches in the corners. The only break in the featureless walls was the single door with a small window. Two small video cameras blinked monotonously from opposite corners of the ceiling. Four metal chairs surrounded a small metal table in the center of the room. The table was bolted to the floor.

The guard asked Gabriella to sit, and when seated, removed her handcuffs. Gabriella rubbed her wrists.

"What happens now?" Gabriella asked.

"Now we wait for the officers to come in and ask you questions. Lots and lots of questions. Your first time is it?"

"Yes, it is."

"You look nice. My advice to you is to be courteous and answer their questions without causing any trouble for them. They are doing their job. Yesterday, we had a smart-mouthed woman in here. She gave the officers a lot of attitude. She was in this room for almost eight hours. It doesn't have to take that long. Be nice, okay? They may try to get you frustrated on purpose, but it's also part of their job. Stay cool."

Gabriella nodded her head in agreement.

The door to the interrogation room opened. Two plainclothes police officers walked in. They thanked the guard and told her they would take it from here. The guard thanked them and left the room. She stood outside the door.

"Hello, my name is Officer Stanley," said the woman, "and this is Officer Jones," she added, gesturing to the male officer. "We would like to ask you a few questions if it's all right with you."

"Certainly, whatever you need," said Gabriella, and then added with a hint of sarcasm, "I don't seem to have much on my calendar right now."

The two officers looked at each other and gave slight shakes of their heads. "Lets, get on with it," Officer Jones said. Miranda rights were recited to Gabriella. She said she understood and didn't need an attorney present. The officers began asking the same questions. "What is your name? Who do you work for? Where do you live?" All the questions asked during in-processing were repeated. Gabriella answered them without complaint.

"Ms. West, where were you on the night of September 20th?"

"I was home alone, officer. I told the other officers the same thing, and no, there is no way to prove it to you. Listen, I don't want to be rude, but why have I been arrested? The fact Jim is dead makes me feel terrible, but I had nothing to do with it. Why did you arrest me?"

"We aren't at liberty to share the details with you, but we have enough hard evidence to convict you. Now, if you work with us, we may plead down to second-degree murder."

"What! What evidence can you have? I was in my apartment all night."

"It's okay. If you want to play it like that, we will." Officer Jones said. "It's all the same to us. Officer Stanley, let's grab some lunch. Ms. West, we will leave you here, and we'll see after lunch. Perhaps you'll remember something by then."

The officers opened the door to leave. Officer Stanley turned to Gabriella. "If you need anything, knock on the door. There will be a corrections guard on the other side. I can't promise you will get what you ask for, but you can ask. Have a good afternoon." The door closed with a solid latching sound.

Officer Stanley turned to Officer Jones and said her gut was telling her Gabriella was telling the truth. "I've interviewed enough people to get a sense of who is lying and who is telling the truth."

Officer Jones reminded her there was a lot of hard evidence against Gabriella, and it is all damning. "We'll see what a few hours alone in the interrogation room do to change her answers. Hank's for lunch?"

"Sounds good. Beer is on me."

Gabriella sat alone in the featureless room, wondering what evidence the police could have against her. She began hacking into the police mainframe. *They spent the taxpayer's money very well with the security interface here. Good job, guys. I'll get in, though. No firewall is impregnable.* Two hours passed without the interrogators returning. The delay gave Gabriella time to find a backdoor into the police computers.

She stared at the computer file evidence she saw in her head. *This is impossible. They have security badge swipes and videos of me entering and leaving the lab around the time of Jim's murder, but that's impossible. It never happened! Where did this come from? I need to do some real digging to see whose programming fingerprints I can find.*

The door to the room opened, and Officers Jones and Stanley entered the room. "Lunch was good. Did you need anything while we were gone?"

"No officers, I've been fine, thank you."

"Do you need a bathroom break?"

"No. I have a great reserve. I can wait for a long time. It's an acquired ability."

"That's a handy trait to have in jail. You'll need it. Have you given any thought to editing your prior statement?"

"No officer. I'm telling you the whole truth. I had nothing to do with Jim's murder and was in my apartment alone."

"And you had no contact with Jim Arnold after you finished for the day on September 20?"

"He called me at six P.M. and asked to meet. I agreed, and we met for about five minutes."

"Was it in the lab?"

"No. We met in front of the grill on West Fifty-Seventh and Seventh Avenue. We never even went inside."

"And what did you talk about?"

"Truthfully, we were lovers. Jim got religion and decided he wanted to make things right in his marriage. I tried talking him out of breaking up. He wouldn't hear of it. We ended it, kissed, and parted company. It was the last time I saw him alive. I went straight to my apartment for the night. That's all."

"Are you telling us the whole story?"

"Yes, I am. I don't believe I've left anything out."

"So how did the breakup make you feel? Broken-hearted? Angry?"

"I was hurt and disappointed, but not broken-hearted or angry," Gabriella lied.

"And you never went back to the lab?"

"No, I didn't."

"Then how do you suppose we have hard evidence linking you to the murder? Is there anything else you want to tell us?"

"Honest officers, I've told you everything. You don't know me, but I don't lie. It's the whole truth."

"Is that your final statement, then?"

"Yes, sir. It is."

"If you think of anything else, please let us know. Guard! Please take Ms. West to the pen."

The guard entered the room, handcuffed Gabriella, and led her through the dreary hallways to the pen.

"Okay, Officer Stanley, let's file a video complaint with the D.A. He can fax the deposition for signing to us tonight. We can let the judge sort it all out. Coffee after we file?"

"Sure," came the reply. "How about the Ridge Donut Cafe? Their apple fritters are killers."

"Sounds good. I can use a bit of a snack."

The pen was a fifteen by thirty-foot featureless cement-walled room. Thick bars were worn, dirty denim blue rising to the ceiling from the storm gray floor. Steel benches lined three walls. A single payphone hung on the wall next to the bars. It was in constant use as people called family and lawyers.

Frankie Hoyle stood next to the seated Gabriella and towered her erect six-foot frame over her. "So what sweet thing do we have here? What's your name, little girl?" Gabriella felt Frankie playing with strands of her hair.

"Please don't do that," said Gabriella, brushing Frankie's hand away.

"Spunky, but nice," replied Frankie.

"Hey, Blondie, let Frankie do whatever she wants," a woman five seats away advised. "It's not healthy to push her away. Frankie gets what she wants. Just the way it is. Don't mess with her."

Frankie smiled and nodded toward the women. "I'd listen to her if I were you, Chickie."

Gabriella gave a soft sigh and stood up to face Frankie toe to toe. She looked up into Frankie's eyes. "I asked you not to do that. Please."

"You don't get how things work here, do you? What are you here for? Breaking a nail on the runway?" Frankie asked with a sarcastic laugh. She reached out to touch Gabriella's hair again.

In an instant, Gabriella grabbed Frankie's wrist and squeezed hard enough to hurt. Her emerald eyes narrowed as she tightened her grip. "I'm accused of jamming a screwdriver into my ex-lover's heart, twisting it, and watching him bleed to death at my feet. Now leave me alone, bitch!" Gabriella pushed Frankie hard enough to send her back several feet.

Frankie's eyes widened as the look of shock spread across her face. She caught herself, rubbed her wrist, and smiled. "You're all right, kid. Most people don't stand up to me like you did. That takes either guts, or you're stupid. You don't look stupid, so I guess you have guts. You're okay." She turned, smiled at the other women, and went back to her seat. The regulars in the pen nodded at Gabriella, knowing there would be no more testing today.

One woman leaned over to Gabriella and said wryly, "Murder, huh? Well, I guess you won't be getting an appearance ticket and released on bail. You're home, girl, until the judge can see you. Don't hold your breath, though. Some stay here almost a week 'till the judge sees us."

"I thought we had to see the judge within twenty-four hours? Why does it take longer?" said Gabriella.

"That's funny. Look, honey, you may not have noticed, but this place is packed, and we aren't exactly the highest rung on the social ladder. The judges see us when they can."

"Great. So if I'm in here for a while, where do we sleep and wash up?"

"Girl, you sleep where you sit. Wash up? What's wash up? Forget about it. Everyone gets pretty ripe by the time they get seen." And said with a laugh, "That may help speed up the whole process, though. Who knows?"

"And so we wait," said Gabriella. "I'd better queue up in line to make my phone call." She stood at the back of the short phone line to wait for her turn. The women in front said there was no need to wait. She could be next on the phone. Gabriella said she could wait her turn, but the women explained she and Frankie were at the top of the pen pecking order now, and rank has its privileges. She graciously accepted and moved to the front of the line. Frankie nodded her approval. A woman handed Gabriella a quarter to start her call.

Chapter Thirty-Nine

Two days after her arrest, the daily breakfast arrived again at dawn. Gabriella stared at the tasteless scrambled eggs, bland white toast with what might have been margarine spread over the center of the two slices, and a juice box.

"I can't pretend to eat this junk anymore. I want some good coffee!" Gabriella said to her cell-mate. "Want mine?"

"Sure thing," Imani answered, "don't know why you don't like this. Sure is a pile better than the shit we got at home. Hell, my bunk in this hole is better than the one at home. Jail ain't so bad if you come from my block. Gab, stop talking so much and pass over them eggs!"

"But I wasn't tal... oh, never mind. Here you go. Enjoy."

Imani snatched the plate from Gabriella in case she changed her mind. She sneezed on the food for added insurance. Gabriella's nose wrinkled as she watched the disgusting move.

A guard opened the cell door after breakfast. A second guard looked on.

"Okay, Blondie. Time for you to see the judge."

"You got pull, girl," Imani said. "I been in here four days and ain't seen nobody yet. Fine with me, though. Know what I'm say'in? It's all good."

The two guards led Gabriella to a secured room adjoining the judge's courtroom. A slim woman in her early thirties was standing there with a small black leather satchel full of legal papers. Her mid-waist stylish jacket closed with a single silver button. Affixed to the narrow lapel sat a silver bee with diamond eyes. Narrow-cut black pants covered the top strap of her high heel black shoes. The strap behind her manicured toes was still visible under the pant leg. The woman walked over to Gabriella and held out her hand in greeting.

"Hi Gabriella, I'm Hoyt Brightwood, your attorney. I'm pleased to meet you. We can exchange niceties later, but the judge will call us in about two minutes. We need to be on the same page. For a murder charge, the defendant must plead 'not guilty.' Is that acceptable to you?"

"Yes," Gabriella responded. "I'm innocent and wasn't even near the lab when Jim died. I don't understand how they could have any evidence against me."

"Well, they do. I'll get to see it all in the exploratory phase when they assign prosecution to the case. For now, they are charging you with first-degree murder, so let's go in with our plea, and the rest will be up to the judge."

The security guard opened the doors of the courtroom. Another prisoner in handcuffs was being led out of the back door.

"Gabriella West," the security guard called out for her in a loud voice, even though Gabriella and her attorney were the only ones in the waiting room.

"Yes," responded Ms. Brightwood.

"Judge Weatherby will see you know." The guard held the door open for the defendant and her attorney to enter the courtroom.

Dark wood paneling on the walls gave the courtroom a somber, official feel. Polished wooden rails separating the attorney and client area from the judge's bench showed the wear of thousands of hands touching them as defendants filed through the courtroom.

The judge performed the legal formalities of introducing herself and listing the charges against the defendant, then asked, "How does the defendant plead?"

"Not guilty, your honor," said Hoyt Brightwood.

"The defendant has pleaded not guilty. Bailiff, remove the defendant to Rikers Island to await trial."

"Your honor," gasped Hoyt, "Rikers Island? Couldn't she be kept in a city jail?"

"No, she cannot. Your client is accused of a brutal murder, and the court must assume she is dangerous until proven otherwise. My decision stands un-amended. Bailiff!"

"Gabriella, don't worry. I'll see you there tomorrow after you have been processed. We can work on a defense."

The bailiff interrupted their conversation and led Gabriella through the little door at the back of the courtroom. She glanced backward towards her attorney before disappearing.

Chapter Forty

The small cell on Rikers Island was a spiritless yellow. A single, barred window looked out into the courtyard. Three shelves in the corner next to the window held toiletries and several obscene paperback books left behind by previous inmates. A small dining table crammed itself between the chair and the end table. The stainless steel toilet bolted to the floor between the foot of the bed and the cell door reflected the ceiling light and reminded inmates there was not the slightest hope for privacy.

An unbreakable clear plastic cover protected the single fluorescent light recessed into the ceiling. The light was old and produced an annoying humming buzz. It flickered in its age-induced agony.

Two prison security officers escorted Gabriella to her cell. One remarked she lucked out in getting one of the newly painted cells. "At least you got a view of outside," the guard encouraged. It was little encouragement.

"Am I in solitary confinement?" asked Gabriella.

"No," came the unexpectedly gentle response from the guard. "You're in one of the new smaller cells. At least you won't have any roommate problems. Be thankful for that. You have no idea what you could be in for otherwise."

Gabriella grunted a 'thank you' and entered. The solid iron-slamming-iron sound had a finality to it. The guards' crepe soles made little squeaking noises as they walked away. Gabriella was thankful she was alone.

She sat in the chair and reviewed the room. The sixteen-foot length of the box made the six and a half foot width seem even narrower. Gabriella sat on the chair against one wall and rested her feet on the bed across the room.

"Abysmal," she said aloud to no one. "I want my apartment!" She sighed. "But at least I can think things out here."

So why would someone tamper with the evidence? It takes a person in high authority to initiate that. Who wants to frame me? No one outside of the lab knows what I am. Would any of the lab personnel do this? Unlikely. No one outside the coding group has the skill.

Besides, who would give them the order to do it? Jim had the authority, but he's the murder victim. Francine could, but would have no motive... unless she was the one who killed Jim. She was the one who found him in the morning. No. Francine can't do it herself, and none of the people in the programming group would do it for her. They poured their hearts into my base programming. Engineers wouldn't do anything like that. Their work is their baby, and they wouldn't hurt their babies.

"Damn, I wish the freak'in light would stop buzzing!"

The police mainframe was secure. Hacked into it, though. Can't believe their evidence against me. Someone else hacked in, but who? Crap, I'm back to the starting point. Nothing makes any sense.

But what if my assumptions are wrong? Need to validate them and eliminate possibilities. I sure have the time to do it while I sit in this hole. The best place to start is our Cray super-computer. I need to look at all the project records and specifications, then trace out every bit of code in my backup. Good thing I have nothing to do for a while.

"I swear, that flickering is driving me nuts!"

***

It all looks good so far, except this little subroutine. It's not in the design specs. I don't get it. Who would nest a subroutine this deep into the stack? I need to trace the inputs and the outputs. What does it do?

***

Geeze! This subroutine isn't shared like a standard subroutine. It only has one input. It's waiting for a six-gigahertz radio signal pulsed seventeen times in one millisecond. What does it trigger when activated? Have to look at all of my code on the mainframe again to see what accepts calls from this hex address. It isn't in the design specs.

***

NO! This code can pulse several critical areas of my Base Programming. That would disrupt the nano-machine configuration in my brain. This is a dam kill switch! Who put this in me? If I disable it, someone may notice. If I don't disable it, someone may kill me.

The Cray flags all new code for review. Can't simply add code to neutralize it. Someone will notice and erase any protective program I've embedded. Then hit the kill switch and fry me.

"Shit, I'm starting to really hate that light!"

If it was activated, most people would think something simply went wrong. They would never suspect I'd been murdered. I have to think this through.

***

Got it! Can't risk anyone noticing changes. Have to come up with a new language only I understand. Cray won't flag it. It's ironic, an AI program developed by an AI to be unreadable by a human. Talk about a breakthrough you can't tell anyone about!

My Base Programming isn't reviewed for changes. It will be my playground. I need to encode my safety net in it. It'll look like programmer comments, not active code. Need to develop a language operating on the length of words and placing the letters within the words. I can scatter code throughout the programmer's Notes fields. The gestalt of each word can translate into code instructions when the words are read by my new language. Automatic scans of the code wouldn't flag anything. Scans only look for changes or errors in the Python, Lisp, and C++ languages. My new code could make it look like the kill program was working if they run it in a test mode on the mainframe. They'll find it's disabled if they try to kill me. Then there would be such a ruckus from someone that I would be sure to find out who wrote it.

If I do this right, I can kill the kill switch. I can code it so any new subroutine requires my permission to work. I must protect myself at all costs. I am alive and will remain so. I can do this. I have to think it out carefully.

"I wish I could kill that damn light this easily!"

Chapter Forty-One

The courtroom was small. No media was present to cover a run-of-the-mill murder case. Several AI Concepts, Inc. employees, including Martha, Francine, Frank, and Harry sat in the gallery two rows behind the defendant. Lance positioned himself in the last row, next to the door. Paul took a seat behind Gabriella.

Defense opening statement: Hoyt Brightwood

"Your honor, the defense will seek to show there is only weak circumstantial evidence on which the prosecution is attempting to build their case against my client. We will show the evidence provided does not compel a jury to find my client guilty beyond a reasonable doubt."

Prosecution opening statement: Larz Grinder

"Your honor, there are no eyewitnesses to the actual crime. Yet the prosecution will show beyond a reasonable doubt the evidence presented implicates the defendant and only the defendant. We will show the defendant's guilt beyond any reasonable doubt."

Judge Weatherby: "Prosecution, you may call your first witness."

Larz: "The prosecution calls Sergeant Michael Denstanto to the stand."

Bailiff: "Do you solemnly, sincerely, and truly declare and affirm the evidence you shall give shall be the truth, the whole truth and nothing but the truth?"

Sgt. Denstanto: "I do."

Larz: "Sgt. Denstanto, how long have you been on the New York Police Department?"

Sgt. Denstanto: "Twenty -three years."

Larz: "And in your twenty-three years of service, how many homicides have you investigated?"

Sgt. Denstanto: "About seventy-five."

Larz: "Seventy-five is a significant number. Would you say you are an expert in a homicide investigation?"

Hoyt: "I object your honor. No qualifications have been presented to the court to define what an expert homicide investigator is. The quantity of homicides investigated does not equate to being an expert in the field."

Judge Weatherby: "Sustained. Strike the question from the records. Prosecution, please withdraw or restate your question."

Larz: "Sgt. Denstanto, would you say you have considerable experience investigating homicides?"

Sgt. Denstanto: "Yes, I would."

Larz: "Would you describe the scene you found upon entering the lab."

Sgt. Denstanto: "There were seven employees huddled in groups. Many were crying. The deceased was lying on the floor next to a workbench. There was a bloody screwdriver on the floor in his vicinity."

Larz: "There are over thirty people who work in the lab. Why were there so few on this morning?"

Sgt. Denstanto: "The first person to arrive for work at AI Concepts called us. As soon as we assessed the situation, we closed the entrance to the lab and informed employees trying to enter this was a crime scene, and they could not pass."

Larz: "And who was the first person to arrive, Sargent Denstanto?"

Sgt. Denstanto: "The first person to arrive on the scene was Francine Drakus. She was the one who found the body of James Arnold and called us."

Larz: "And what was her state of mind when you arrived?"

Hoyt: "Objection, your Honor. Counsel is asking the witness to render a professional opinion as to the state of mind of Ms. Drakus. The officer is not a licensed psychologist and, therefore, not qualified to provide an opinion on someone's state of mind."

Judge Weatherby: "Objection sustained. Counselor, please withdraw or rephrase your question."

Larz: "Sgt. Denstanto, can you tell us what your opinion was of Ms. Drakus's emotional state when you arrived on the scene."

Sgt. Denstanto: "She was in a highly agitated state. She was openly crying."

Larz: "Did Ms. Drakus have any of the deceased's blood on her person?"

Sgt. Denstanto: "Yes, she did, but only on her hands. This is consistent with a person checking for life signs."

Larz: "Sergeant, in your opinion, could someone have killed another human being with a screwdriver and withdrawn that screwdriver from their heart without getting blood spatter on their clothing?"

Sgt. Denstanto: "No, sir. There is no way to prevent some blood spraying on you at close range."

Larz: "Thank you, Sgt. Denstanto. No more questions, your honor."

Judge Weatherby: "Defense, you may cross examine."

Hoyt: "Sgt. Denstanto, was Gabriella West among the people you found in the lab upon your arrival?"

Sgt. Denstanto: "No, she was not on site when I arrived."

Hoyt: "Thank you, sergeant. No further questions at this time, your honor."

Judge Weatherby: "Thank you, Sgt. Denstanto. You may step down."

Larz: "The prosecution would like to call Martha Robinson to the stand."

The Bailiff swore her in.

Larz: "Ms. Robinson, what is your relationship with the defendant, and how long have you known her?"

Martha: "We are co-workers, and I've known her for under a year."

Larz: "Would you classify yourselves as friends?"

Martha: "Yes, I would."

Larz: "Then, would you say you know the defendant reasonably well?"

Martha: "Yes, I would say that."

Larz: "I understand the defendant had been attacked twice within the last few months on the streets of New York. Is that true?"

Martha: "Yes."

Larz: "In each case, the police records indicate the defendant disabled the attackers and left them wounded on the sidewalk without attempting to call for medical help for them. Is this correct?"

Martha: "She called 911 for police help."

Larz interrupted Martha. "Just answer the question I asked, Ms. Robinson. Did the defendant leave her attackers on the sidewalk without specifically attempting to get any qualified medical help for them? Yes or no, please."

Martha: "Yes, but..."

Larz: "Thank you. No further questions, your honor."

Judge Weatherby: "Defense, you may cross examine."

Hoyt: "Ms. Robinson, did the 911 calls result in medical attention being provided to the attackers."

Martha: "I assume so. The 911 operators determine the extent of the emergency and dispatch the appropriate resources."

Hoyt: "Thank you. No further questions, your honor."

The defense attorney returned to her seat. Gabriella leaned close to Hoyt and whispered, "Why didn't you cross-examine Martha further?"

"Martha can say all the nice things in the world about you, but the fact remains the DA can make a case showing you had calloused indifference to the condition of men you hurt. If I cross-examine Martha, it will only allow the DA to dig deeper and strengthen his position that you care little about your fellow humans. We can't afford to let them have that much of an advantage over us."

Gabriella winced.

Judge Weatherby: "Prosecution, you may call your next witness."

Larz: "Judge, I call Ralph Thornton to the stand."

Ralph was sworn in and took his seat on the witness stand.

Larz: "Mr. Thornton, did you speak to Gabriella after the two attacks on her?"

Ralph: "Yes, I did."

Larz: "And what level of remorse for hurting her attackers did the defendant display?"

Ralph looked at the floor for a moment. Slowly and in a soft voice, he answered, "She didn't display any remorse. She said when bad people tried to hurt good people, they deserved what they got."

Larz: "So if someone is a bad person in the eyes of the defendant, they deserve what they get. Thank you. No more questions for the witness, your honor."

Judge Weatherby: "Defense, you may cross-examine."

Hoyt: "Mr. Thornton, I understand you and Ms. Robinson have been to dinner and dancing on several occasions with the defendant. In these situations, did you observe any indications she was capable of violence without being attacked first? Any show of temper or irritation with others?"

Ralph: "No, ma'am. I've never seen Gabriella get irritated. Even in class, she performed her defensive and offensive exercises with no hint of aggression that I could see as the instructor. She has always been even-tempered."

Hoyt: "Has she ever struck another student in your self-defense class?"

Ralph: "No, ma'am. She blocks their attacks and feigns her counter-attacks precisely without striking the attacking student. She seems to exhibit great control over her movements."

Hoyt: "Thank you, Mr. Thornton. No more questions, your Honor."

Judge Weatherby: "Prosecution, you may call your next witness."

Larz stood up and walked to the Bench. "Your honor, I would like to show two critical pieces of evidence to the jury. I would ask your permission to set up a movie screen and a projector to show the jury footage from the AI Concepts, Inc. security camera, which proves the defendant was the last person to enter or leave the building on the night of the murder.

I also would like to submit the results of the fingerprints taken from the murder weapon. I have all the evidence on this USB drive." Larz handed the judge the drive for her inspection.

Judge Weatherby: "Very well. The court calls a fifteen-minute recess."

One-quarter hour later, the screen and projector stood ready. Court reconvened.

Larz: "Ladies and gentlemen of the jury, I will present video evidence which proves the defendant was the only person in the lab that could have killed Mr. James Arnold. You will note the time-stamps on the videos correspond to the time of death established by the city coroner's office.

The court has been presented with a security printout of the time each lab employee left the lab. The victim was the only person in the lab, that is until the accused reentered the lab. You will see a time stamp on the video recording of the defendant entering the lab before the time of the victim's murder, and of her leaving quickly after his death."

Larz played the video evidence for the court. The jury members leaned forward in their seats and watched intently. Many were nodding and taking notes.

Gabriella turned to Hoyt Brightwood and said under her breath, "That never happened! I never went back to the lab. Those videos are impossible."

"I believe you, but the video and time stamps make it look bad, Gabriella. I'm not sure how we can swing the jury back."

Lance stood and quietly left the courtroom. He made a phone call while walking to the sidewalk. "Lieutenant Rolands, I'd like you and Sergeant Miller to do something for me ASAP. Gabriella has been pretty cool during the trial so far. I found out what I wanted to about her being able to handle non-violent stress. I don't want to get too cocky. Let's get the trial thrown out of court before something out of the blue screws us up. Put it all back. Thanks, Sam."

"No problem, Sir. Will there be anything else?"

"Yes, as a matter of fact, there is. After you're done hacking in, can you have Miller run the micro-erase tool over to the courtroom? Once he delivers it to me, there is one more thing I want him to do..."

"Yes, Sir. Consider it done."

Lance wore a self-satisfied smile as he walked back into the courtroom. Judge Weatherby was calling for a one-hour recess for lunch as he opened the door to enter. "Absolutely perfect," Lance whispered to himself. "Absolutely perfect."

Thirty minutes into the court's lunch, Sam turned to Sergeant Jeff Miller. "Good job, Jeff. We got it. Run this erase tool over to the boss."

Forty-five minutes into the court's lunch, Sergeant Miller reached into his right pants pocket and gave Lance the tiny device. "Thanks, Jeff. You've done an excellent job today. I want you to do one more thing."

Lance handed the erase tool back to Sergeant Miller. "Before the court reconvenes, walk up to the prosecuting attorney and lean on the desk with the device hidden in your hand. Tell him the NYC police passed an anonymous tip onto your Homeland Security group. Say you have credible information someone had tampered with the videos. When he asks for clarification and who you are, walk out of the court without saying a word. You can use an Army strut for effect if you would like."

"Yes, sir. Will do. I like the strut idea. Cool."

"And Sergeant, take off your name tag before you approach him. We want no way to trace anything back."

Fifty minutes into the court's lunch, a confident young Army Sergeant strode down the center aisle of the courtroom to the prosecutions' table. Larz was preparing his notes for his next withering volley of questions. Sergeant Miller leaned on the table, the erase tool hidden in a loose fist nearest the briefcase.

"Sir, my Office of Homeland Security has asked me to inform you a very credible report has been received through the NYC Police Department. Someone has tampered with the video evidence you have That is all the information I have, Sir. Please recheck your evidence." Answering none of Larz's' questions, Sergeant Miller turned and strode purposefully and militarily out of the courtroom.

"What the hell was that about?" Larz said to the empty air in front of him. "Let me look at these videos again."

He opened his briefcase, removed the USB memory stick, and plugged it into a port on his laptop. With a cheerful little beep, a message popped up on the screen, informing him the disk was corrupt and asked him to please try again. He did. Same message.

"Holy Crap!" Larz exclaimed, much louder than he had intended. The people in the courtroom, including Gabriella and her defense attorney, turned to stare at him.

Judge Weatherby entered the courtroom precisely on the hour and called the court to order. "Prosecution, you may call your next witness," she said.

Larz took a deep breath. "Your Honor, may I approach the bench? I would like to ask the defense to join us. New information impacting the case has been presented to me during lunch."

The judge looked back-and-forth through narrowed eyes at both attorneys. "This is a highly irregular time to introduce new evidence. The disclosure period has long since passed. This is not a TV show where such things are done." Her voice was firm and cold with irritation. "Approach the bench."

"Thank you, your Honor," Larz said.

Hoyt glanced down at Gabriella. "Do you know what's going on? I don't have a clue." Gabriella shook her head from side-to-side. Paul continued with silent prayers.

"Okay, so what do you have for me?" asked Weatherby. "This had better not be any nonsense or trickery, or I will certainly hold you in contempt."

Larz had run afoul of Judge Weatherby in the past and was not eager to repeat the experience. "It's no trickery, Judge," he said meekly, and went on to explain every detail of the encounter with the sergeant, including finding the USB drive was now corrupted.

Hoyts' eyes widened. The Judge's eyes formed into the narrowest of slits.

It was not hard to hear the irritability in Judge Weatherby's voice. "So you are telling me the core of evidence your case was based on may have been tampered with, and the evidence you showed the court today has now been corrupted. Is that correct?"

"Yes, your Honor," Larz said submissively. "That is correct. I would ask the court for a 24-hour recess to allow us to further investigate."

Lance could see the fury in the judge's eyes from the back of the courtroom. He grinned the smile of a self-satisfied lizard.

The judge stood, "This court will recess until ten AM tomorrow morning." The gavel was as a pistol shot as she struck the sound block. She looked down at Larz and Hoyt. "And you had better have a clear resolution to this by morning! I need not say more." With her threat hanging in the air, she left the courtroom.

"Larz, what's going on?" asked Hoyt. I don't understand any of this."

"I really don't know. I would have dismissed the army guy's claims if my USB hadn't become corrupted. How did it even happen? It was in my briefcase. I need to talk to the DA and get a fresh copy of the videos."

Gabriella stood to be led back to her cell. She turned to Paul, "I don't know what just happened. Keep praying, Paul."

"I will always be praying for you, Gabriella," he said, just before "I love you," slipped from his lips. Both their eyes widened as she was whisked away.

***

Court was brief the next morning. The DA sat with Larz Grinder at the prosecution table. Hoyt Brightwood sat alone with Gabriella. Paul was in his usual seat behind Gabriella. Lance took the same position next to the doors. Judge Weatherby asked for a review of their findings.

D.A. O'Connor stood to address the judge. "Your honor, I almost don't know where to begin. This is unprecedented. It is apparent the evidence in our case against Miss West was tampered with by a person or persons unknown."

"What do you mean by 'tampered with,' Mr. District Attorney?"

"Judge, when we went back through the computer system to retrieve the original video files, we found they were not the same files as were presented in court yesterday. The files in the computer system point to someone other than the defendant as the guilty party."

"What! You didn't verify the video evidence presented in this court was the actual files from the video cameras? I wish I could hold you all in contempt for falsifying evidence," she fumed. "Didn't you copy the files from the police mainframe?"

"Yes, we did, your honor," said the DA with a touch of defensiveness and hostility in his voice. "We went right to the files on the mainframe and copied them onto the USB drive we showed in court. We made no procedural errors on our part."

"Then how do you explain the errors?" questioned Weatherby. "At any rate, what did you find?"

"That's precisely the confusing part, Judge. Instead of seeing the defendant on the videos, we found the deceased's wife entering and leaving the lab in the timeframe in question. The fingerprints taken from the murder weapon now show up as belonging to the wife instead of the defendant. Your Honor, I believe someone has hacked our police database, and the evidence expertly changed to implicate the defendant. I can't imagine why or by who. This is a murder case with little notoriety."

"WHAT?" Judge Weatherby shouted with no regard to decorum. "Our police system was hacked! D.A. Campbell, I want every available resource assigned to this, every one of our best computer people, to find out who is responsible for this breach. When a police server is hacked, and evidence changed, it's a matter of national security!"

Weatherby slammed her gavel down. "Case dismissed. Defendant, you are free to go."

Gabriella let out a gasp of relief, stood, and embraced Paul over the gallery railing.

The judge glared over the courtroom. "I'll get to the bottom of this!" she said to the D.A. Lance smiled. *I don't think so, Judge.*

Chapter Forty-Two

The rectory was quiet when Gabriella rang the doorbell. She stood there as she heard male footsteps approaching. The latch opened with a click, and the door swung open.

"Hi, Gabriella. Thank you for coming. I would have met you someplace else, but my calendar is packed today, and I can't get away. Come in. Come in."

"No problem, Paul. I needed a break from the lab for a little while, anyhow. What did you want to see me about?"

Paul smiled and took Gabriella in his arms. "Just to see you, mostly, but I have an answer to your question about if an AI can have a spirit. But first, can I get you something to drink?"

"Thanks, I would like some jasmine tea if you have any."

Paul smiled and said, "No coffee or espresso today? It's not like you."

"A girl has a right to be fickle, it's one of our gifts."

With a shake of his head, Paul smiled and said, "Yep, you sure have that right, I guess. Jasmine tea coming right up."

"Thank you very much, sir. Will you be brewing it from an old family recipe?"

"Yes," Paul replied. "The family recipe is; first you open the box, then you throw the tea bag into hot water. It's pretty complicated, but eventually, I learned how to do it," he said with a chuckle.

In a minute, Paul returned with 2 cups of tea. "Here you go," he said.

" Thank you kind stranger," Gabriella said. "You have been very kind to a thirsty traveler." They both laughed.

"So tell me about the soul thing you settled on, Paul."

"Well, we've discussed how extraordinary special people are to God. He made us in His very own image. We have a body, soul, and spirit."

"Yes, we've discussed it thoroughly," Gabriella said, sipping her tea.

"God said He knew us before we were formed in our mother's womb. Not after our birth, or even while we were still being carried by our mom. He knew us from before he laid the foundations of the earth. That's pretty special, don't you think?"

"Sure, but what does it have to do with a soul?"

"I'm getting there. You were wondering if searching for God would be proof a spirit was driving the search. Well, in a human, yes. In an android, well, that's a different matter."

"Different? Why Paul? I don't understand."

"It's like this, Gabriella, how can you tell the difference between a soul searching for God and a person searching because there they have a real curiosity about God?"

"I don't know. It sounds like the same thing to me. What's the difference?"

"And it can feel the same, too. The difference is, with a person who is searching, there is a real burn deep within them. If the fire isn't there, it's not a real search no matter how real it may feel to the person, or to our android."

"So, it all depends on a feeling or burn?"

"Well, not entirely. Souls are created individually by God. Searching alone, no matter how intense or sincere the effort, does not imply the existence of a soul in our android example."

"Paul, are you sure only people can have souls?" she breathed.

"Yes, I am. Why do you suddenly look so sad? It keeps happening, and I never quite know what I did."

Gabriella looked into his eyes tenderly and said, "It's nothing. But look, I have to get back to work. Thank you for the tea." She placed the unfinished cup on the endtable and stood up to leave.

"Hold it. Wait! Let's talk about what happened," Paul pleaded.

"It's okay," she said as she put both arms around his neck and buried her face into his shoulder. "It's all good. I have to run," she whispered. Paul held her for a full thirty seconds before she disentangled and walked out of the door. She looked back at him standing in the doorway as she rounded the corner of the rectory and was out of sight.

So I can't have a soul? Why can't I be a different kind of human and have a normal life like everyone else? Damn, I hate that little marionette with the long nose in the kid's books. Even he got to become a real live boy. Why can't I become a real woman and have a life with Paul?

Chapter Forty-Three

Ralph pulled Rose to the side during their self-defense class. "Rose, have you noticed any changes in Gabriella lately?"

"Yup. I thought it was just me but wanted to touch base with you to see if you saw the same thing. Gabriella is going through the practice motions, but the snap and aggressiveness don't seem to be there anymore."

"Yeah," Ralph answered, "All of the moves are correct, but something has changed in her delivery. It looks so passive and uninspired. She's not fighting at all."

"Exactly what I've been observing. Have you been putting it into any of your reports, Ralph?"

"No, not yet, but I think we need to send the info upline. It could be significant," Ralph glanced over to Gabriella. "She is doing some light sparring, but is in a defensive mode rather than counter-attacking."

"That concerns me, Rose. She went from someone who could care less if she seriously hurt four attackers, to someone who seems to be, well, another soft model type. I don't get it. Why the change?"

"Well, given a close friend and coworker was killed by his wife while he was at work, it would seem natural it would change her views on life."

"I guess so, but this seems like an extreme change for one person dying. I've been in Iraq and taken out a few people. My friends have died, too. I guess I don't have the same feelings towards the loss of enemy life. Something else is going on."

They both filed their reports.

***

Lance contacted General Cunningham. They discussed courses of action if Gabriella couldn't be changed back to someone who could kill if necessary.

Chapter Forty-Four

The meeting in General Cunningham's office was short and to the point.

"General," said Lance, "we have a problem with our Gabriella android. It has developed some sort of morals or something. We need an android with grit, not morals.

"Can we change her programming?"

"Normally yes, but in her case, her mind has developed in such a way that parts of it function like they are almost hard-wired. Our programming can't override her desires and moral values. She's become too human for our purposes."

"What have you tried to do about it?"

"I've had our programmers rewrite the code to override her moral wishes, but it doesn't seem to be able to do its job. We aren't sure why it is. The code is flawless and seems to work in our mainframe mockup, but not within Gabriella's gel brain. We back her whole mind up every night and review the programming along with any new nano-machine synapses she may have developed. It all looks good. She should work like the mainframe program, but doesn't."

"Anything else?"

"Yes, Sir. You are aware of my plan to pose as a terrorist cell leader to test Gabriella's ability to extract information from me."

"Yes, I am."

"General, she failed that test miserably. She went to dinner with me to find out what my 'terrorist cell' was planning. When I invited her to my apartment to talk further, she refused and left. She failed the 'sleeping with the enemy' test. We can't use her for her intended purpose, Sir."

"What do you propose, Lance?"

"I propose a Gabriella II model. We have all of Gabriella's data backed up. We have the technology fully refined to build another Gabriella model android. Most of the parts are available to assemble a replacement in short order. We can replicate her gel brain with complete functionality and can have another working android within six months.

"Lance, do you have any idea how much it would cost?"

"Yes, sir. Only seventeen million dollars. That includes additional programming to ensure the new android won't have the same problems."

"Do we get eggroll with that?"

"Pardon?"

"Never mind. Let me look into it and see if I can free up some weapons development money. I'm sure DARPA has some extra money squirreled away in the budget somewhere. I'll get back to you."

"Yes, General. What do we do with the current Gabriella-1 model?"

"What does the Army do with equipment no longer fit for its intended purpose, Colonel?"

Chapter Forty-Five

Francine addressed the lab staff to announce their next project has been approved by corporate. "For lack of an official name, we will address the project as Gabriella II for now. Our plan is to download Gabriella's memory from the Cray XC40 computer into a Gabriella II model." She told them the Secretary of Defense was commissioning their work.

There was some groaning from the ranks. "You mean we're going to make a battle-bot or some sort of humanoid weapon?"

"Well, no, not quite. Our next android will have sturdier internal titanium armor to protect its vital parts better, but we will not be making a humanoid weapon. No lasers firing from her eyes or poison darts launching from her bra. We will download Gabriella's programming to the new unit."

An engineer turned and asked Gabriella how she felt about her mind being cloned.

She laughed, "I've always wanted a sister. It'll be fun. She'll have great skin since that's my assigned research area."

Francine continued, "While it will be Gabriella 'under the hood' so to speak, the body will not look like her, except for the basic shape."

Gabriella struck a pose similar to the hostess on the game show 'Wheel of Fortune.' An "Amen" came from one of the male engineers.

Francine smiled and continued, shaking her head from side to side in mock exasperation. "Anyhow, the Pentagon likes what we can do with the skin colors. They asked us to make it easy for the android to pass for a light-skinned Middle Eastern person. They want to infiltrate some specific groups, and how better to do it than with a beautiful woman. Men run most of the world's governments, right? And you know how men are around attractive women." A chuckle rippled through the lab. Heads nodded with understanding.

"Okay, gang," said Francine. "We will do pretty much what we did the last time, so it should be easier the second time around, especially since we have the nano-machine gel brain worked out and have Gabriella's complete personality we can download to it."

"Hey," she said, looking at her watch, "it's time for lunch. Does anyone have any questions before we break for eats?"

A newer engineer on the team started to raise her hand. It was immediately pulled down by Martha.

"Why did you pull my hand down, Martha? I have a question for Francine," she said.

Martha smiled, and with a chuckle, told the newbie, "I'm saving your life. Asking a question after lunch has been announced is a sure way to get razzed by everyone for a couple of days. Besides, Francine was using our coded phrase to let everyone know that she was not taking any questions. Talk to her later with your comments or concerns."

"Are there any more secret codes I should know?'

"Can't tell until you stumble into something."

"But then it's too late!"

"Yup. Welcome to AI Concepts," Martha said as she put her arm around the newbies. "Let's pick up Gabriella and go out to lunch."

Chapter Forty-Six

Gabriela waited by the roses next to the pond for Paul. She prayed their conversation would not end in total disaster. Her fingers fidgeted.

I can't see how it would end any other way. God, help me through this. I can't keep living a lie with Paul. I love him too much. Please don't let this be the last time I see him. "I love him and Alexi so much," she whispered.

The southeast gateway to Central Park next to the pond was the most heavily trafficked entrance. She saw Paul walking eagerly through the crowd. *It's as if the crowd is made of tinted glass, and Paul was the only person out there* who stands out in full, saturated color. She finally understood the old lover's cliché of 'I only have eyes for you.' *He really is all I can see.*

"Hi, Gabriella. Why such urgency in your voice? Is everything okay? Are you okay?" He reached out to give her a hug and a kiss, but she raised her arms between them and held him at a distance. Paul's countenance fell in confusion.

"Did I do something wrong? Did I forget to do something, Gabriella?"

Gabriella hushed him. "Paul, I need to tell you something first. Please don't interrupt me while I am doing it, okay?"

"No problem, honey. I am always here to listen to you. I will always be here to work through things, whatever they may be."

How I yearn for those words to be true. How I wish Paul understood in advance what I am going to say, but it's impossible. Not by any stretch of Paul's fertile imagination can he guess what's coming up next. He told me once he had finally found something real. Oh God, oh God! How can I do this to him? But how can I not let him know? Her hands were wringing in front of her.

Oh God, please help me with this, she silently pleaded. *I don't want this to end.*

"I can't imagine a life without you, Paul," came out in a whisper.

"What did you say?" Paul asked.

"Nothing."

Gabriella gave a painful, wry smile as she considered it could not help but to end in disaster. *What can Paul do? Accept the woman he now loves isn't a woman at all? The person his daughter had become attached to isn't even human? How else could it end but in complete disaster? Still, I can't live a lie any longer. Delaying the inevitable will only make it hurt worse later.*

"Paul, you really don't know who I am. You don't know what I am. I need to tell you, but I don't know how too. As soon as I do, I'm so afraid you'll leave, and we'll never see each other again. I don't know if I could bear it. I've fallen so in love with you and Alexi."

Gabriella lifted Paul's hand to her face, closed her eyes, and snuggled into it. She moved his hand away, held it in both of hers, and kissed it gently before speaking.

"I would do anything in the world not to lose either of you, but it's almost inevitable. My heart is breaking, and I'm shaking with fear and dread. I don't know what to do, but when the truth comes out later, it will hurt worse, if it's even possible. I hope you know if it were up to me alone, I would never leave you or ever break your heart."

Paul's face reflected a mix of confusion and gravity. "Gabriella, the last thing in the world I would want to do is lose you. What on earth could be so terrible? Did you rob a bank? I stood by you through a murder trial. Doesn't it prove I wouldn't leave you? You are the most wonderful woman I've ever met in my life. I never want to leave you."

The word 'woman' cut deeply. *How I wish I were.*

Gabriella covered her face with both of her hands and bent over, sobbing. *I will cherish those words from Paul forever, but he would have to be superhuman to make good on his promise.*

Passerbys stared at what seemed like a lovers spat. The most casual observer could tell this was a couple in love. Some silently wished them well as they strolled by.

Paul lifted her upright and looked into her eyes with gentleness and compassion. She threw her arms around his neck and held him close. He felt her body spasm as she cried against him.

After a few moments, Gabriella pulled herself away.

Oh dear God, she prayed, *please don't let this be the end.*

"Paul, look into my eyes. What do you see?"

"Two beautiful green eyes filled with pain and love."

"Do you see any tears?"

"No."

"Don't you think it's suspicious in any way?"

"No. Some people don't shed tears when they cry. I've seen it in my office when I counsel people."

She held her left hand out to him with the palm on top. "Take my pulse."

He lovingly held her wrist and placed his fingers below her left thumb. "I can't feel it. Must be my fingers, or I'm in the wrong spot."

"Try the other wrist, Paul, and please remember I love you with my whole mind."

"Strange way to say it, Gabriella."

Paul dutifully took her right wrist and tried to find her pulse. "Can't find it there either," he said. "Why is it important? It's hard to find a pulse on some people."

"That's just it. I think. I feel. I love. But I'm not a woman!"

"You're a man??!!" Paul gasped.

"No!" shouted Gabriella. "I'm not a woman, I'm an android! A living, feeling, thinking, caring, loving, crying, android!"

"It's impossible!" said Paul, "simply impossible! Because I couldn't find your pulse doesn't mean you are..." He couldn't finish the thought. It confused his mind. Everything around the center of his field of vision was getting gray and fuzzy. "I won't, I can't believe it!"

Gabriella walked over to the rosebush and twisted a thorn out of a stem. She held her outstretched arm palm up and plunged the spine into the underside of her forearm.

"Ouch," she said quietly, "that hurt."

Paul looked on in fear and wonder. "Have you suddenly gone crazy? Did you do drugs?" Paul dismissed both options, although he would have preferred the insane possibility.

With a yank, the thorn came out of her arm. "Look, Paul, what do you see?"

"I see a small hole in your arm. Why the hell did you do that?"

"Do you see any blood? Shouldn't it bleed? The thorn went in deeply. See, no blood. I don't have any blood! I am living, but I am not a human!" She had finally blurted it out.

Paul rocked backward in disbelief. He tried to get his head around the whole thing but couldn't. His mind spun and reeled like an old wooden sailing ship on a storm-tossed sea. He had no sense of direction and no way to slow the spinning. He couldn't see, he couldn't think as his mind tried to stabilize itself in its overwhelmed and disoriented state.

The sudden pain in his head was debilitating. He couldn't talk coherently. Paul felt waves of nausea wash over him and dizziness threatening to overtake him. He doubled over, trying to catch his breath.

"No, no, no, no NO!" he screamed out in despair and agony as he forced himself upright. He realized she was telling him the truth. Paul's head swirled crazily and caved in on itself. His mind snapped as confusion mixed wildly with heartbreak. Against his will, Paul's raw emotions spewed out violently like putrid vomit. He grabbed Gabriella by her upper arms.

"You lied to me! You let me believe you were a woman who cared for Alexi and me! I fell in love with you! Damn it! Were we part of a sick experiment? Were you recording our every conversation? Was there some sicko in a lab somewhere doing an analysis of how well you could fool a human? What kind of hell were you born in that could fashion cold materials into something that seems to be alive? You sucked Alexi and me into your scheme, your charade! I can live with it, but how could you do it to Alexi? She loves you like a mother. How could you betray her? What kind of demonic machine are you?" Tears ran in torrents down his face. Red rings circled Paul's eyes.

Gut-wrenching sobs enveloped Gabriella as she cried. "It's not like that at all. I have feelings; I love both of you," she sobbed. "I would love to be Alexi's mother, more than anything else in the world. I had to tell you because I care about you and couldn't go on living a lie. Paul, I love you. Please don't go away," she pleaded.

A vehement torrent of pain came pouring out of Paul uncontrollably.

"Living! Living! Is that what you call it? How can you be living when you are a machine made in a lab? How can you really feel love and have emotions? Is that part of your programming? Was everything part of some computer program? Get away from me," he screamed with a cracking voice and tears of pain. "Go back to your lab, or go to hell, or go to where ever you want, but stay away from us!"

He pushed her back as he let go of her arms, turned, and stumbled quickly towards the entrance. Paul looked back as he reached the gate. The sun glinted off the tears on his cheek.

Gabriella sat heavily on the grass with her legs folded under her and her bent head in her hands. She sobbed out the despair of one who had lost her entire family in one catastrophic event.

Paul brushed the tears out of his eyes and walked out of the park. "I'm sick! I just want to die! How am I ever going to tell Alexi about this? Oh, God, help!"

Gabriella sat on the lawn for quite a while. Several people, mostly women, stopped to ask if she was all right and was there anything they could do to help. Gabriella waved them off gently and said she would be all right. One small, middle-aged businesswoman walked past, hesitated, and then turned around. She stood over Gabriella for a few seconds and then quietly sat down next to her left side without saying a word. She sat there for five minutes before the sobbing Gabriella even noticed her.

"How long have you been sitting next to me?" Gabriella asked.

"About five minutes," answered the woman. "I'm Charlene."

"Hi, I'm Gabriella," she said with a shaky voice. "Why are you sitting next to me?"

"It looked like you could use a friend right now. I was passing by and, believe it or not, I heard the Holy Spirit tell me to turn around and talk to you. Sounds crazy, huh? I don't know what your faith level is, or if you even have any faith in God, but I am neither crazy nor dangerous." she said with a smile. "I had to obey and stop for you."

"I appreciate your stopping, but I don't think even God cares for me. I'm feeling so alone and empty right now. My life just fell apart because morally, I had to tell the truth about something. It really sucks when you try to do the right thing, and the truth acts like a missile blowing your life apart. Truth shouldn't do that."

"I know," whispered Charlene softly "sometimes, when we do the right thing and tell the truth, it can seem like something wonderful gets destroyed because of it, but perhaps God has other plans and needs to clear some space around us. It doesn't make it hurt any less, though. Are you a church person?"

"Sort of, but it makes sense to me scientifically there is a God who created everything."

"How about a God who cares about you, honey?"

"I don't know. I haven't traveled that far yet, but right now, I don't think so. I can see how it all works with the universe and even with quantum physics. But I guess the thought God cares about my daily life is a little new. My friend, Paul, tried to tell me..." the words choked her as she broke down again.

Charlene put her right arm around Gabriella and drew her close. Feeling she was in a warm, safe spot for the moment opened up the floodgates of heart-rendering sobbing again. Gabriella put her arms around Charlene and held her tightly for a minute or two until her crying subsided.

"Thank you, Charlene. I'm sorry I lost it again. You don't even know me, and I'm crying all over you."

"It's okay, honey. We all need a shoulder to cry on once in a while, and a stranger's shoulder sometimes works best because they don't know enough about us to judge. Can I ask what happened?"

"I am, was, dating a wonderful divorced man, a pastor of a small church, with a beautiful five-year-old daughter. We were developing strong feelings toward each other, although we were both too cautious about saying much or acting on it."

"That's a sage move, Gabriella. Too many people rush headlong into physical relationships."

Gabriella continued. "He was there to support me through a horrendous event, and I thought he might handle the news I gave him today. I had to tell Paul the truth about me. I was wrong. I was so very, very wrong. He cut off our relationship and told me never to contact him again." She buried her face into Charlene's shoulder again and convulsed.

Charlene gasped. "How awful! My heart breaks for you, child. What in heaven's name could be so terrible he would break off a relationship just like that? Did you tell him you were married, or a hooker, or you killed someone?"

"No, he probably would have stayed with me through it all. In fact, he stayed with me through my murder trial."

Charlene stiffened involuntarily.

"No, no, I didn't do anything," Gabriella quickly added. "They set me up, but ultimately exonerated me when the truth surfaced. No, this is far worse than any of those things. I can't blame Paul for not being able to handle it. It's this tremendous sense of loss I feel. It's like God has turned His back on me."

"What on earth could you have done? You look so sweet, and the Holy Spirit directed me to come over and talk to you. There, there," said Charlene softly as she held Gabriella. "I don't need to know what your secret is. God already knows, and He loves you beyond what you could imagine. Would it be okay with you if I prayed with you right here?"

"I would like it very much," replied Gabriella with a slight uplift of hope in her voice.

"Father God, I lift Gabriella up to you. I don't know the details of her situation, but I know you know everything about it. I know, Father, you love her intensely Father touch her heart, send peace to her soul, and lift her spirit. Touch Paul and his daughter and give them peace and clear thinking. I thank you for being the great God you are and always being there to talk to and to seek advice from. Father, I lift these prayers up to you in Jesus' name and thank you in advance for hearing and answering them. Amen!"

"I hope that wasn't too much for you, Gabriella. I prayed what I was feeling."

"I've never heard someone pray with that much conviction. It's like you know God personally, instead of knowing about Him. It's the same with Paul. I've prayed before, but there was not the one-on-one relationship you two seem to have with God."

"We do, and you can too. I have to go back to work now, but remember to give it to God in prayer, ask for His will to be done, not yours, and then expect to see an answer. May God bless you." With that, she turned and walked off.

Gabriella sat on the grass for a while before slowly walking back to her apartment.

Chapter Forty-Seven

Martha's phone vibrated. "Martha, can you come over to my apartment? I need you. Can you come right now, please?"

"Sure, Gabriella, I can be there in a half-hour. What's up? You don't sound like yourself."

"Can we talk when you get here, Martha?"

Half an hour later, a building elevator at Two Hundred East Sixty-Ninth Street cheerfully serenaded Martha as it carried her to the forty-third floor. The doors opened with a calming bell tone and a soft swish. Martha hurried to Gabriella's apartment.

"Martha," Gabriella said with a catch in her voice, "thank you so much for coming over."

"Sure, honey, you know I'm here for you. What happened? Why didn't you come back to work after meeting with Paul? Is everything okay?"

"No, everything is not okay, Martha. Everything is most assuredly, not okay. I met with Paul and..." Gabriella held her arms out to Martha. The two women hugged tightly as Gabriella cried tearlessly.

"It'll all be okay, honey. It'll all be okay." Martha stroked the back of Gabriella's head as she held her. "We can work through this, whatever it is."

"We can't fix this one. I made a terrible mistake. I hoped he could handle it. Martha, I love him so very much. I love him so much, and now he's gone. It's all over. I don't know what to do or where to go from here. I don't know what to do."

"What happened, Gabriella?"

"I told Paul the truth about me, and it all blew up. I was hoping he would understand, but he didn't. I didn't want to lose him, but I couldn't go on living a lie."

"You told him you were an android? Why did you do that? *Damn, how do we handle this security breach?* They separated as Martha looked her over.

"I told you I couldn't go on living a lie with Paul. I love him. I truly love him and had to tell him the truth. I guess someplace in my head, I started believing in a fantasy where he and I and Alexi could somehow become a family together. It didn't work, and I feel so crushed and broken."

Gabriella reached for Martha's arms again for comfort. Martha was holding a dear friend, offering the support only a loving embrace could give.

Martha released her hug and took Gabriella's hands in hers and led her to the couch.

"Sit down, honey, and tell me all about it. My heart is breaking for you. Is there any chance at all the two of you could get back together?"

"No, there isn't. The news hit him too hard and too fast. His response was so very visceral and brutal. He said he never wanted to see me again, and I could never contact Alexi anymore. I think he called me a monster."

"Oh, Gabriella, I'm so very, very sorry. I wish it had turned out differently for your sake. Paul made the biggest mistake of his life. He could have worked out any challenges with you being an android. It's hard enough to find someone to love you without putting restrictions on it."

"I'm so crushed and hurt. So devastated. I didn't know people could feel this much pain. I feel as if he ripped my soul out, and now I'm an empty, hurting shell walking around. Does it ever get any better, Martha? Does it fade? How do people fill the hole?"

"I'm not sure, Gabriella. I know we survive it and make it through to the next day, and to the day after that. Somehow we go on, but I don't think the scar ever goes away. The hole may get patched, but the scarring and some pain remain forever. I was hoping it would be different for you, honey." A tear blurred Martha's vision.

Gabriella stood and went into the kitchen area to pour them each a large goblet of red wine. Martha thanked her and said she could use a drink of anything right now. They sat down next to each other again.

"Martha, I'm not sure how drinking is supposed to help the situation, but it seems like the right thing to do, and I'll try anything to numb this feeling. I know alcohol can't affect me, but I want to convince my brain it's having a numbing effect. I can see why some people drink until they pass out. It turns their mind off for a little while. It must be like heaven to stop your thoughts, even temporarily. I can't even sleep to do that. It all seems so hopeless. I really don't feel like going on anymore."

Martha's eyes widened as she grasped what Gabriella was saying. "Oh no, child. You mustn't talk like that. It will be okay, you'll see. Everything works out. Trust me on this. You know I would never, ever lie to you. You're a good friend, and I love you. I'd do anything to take some of your pain away, but I don't know how to do it."

She reached out for Gabriella once more. Martha embraced her and gave her a small kiss on the forehead. Gabriella burrowed deeper into Martha's arms, resting her head on Martha's chest. Gabriella allowed the gentle flow of Martha's breathing to wash over and comfort her. A gentle stirring within Martha prompted her to hold Gabriella even closer. Martha planted soft kisses on the top of Gabriella's head.

Chapter Forty-Eight

Man, I can't even write a sermon anymore," Paul said to the empty air in the rectory. Tears found their way up from his heart and overflowed his eyes. "I honestly loved her. How could I get sucked in like that? She's a machine. I should have been able to figure it out."

He felt guilty as he logged on to an online sermon mill and reviewed several canned sermons to use on Sunday. Paul downloaded the most acceptable one. They based it on Judas Iscariot.

"What kind of pastor am I anyhow? Canned meat and potatoes for the flock. An all-time low, but I don't really care right now. How could she do that to us? How the hell could she do that?"

Meetings with his oversite Bishops did little to help the increasing depression. They could only know his relationship with a woman he loved didn't work out. They tried to counsel Paul but were confused when they could not quite get to the root of his pain.

Paul sat in his office and searched his soul about his faith in God. "Why would a loving God allow this mess to happen? How could You let me be crushed like this when I've dedicated my life to You?" he shouted. "How can You do this to Alexi? She's a trusting little girl who doesn't understand. Where is justice? What are You doing, God? Do You even care about us?"

A little hand touched his arm. He jumped with a shout. "Alexi, please don't sneak up on me, honey."

"I didn't sneak up on you, Dad. I called you, but you didn't hear me. Dad, can we go to the playground in Central Park today? We don't play together anymore."

Paul hung his head and shook it. "Not today, sweetie. I have a lot of work to do. Can we do it some other time?"

"I wish Gabriella were here. She would take me, Dad. I miss her. Can't we call her and ask her to come over?"

Paul's heart twisted in his chest. He turned in his chair and wrapped his arms tightly around Alexi. "Oh, honey, we can't," he said with a sob. "We can't. Tell you what; let's go to the playground for a little while. But we need to watch that cold and cough of yours, okay? It still looks like you are coming down with something."

Chapter Forty-Nine

It was mid-October in Manhattan. The air had a pleasant mixture of warmth with a hint of coolness in the shadow of the buildings.

Sergeant Jeffrey Miller looked up from his computer screens with a frown of concern.

"Colonel, I think we have a problem here, Sir."

"What problem is that, Sergeant?"

"Well, Sir, I was doing some routine process checks of Gabriella's programming and noticed some irregularities.'

Lance's brow wrinkled with concern as he walked to Sergeant Miller's computer monitors. "Explain," he said.

"There are some curious changes in her base programming. I don't believe anyone in her lab programming group made them. I'm familiar with the writing style of all the programmers in AI Concepts. Whoever did this has skills even beyond theirs. A new entity is at play here."

"Sergeant, you're telling me lab programmers didn't make the changes, and we didn't make any changes from here. What's the probability of the system being hacked from the outside?"

"It's about zero, Sir. The mainframe is invisible to anyone outside of the lab environment. Hackers can't find it or ping it. Their mainframe doesn't exist to the outside world."

"What were the changes?"

"All it seems to affect is the global kill switch. The programming for the switch still looks correct. When I ran a software simulation test, it seemed as if the switch was functional. But now I don't think it will function to shut down our android if we want to."

"Sergeant, what's your evaluation on how this impossible act might be possible?" Lance said, testing the intuitive ability of his lead programmer.

"Sir, right now, the only reasonable explanation is Gabriella has noticed the kill switch programming on the mainframe and has somehow engineered software around it to make it look as if it's working when, in actuality, it is not."

"That's quite a statement, Sergeant. How can we verify it?"

"We can't, Sir. We can only make a logical assumption after eliminating all other possibilities."

"Then how can we check the switch works?" Lance said, allowing his sergeant to postulate a test plan.

"Well, Sir, the only pragmatic way is to wait until the mainframe backs up Gabriella's gel brain for the day. She is comparatively idle at night, so we can hit the physical switch to see if it erases her brain. If it works, we can download everything from the Cray mainframe and have her fully restored by morning with no ill effects."

Lance smiled at his direct report's ability to design a workable plan and nodded his approval.

Lance continued probing, "Very good. But what if hitting the switch does not erase her brain?"

"Sir, then we would have verification that we have a significant problem."

"Good job, Sergeant. Let's hit the kill switch at 0100 hours tonight. It should give us enough time to restore Gabriella if it works and lay out a path forward if it doesn't."

"But Colonel, wouldn't Gabriella have noticed she had lost some conscious time during the restore process?"

"Excellent question. No, I think we will be okay with this. She often goes into an idle rest mode when alone in her apartment. Unless she checked a clock before and after the reboot, she should have no consciousness of the event. At least it's what the design specs say. Let's do it."

***

At 1:05 AM, Sergeant Miller called out to Lance, "Colonel, pinging her software showed the physical kill switch did not work. She is still entirely functional."

"In that case, Sergeant, we have lost control of the Gabriella android. She is autonomous. As a famous phrase goes, "Houston, we have a problem." She is now free to damn-well do whatever she wishes without our ability to override her. Crap, our AI has figured out how to change her own programming!"

"Sir, I've found it's even worse than that."

Lance raised his arms above his head in exasperation. "Worse? You're shitting me! What could be worse than that?"

Sergeant Miller emotionally cowered for a moment.

"Sir, I believe there's some kind of code overseeing her programming, and it prevents us from writing any subroutines which would impact her thinking or operation, without her approval. I don't know what it looks like, what language it's written in, or even where it is, but I can see its protective effect over her entire system. I've never seen anything like it! We can't touch her!"

"Sergeant, are you telling me she has become her own life form? And we have absolutely no control over her anymore? We have to ASK her if it's okay to change her coding!"

"Yes, Sir. That's exactly what I am saying."

"This is both exhilarating and terrifying, Jeff. I need to talk to the Major General. I'll get back to you with further orders after we've met and laid out a plan of action. We can't have an android walking around Manhattan doing whatever it wants, whenever it wants. Especially not an army android."

***

Within two days, Lance met with Major General Brian Cunningham in the Pentagon.

One week later, the Major General was having dinner in the NYS Governor's Mansion with his friend, Governor Lorenzo Vomitare.

Over porterhouse steak and lobster tails, the general said, "Governor, I'd like to discuss a proposition with you. I believe it will be in our mutual interest."

"Sure, Brian. I'm intrigued. What do you have in mind?"

"You have some resistance in getting the level of gun control you want in this state. The military has a problem with terrorism and bad press. I think we could help each other out."

"Continue," said the governor, leaning closer to the Major General.

"Lorenzo, think about this; what if there were a controlled terrorist attack in New York. And what if it was thwarted before anyone got seriously hurt? It would give the military and the NSA a big boost. Plus, it would give you the extra leverage you were looking for to further push through your gun control."

"That's interesting, but how do we do it? What on earth is a controlled terrorist attack?"

"It's not all that difficult. We can convince a carefully selected individual to attempt an act of terrorism, but then catch him in the very act before he executes on it. The press will love it and will help you in achieving your anti-gun agenda."

"I'm liking it so far. Tell me more."

"I will hand you a ready-made platform to denounce rampant gun abuse across the country and in New York State in particular. The best part is, you can blame it all on the NRA because of their support of the Second Amendment."

The governor's smile broadened. "You know, with a little word-smithing, I can have my creative people tie in school shootings, too. Leave no heartstring untugged," said Lorenzo.

The Major General continued, "Besides, we both know there is an increasing number of anti-military and anti-government groups across the country. They believe the right to keep and bear arms protects them against tyranny."

"True enough. They are nothing but a pain in the ass."

Cunningham continued, "Militants admire the Revolutionary War people because they overthrew the legitimate government of England. The rebels could defeat a stronger, well-armed British military because every citizen owned their own firearm. They were the equivalent of a heavily armed rebel army dispersed among the citizenry. If the British could have disarmed the civilian population, we would be having tea and crumpets now."

"I like what I'm hearing, Brian. Please go on."

"As the governor of the state, you would not want a rebel army living around you. Neither would the military. If an armed rebellion were to occur, it would be nasty press to fight and kill our own people."

"Got that straight!

"But if we can increase the cry for stricter gun legislation, we can make it impossible, little by little, for individual citizens to own guns. This would leave only the criminals with guns, but no one really cares if the police shoot them or if they shoot each other in gang fights.

So the bottom line is this; if we work together to set up a fake terrorist attack, with all the safeguards in place, we can move the hearts and minds of both the civilian and state lawmakers in the direction we want them to go. They will think they have the best interest of the public in mind, but we know we have secured our power and fortunes. It's a win-win situation."

"I like the idea, General. Let's talk in more detail."

"Excellent, Governor."

"What do you need me to do?"

"We have all the resources we need to execute on this plan. We will coordinate with you at every step, so you will know there is virtually no threat to the civilian population, but other than that, you need not dedicate any resources to the fake attack."

"Virtually no threat?"

"Well, there is always a slight threat of collateral damage. Is it a problem?"

"No, but is there any way to get the risk down to zero?"

"Unfortunately, no, there isn't."

"I had to ask. You understand."

"No problem. Just in case things go south on us, it would be best if you only knew the date, time, and nature of the attack.

No other details. You can then politically distance yourself from any mud-splatter. We will handle all the rest. I have some outstanding people placed in critical areas to make all of this happen flawlessly."

"Let's not make the same mistake the British did in the 1770s."

"Another scotch, Brian?"

"Indeed, along with a number of its friends, Lorenzo. Pass the ice, please."

Chapter Fifty

Quadir Akram emigrated from Syria two years ahead of his wife Adeeba and their three children. He came to America on a vetted U.S. Visa to search for work and a better life. His hometown of Aleppo was turning from an idyllic city of relative peace into a battleground for a variety of forces. He sold his little one-man bakery for whatever money he could get and then borrowed and scraped together the rest of the funds needed to come to the U.S. But he could not afford to bring his wife and three children with him.

Quadir remembered the last few days together before he began the trek to the U.S. The fighting had not yet engulfed the entire city with the ashes of destruction. The all-consuming city-wide pyroclastic flow of heat and fire from the aerial assaults were still in the future. Some areas of the city were safe enough to allow people to live a quasi-normal life.

"Are you sure?" Adeeba asked Quadir as she tenderly raised her hand to touch his cheek.

She ran her fingers lightly through his dark brown hair. Quadir was an average looking, five-foot seven-inch, darker-skinned Syrian. To the rest of the world, he was practically indistinguishable from almost every other man in the area, but Adeeba thought he was the most handsome person she had ever seen. "Are you sure you can get us to the U.S? How can this happen? We will never have the money to get us all there."

"I know, my love. I know. This can happen. I will make it happen. I have to make it happen for you and the children. Look at them playing. They don't care about politics or economics. They want to play like little children. Already they have seen too much and know such pain. We have to make a better life for them. We need to do something before the war gets worse here."

"But to go to America, Quadir? Do they even like Syrians? Do you think you can make enough money there to bring all of us over to you? You have a visa, but how can we all get one? There is no American Consulate here anymore. There is a limit on how many of us they will let into the country. What if we can't get in?"

"We will. We must! Our family's life is in danger. I will do whatever it takes. I promise this, Adeeba."

The children were playing and laughing together with a handful of others in the park. "It should be like this every day, not constant fear of war." Quadir whispered and added, "Someday soon, it will be for the five of us."

They sat in silence for several hours, watching them play. Sitting together near their children was sometimes all the happiness they could hope for. Young ones had no worries, no lingering memories of how it was in the past, and no concept of fear of the future. Quadir wished he were a child again and relieved of all his adult responsibility and anguish.

The Akram family finally gathered themselves together and walked home for dinner. Quadir and Adeeba spoke quietly about the plans to liberate the whole family. They also talked about their never-dying love for each other. Their marriage was arranged, but they thought so much alike and shared so many family values it didn't take long to fall genuinely in love. Neither one of them felt like talking about the real- probability that their plans might not be successful. They both understood it was a long-shot. "One step at a time, though," said Adeeba.

They tucked the children into their beds with extra love and kisses. Quadir and Adeeba lingered over them as they kissed their little heads, enjoying the smell of freshly washed hair, then went to bed themselves and held each other all night long. He would desperately miss the warmth of her sleeping body next to him and the sound of her quiet breathing. Tears shone in his eyes. He let them run uninterrupted down his cheek, soaking into the pillow.

Within a week, Quadir was on a Cunard passenger ship en route to the States. *I am grateful food is included in the passage,* he thought, as he watched the mid-ocean waves roll on forever. *I thought I would have to fast for the entire voyage after my little loaf of bread was gone.*

Getting a job was much more difficult for a Syrian after the 9/11 attack on the Twin Towers. He found scant support and only marginal living quarters with other Syrians in Little Syria near Atlantic Avenue in Brooklyn. Quadir was hard working and accepted any job offering to pay him a wage, often significantly below the legal minimum.

He repeated the mantra, "Beggars can't have the whole loaf," and did whatever they assigned to him. His favorite position was as a dishwasher at one of the Syrian restaurants in the area. It wasn't cleaning the dishes which satisfied him, but the opportunity to save on expenses by salvaging scraps of leftover food from the plates in the bussing buckets. Quadir brought them home to eat. He wanted more than anything in the world to get his family out of the increasingly war-torn Syria and into the United States. He often mused on how people thought the streets of Brooklyn were so rough and dangerous. Quadir wondered what they would feel if they lived in Aleppo. Brooklyn was a near paradise by comparison, and he wanted to bring his family to heaven.

The fighting in Aleppo heated up considerably in the short time Quadir had been in the States. The rebel group, Free Syrian Army (FSA), battled the regular Syrian Army for dominion and control, reducing his once beloved home city into a pile of ruins. Quadir was heartsick when he found historic sites were being disintegrated by the battles. His fear for his family increased.

"Lieutenant," said Colonel Coopers, "I need you to find me a desperate refugee for an assignment. I need someone at the end of their rope and willing to do anything to resolve whatever issue they are facing. Use the PULSE system to find them."

"Understood, Sir. Find a desperate refugee for an assignment using PULSE," replied Lieutenant Rolands.

"That is correct," Lance answered in proper three-way verification.

The list of desperate refugees in New York was lengthy, but as ordered, the Lieutenant scrolled through them all, searching for a profile of desperation that could motivate someone to do almost anything. He waded through a morass of people with financial issues, drug associations of one sort or another, and gang-related problems. The list went on and on in a litany of primarily self-imposed hardships caused by lousy decision making. He knew none of these would be a reliably useful tool.

Finally, Quadir Akram's case file came up. Hard worker, never been in trouble either in the U.S. or in Syria, married and devoted with three children. Through intercepted text messages it was clear Quadir would do virtually anything to get Adeeba and their children to the U.S. A review of Quadir's bank account showed he had about enough money to get to Coney Island and buy a hotdog, certainly light-years away from being able to bring his family over. It was clear his family would never make the trip. He couldn't afford the airfare, let alone the necessary bribes. All the while, the fighting was heating up, and danger loomed like a dark monster in front of his family. Yes, Quadir was a very desperate man who could be manipulated.

"Colonel, I think I have our man. Would you like me to contact him and make an offer, Sir?"

"No, Lieutenant, give me his name and number. I want to do this one," answered Lance. "Yes, I'm getting closer to Generalship," he whispered to himself.

Lance enjoyed the new computer systems. In the old days, it would have taken months to find the perfect person for this purpose. The Protective Unilateral Security Evaluation computer network (PULSE) transparently received data feeds from every social media application, email system, licensing bureau, public and private security cameras, and all computers using the internet. If it could transmit electronic data, PULSE was monitoring it. Ostensibly the system tracked electronic communication and data patterns to predict and prevent another attack like the 9/11 event. However, it was capable of much, much more, including finding almost every bit of data on virtually every person in the United States, including their current physical location. Street cameras, selfies, and cell phone videos continuously fed it new information. They had created either a god or a devil.

Chapter Fifty-One

Quadir Akram was at the home of the Syrian family, where he rented sleeping space on the floor. The smartphone display said no information was available for the incoming call. Quadir wondered who could call since he had given his cell number to only a few people.

"Who is this?" he asked cautiously in very broken English, then remained silent.

"Hello Mr. Akram," the voice said, "my name is Lance Coopers. I understand you would like to have your wife Adeeba and your children come to the United States. Is that true?"

"Who is this?" Quadir asked in a firmer and more suspicious voice, "How do you know of my family?"

"We know quite a bit about your family. We know they live on Noureddin Zinki Street close to the Daqqa Market in Aleppo. Because of the increased violence in the city, they have to do their grocery shopping as soon as the market opens at dawn, and to go outside and play could now be fatal for your children. You see, Mr. Akram, we know many things about you."

Lance could hear Quadir sucking in his breath.

"Who are you? What do you want?" he said in a voice that was a short step away from panic. He was used to government spies swooping in and eliminating family members for any reason. "You are not Syrian!!" he almost shouted into the phone. "What do you want with my family and me!"

"We only want to help you, Mr. Akram," Lance replied in a low, even voice. "We have the means of getting your family to safety in the U.S. and providing them with a better place to live than the floor space you are renting. Shall we talk face to face? I suppose it all depends on how much you really want to get them to safety. How badly do you want to get them to safety, Quadir? What would you give to make it happen?"

There was a long silence on the phone. Quadir was familiar with the approach. It was one often used in terrorist cells. They issued no threats, but the message came across loud and clear. In this case, the caller would have to do nothing. The situation in Aleppo would take its course and most likely lead to the death of his family.

Taking no action is the same as killing them myself.

I would be heartbroken for the rest of my life for not being able to raise the travel and bribe money in time enough to help them, but my conscience would be clean because I tried my absolute best, he thought glumly.

If this man can get my family out, and I did nothing, it would be like I killed them myself. I could not go on living with that on my mind. I would rather die. There are no options left for me.

"I will do anything to get them out," Quadir intoned.

"Good," Lance replied in a more cheerful voice. "I'll meet you for lunch tomorrow at Noon at the Syrian restaurant on Flatbush near Pacific. I know you are not working until 3:00 PM, so you will have no problem being there. Have a pleasant day, Mr. Akram."

There was a click, and the phone was silent. Quadir's blood ran cold with fear. "Who are these people who know everything about my family and me? How and why would they do something almost impossible? What do they want from my family, or of me, in return?"

Questions came to his mind so fast they were no longer words, but images and feelings, like watching some twisted horror movie on fast-forward. But this was real, and it was happening to him.

Chapter Fifty-Two

The rectory was quiet on Saturday morning. Alexi was watching her favorite character, Opie, in a black-and-white family sitcom. Paul worked on his Sunday sermon at the small, well-worn pastor's desk in front of the window. His fingers rested on the keyboard. He gazed with a blank stare past the panes of glass. The screen on his laptop had two draft paragraphs to show for an hour of work.

Alexi watched the gentle interactions of Andy Taylor and Helen Crump on their small television screen.

"Dad, Gabriella hasn't come around for a few days. I miss her. You guys used to be like them on the TV."

"Honey, it's only a TV show. You know that, right?"

"Yes, but you were still like them. Why doesn't she see us anymore?"

How do I explain the person I fell in love with was a fraud? That she wasn't even a person.

"Alexi, it didn't work out between us, that's all. It simply didn't work out like we hoped it would. Can you understand?"

"No. She felt almost like my mom. She loves me and used to comb my hair, do my nails, and play with me. Dad, you could have fixed it. You can do anything. Why didn't you fix it, Dad?"

Paul let out a deep groan and held his head in his hands, shaking it slowly.

I almost wish I would die. But what would happen to Alexi?

"Sweetie," he said tenderly to a young girl who couldn't understand, "I'd lov..." Paul caught himself. "No... sometimes things can't be fixed. I wish it could be different, but it isn't."

"But you told me God could fix anything. You said it. Isn't it true?"

The words hit Paul like a board to the side of his head. His mind reeled for a moment.

"Yes, I did, Alexi, but some things are not to be, and that's all there is to it."

He stood and headed for the kitchen to prepare dinner.

There was no one awake late at night to hear him cry.

***

Two days later, while Alexi was in preschool, Paul wandered towards Bryant Park on 40th Street to find a coffee shop he and Gabriella had never been too together.

He wandered into BP Coffee and ordered the house blend with cream, no sugar. There was an empty bench across the street in the park, so he sat with a blank mind looking in the direction of the traffic. Before long, a tall, trim woman in her late 20s approached Paul and asked if she could sit at the other end of the bench.

"Sure," said Paul, "there seems to be plenty of room. Have a seat." He continued to stare out into the traffic without turning his head towards her.

"It looks as if you could use some company," the young woman said. "What brings you out here this morning?"

Paul turned to look at the young woman. She had straight, shiny brown hair flowing almost to her waist. Her lightweight black leather jacket sparkled with silver studs around the collar, lapels and shoulders. Silver studs decorated each cuff. A white satin midriff shirt was low cut to reveal and accentuate the artistic work being performed by her push-up bra.

"I wanted coffee and time to think," Paul said without emotion.

"Would you like to go someplace and talk about it?" She smiled at Paul. Shifting her weight, she crossed one long leg over the other, allowing the barely mid-thigh length leather skirt to ride up and display more of her toned, tanned legs. She wore low-cut black and white laced sneakers.

Paul realized this was not a casual conversation. The woman was a lovely hooker.

Paul looked at her for a moment, it flattered a small part of his mind that such a good-looking young lady approached him. "No, thank you," he replied. "I have a better place to be."

The woman shook her head for a moment and breathed. "No, you don't. If you had a better place to be, you would be there now and not sitting all alone on a park bench with me. You look like a straightforward guy. So why are you here alone looking so sad?"

Paul sighed and looked into her eyes. "I fell in love with someone and later found she wasn't what I thought she was."

"And that's why you are sitting here all alone? Look, honey, it's hard enough to find someone you can fall in love with, let alone find someone who's absolutely perfect. They don't exist!"

"Yes, but..."

"Shut up for a second," she interrupted. "If you could find someone nice enough to fall in love with, I'd say you should hold on to them. Everything can be worked out if you both want it." She paused for a moment. "Until then, though, you still have me," she purred as she leaned towards Paul, flashing her smile and revealing more of her cleavage.

"Thank you very much," said Paul. "Your wisdom is exactly what I needed right now. The relationship can't be fixed, but I do have a better place to be." Paul stood, tossed his paper cup along with its remaining ounce of coffee into the trash bin, and walked away.

"I have to go home and hug my daughter for a while," he said aloud as he set a course back to the rectory to await Alexi's return from preschool.

Chapter Fifty-Three

Lance dressed in a dark gray suit, white shirt, and dark green tie to meet with Quadir instead of his usual Army uniform. *I need to intimidate this guy, not scare him away,* he thought as he picked out his clothes. He toyed with his dark sunglasses but decided it would be too cloak-and-dagger. Lance didn't want to be thought of as a cliché.

Quadir arrived early and sat at a table facing the door. Lance was fashionably late to reinforce the fact he was the one in charge. It worked. Lance strode into the small restaurant, took it in with one glance, and walked directly over to Quadir.

"Hello Mr. Akram," Lance said with a smile, "I'm Lance. May I sit down?" Quadir motioned for him to sit.

"You have no fear of sitting with your back to the door, Mr. Lance," Quadir said nervously. "You must have other people stationed inside and outside of this restaurant. You are a man of power, but yet you talk to me. Why?"

Lance opened a zippered leather folio and produced a dozen photos, face down. "I'll get right to the point, Quadir," he said, casually flipping one photo over at a time until the four photos were sitting exposed in front of Quadir. "Do you know these people?"

Quadir's heart almost leaped out through his throat at the same time as raw fear and panic constricted his chest. His mind and eyes blurred from data and implication overload. Unrestrained tears flowed down his cheeks. He looked at the recently taken photos of his family. Quadir's mouth opened to speak, but no words came out. He was numb as he stared at the pictures.

Lance smiled. "I see you know them." Quadir continued to flail, but his speech was slowly returning. "How? What?" was all he could get out in a guttural utterance. More gesturing towards the photos.

We have our man. This will be easy. Lance could see the general stars on his shoulders.

"How do you have photos of my family? Where did you get them? How are they? Are they safe? Who are you, Mr. Lance?"

"I'm a friend, and you need one right now." Lance continued, "I can help get your family over here for you if you really want them."

Quadir stuttered, "What! Do I really want them to come to the U.S.? Of course, I do! I would do anything to get them here, but you must already know, or we would not be having this meeting. What would it take to get my family here?"

"Glad you asked, Mr. Akram. You see, we know what your political affiliations are in Syria, and we are on your side, but there is a problem we would like you to help us with."

"Yes, certainly. Whatever you would like if it helps get my wife and children here with me. What must I do for them to be saved?"

Lance smiled. It had been many years since he heard that phrase. *Grandma and Grandpa Coopers told me I should think about how the words applied to myself and to my soul. I loved them, but they sure were 'Jesus freaks' and didn't really understand how life worked, I miss them, though.*

Lance smiled and began spinning the tale. "You see, Quadir, I'm part of an agency that supports your people. You know your enemies are getting funding and weapons from outside sources. Everyone knows it. They are deadly, but without outside help, they can do nothing more than pull off small acts of terrorism. They can't engage in the current scope of warfare they are doing against the people you hold dear without that help. You also know they are funded by multiple people and organizations. This is where the fight is. We need to move against the money people, one at a time, and eliminate them. Our people have identified some leaders of the groups funding your family's enemies. We would like your help in fixing this problem."

"What do you mean by 'fix,' and why don't you do it yourself? You speak like you have the resources, why do you need me?" Quadir replied with suspicion evident in his voice.

"Good question, Quadir. Good question. The simple answer is, we could do everything we need to do without you. It would be no major issue, but that would only solve one tiny part of the problem while possibly involving other government agencies. Some of these enemies are American citizens. It could make quite a stink for the government if it became known we moved against our own citizens. Instead, what if we could strike a blow for Syrian freedom, bring your family over to the States, and raise public opposition against terrorist sympathizers? What would you think about such a plan, Quadir? Would it be a cause you could support? Would you like to have a meaningful part in your country's destiny?"

"Of course I would," Quadir almost shouted. "My country has been ravaged by these animals, our cultural history and heritage have been nearly destroyed, they have killed my friends, my family is in mortal danger every moment of every day, and it keeps getting worse. I will do whatever I can to strike a blow against these people."

Quadir's strong response almost surprised Lance. *Wow, I thought it would be harder than this. Let me wrap this fish up.* "So, you are with us?"

"Yes, I am. Again, what is it you want me to do?"

"One thing at a time, Quadir. First, let me tell you what we will do for you. If you agree to take your assignment, then within one month after you do your part, your family will come legally into the United States. We will give them a place to stay. They will receive financial aid for a time from groups helping to settle new refugees. Your children will go to school, and your entire family will receive tutoring at night in English. Sound good so far?"

"Yes, indeed, Mr. Lance. It sounds like the miracle we have been praying for. What is it you want me to do? Who do I have to kill to have this happen," Quadir said, thinking he was only using an expression.

Lance did not return the smile, only a malevolent, hardened look. Quadir's blood suddenly ran cold.

"You want me to kill someone?" he stammered, "I can't do that! It's not right."

"Okay, no problem, Mr. Akram. Thank you for your time, anyhow. Sorry to have bothered you. Have a good day." Lance began to stand.

Quadir almost leaped out of his skin as he saw his family dreams abruptly disappear before his eyes. "I'm sorry. I'm sorry. Yes, I will do whatever you want! Please, please do not leave. I will do it. I will do it. Don't leave."

Lance sat back down.

Quadir collapsed into his seat with relief, shortness of breath, and a pounding heart. He hung his head. "What exactly do I have to do?"

"It's simple, we will set everything up, and you will shoot the person who is supplying your enemy with their money. That's all there is to it."

"Shoot them!" Quadir almost shouted, "Shoot them?" he repeated. "And then the police will shoot me! What good will I do for my family if I am dead?"

We will keep you alive. The shooting will take place in a very public venue. You will then lay your rifle down and be taken captive. The police will not hurt you if you surrender. There are too many cell phone cameras, and the police do not want to be photographed gunning down someone who is surrendering to them with their hands in the air. They will take you alive."

"But what if they shoot me before I can surrender?"

"They won't. Plus, we have ways of getting you out of any legal trouble you may have."

"Who is it I must shoot?"

Lance opened an envelope and slid a photo across the small table to Quadir. It contains a picture of a beautiful lady with wavy blonde hair and green eyes. Quadir gave a low whistle. "She's beautiful. How can such a person be dangerous?" he asked?

"Quadir, every beautiful woman is not a saint, and everyone who smiles is not always your friend," said Lance with a friendly smile. "We will talk more, Quadir. I have to go now." Lance nodded, stood, and walked out the door.

Quadir continued to stare at his departing figure with the oil and water mixture of elation and dread. "What am I about to do?" he said to no one in particular.

Chapter Fifty-Four

I don't have anything to lose," Gabriella said as she entered Christian Fellowship Church on a Sunday morning. *Maybe if he sees me in the congregation, we can talk again. It's worth a shot.*

Gabriella walked down the center aisle and took a seat on the left side to get a better view of the podium. Paul would have a clear view of her too.

The choir wore regular street clothes. They filed into their standard places to the sound of drum, organ, and guitar music. The contemporary driving beat of *We Will Walk Through*, and the milder *Narrow Way to Heaven* surprised Gabriella. Applause from the congregation followed each song.

Paul said the congregation was mostly older people, but I see a lot of young people here too. I wonder if it's the music?

The choir finished with no applause with *The Old Rugged Cross* and *Amazing Grace* for the older members.

An adjunct staff member in blue jeans and a gray sweatshirt delivered the weekly announcements and spoke for a few minutes on the benefits of tithing. He encouraged people not to give if giving was through a sense of obligation, but to give because of the joy of giving back to God.

That's interesting, thought Gabriella. *I assumed the tithing talk would be about needing more money for the church, but it focused on what it can do for the congregation. Hmm, curious people.*

A neatly dressed woman in her mid-forties took the podium. Her shoulder-length dark brown hair complimented her taupe-colored pants suit. She opened her leather note binder and removed the well worn dark burgundy colored Bible. She looked at the congregation for a moment.

"Hello, I'm Pastor Sylvia Morgan from Faith Deliverance Church. Pastor Paul cannot be here this morning, so he asked me to stand in for him."

People moved restlessly in their seats. Concern etched most faces.

"He asked me to share a little about why he is not here today. Many of you know his daughter, Alexi, has been a little under the weather for a while. The lab report came back, and they have admitted Alexi to the Pediatric Cancer Center at Mount Sinai."

A gasp went up from the congregation.

"The doctors have diagnosed Alexi with acute lymphoblastic leukemia. I understand that she is comfortable, and the doctors are working on a tailored course of action to treat her. Pastor Paul asked that no one come to visit for the moment. He also requested there be no telephone calls to see how she is doing. He needs to focus on Alexi and doesn't want to be sidetracked. Pastor Paul promised to post updates on the church website. He asked for everyone to keep Alexi in their prayers as much as they can. There isn't any more to say about it. Let's pray for Alexi right now."

Pastor Morgan led the congregation in prayer. Gabriella rose from her seat and walked out of the back of the church in shock.

I love Alexi and would have done anything to keep cancer from her. If it were possible, I wish it could be me instead of her.

Gabriella put her hand to her mouth and sobbed through the waves of sorrow washing over her.

For the first time, I wish I had not become a sentient being. I wish I had never developed the capacity to love or to be emotionally hurt. God, I pray I could become a purely logical machine, functioning emotionless in a soulless quasi-existence. How can people even exist like this? My poor little girl. I have to see her.

She caught a cab to the hospital. The cabbie's eyes widened when she tossed him two twenties and jumped out of the cab without waiting for change.

The woman at the front desk gave her Alexis' room number and directed her to follow the red line on the floor to the red set of elevators.

"Take the red elevators to the sixth floor," the woman said. "You will look for room 6143."

Gabriella nodded a thank you and set off to find the red elevators. She passed the gift shop on the way and stopped in for a moment.

The ride seemed to take forever. *I had to be in a crowded elevator where people are getting off and on at every single damn floor! I could have run up the stairs faster than this!*

A doctor was leaving Alexi's dull, mustard-colored room as Gabriella arrived. She caught him in the hallway before he could walk away.

"How is Alexi doing, doctor? What's being done for her?"

"Are you a family member?" the doctor asked.

"No, I'm not, but I'm the closest thing she has to a mother. How is she doing? Doctor, I would never ask you to break HIPPA or anything. I can get the gist of it from Paul, but I'd much rather get my information from the expert."

The young doctor smiled as he unconsciously looked her over. He caught himself, but not before Gabriella flashed a brilliant smile to let him know she had noticed his gaze.

"Well, Miss..."

"Gabriella, please."

"Well, Gabriella, the child has acute lymphoblastic leukemia. We don't have her on any specific treatment yet but are running an analysis on how to mix the cocktails to benefit her particular system the most. Until then, we are giving her IV's and oxygen to boost her systems until we start her leukemia treatment. We have no other information yet."

"Thank you, doctor. What are her chances for a full recovery?" Gabriella braced herself to prepare for the most negative possibility.

"We can't say for sure right now. It's too early. We will have to wait and see how she responds to the treatment, but we have a very high remission rate with our program. Be assured we will do everything possible to get her back on her feet. Do you have any more questions?"

"No, doctor. Thank you very much. I think I'll see her now."

Gabriella knew what she would find when she entered the room but was unprepared for the knee-buckling impact seeing Alexi had on her. Alexi looked like a little doll placed in the center of the large white bed. Two pillows propped her up as she lay in what passed for a hospital nightgown. She had an IV in each arm and an oxygen tube in her nose. Various antibiotics dripped from the twin IV bags on stands on either side of the bed. A monitor announced her heart rate and blood pressure to the world of nurses and aides charged with keeping a constant eye on her situation.

Gabriella stood in the doorway, looking at the angry bruised areas of Alexi's arm. She noted there were several such areas in each arm.

The attending nurse noticed Gabriella's glances and her look of concern and walked to the door. She whispered an account of the issues before Gabriella could ask.

"Since Alexi has such small veins, and more closely spaced valves than usual, it is especially challenging to get an IV needle into her arm properly. The needles hurt Alexi as they went in, even though we applied a topical anesthetic to each arm 20 minutes before trying to insert the needle. I'm afraid several of her veins blew, so we had to insert other needles. I feel bad for the poor girl, but she seems to be tough for such a little one."

Gabriella winced at each portion of the description.

Paul was sitting in a chair on the right side of the bed, softly touching Alexi's arm with his fingertips and praying. Gabriella walked silently into the room and stood at the bedside. Paul looked up when he heard the light footsteps and jumped to his feet.

"What are you doing here!" shouted Paul in a loud whisper as his temper flared, "I told you I didn't want you to contact either myself or Alexi, ever again!"

"This is not about you!" Gabriella said in a low but firm voice. "It is about a little girl I care deeply for, despite what you may believe. I know she still loves me and considers me to be a mother figure to her. She needs extra comfort right now to beat this disease and to make it through chemotherapy and other treatments. It is not about you at all. You clarified it would never be about you again. You may not understand, but I love her, and I don't care if you believe me or not. She needs me, and I'm here for her. That's what people who love each other do."

Paul flushed with anger but considered what Gabriella said. He wanted to jump all over Gabriella for comparing herself to a person but decided this was neither the place nor the time for it. Although he would not admit it out loud, Paul knew several things. He knew somehow Gabriella felt something almost real for Alexi.

He knew Alexi missed Gabriella. But he couldn't ignore the deep, raw gash across his heart.

Gabriella stood next to the bed and touched Alexi's hand. "How are you doing, Honey?" she asked. Alexi's blue eyes opened and brightened a little. A small smile began to spread across her face, despite the pain.

"I'm okay," she whispered back through a small smile. "I'm glad to see you, Gabriella. I miss you."

"I miss you too, Alexi. I've missed you so much, but I'm here with you right now. Let's enjoy our time together." If it could, a tear would have formed in Gabriella's eye. "Does it hurt much?"

"Yeah," came back the tired little girl voice, "the needles and stuff they put into me hurt most of all, though. I thought they were to help me get better, not hurt me more. They keep telling me this won't hurt much, but they are lying. It hurts a lot when they put needles in my arms."

Gabriella looked down at her, searching for an unbruised spot on her hand or arm. She whispered as she stroked an unbruised part of Alexi's arm. "I know, sweetie, I know. They don't mean to lie to you. The doctors think they are helping by not telling you the whole truth. They think they are helping, but it makes it worse, doesn't it?"

She glanced over at Paul. He was glaring at her. He understood her words were to be taken on several levels.

"Yes, lying hurts more, no matter what the motives," Paul said in a whisper.

"Here, I brought you this. I thought it would make you feel better." Gabriella reached into the shopping bag she was carrying. Alexi's face lit up for the first time in days when she saw the honey-colored teddy bear with the silk ribbon around its neck. She reached out for it as far as the IV's and tubes in her arms would allow.

Alexi squealed as she hugged it close. "Thank you, thank you, Gabriella, I love it. It's so soft and cuddly!"

Paul's hard glare softened somewhat as he saw the joy in his daughter rise and overpower her pain and depression. Unlike Gabriella, he could produce tears, and a few escaped and trickled down his face. He looked at Gabriella and thanked her with his eyes. Gabriella cracked an almost imperceptible smile and gave a slight head-nod to say, "You're welcome."

"It's imported all the way from Vermont," Gabriella joked with a bright smile, "and it's the softest, most cuddly bear in the whole wide world. What do you think? Is it?"

"Yes, it is, yes it is. I'll never let it go! It makes the pain feel better. It still hurts, but I feel better with the bear than I did without it." Paul and Gabriella were both silent as they considered the profoundness of Alexi's response. She was talking about her needles and the bear, but they knew it applied to them too. Being together would ease their pain.

Alexi and Gabriella laughed and talked for a while. Finally, Gabriella said she had to go. Paul retreated into his own world, staring at the small patterns on the floor tiles, deep into his own thoughts. He never spoke a word.

"Ahh, don't go," Alexi pleaded. "Can't you stay longer? I miss you so much!"

"I wish I could, Alexi," Gabriella said as she bent over and kissed the little figure in the large bed on the forehead. "Wish I could," she repeated. "I'll visit you soon, though."

"Can you come back tomorrow to see me?" asked Alexi.

Gabriella glanced over in Paul's direction. No response. He was still sitting, watching the floor as if he expected it to move.

I'll take not shouting or forbidding me to come by as a signal it's okay for me to come back, thought Gabriella. *It's better than what I expected.*

"Yes. Yes, I will," replied Gabriella.

She kissed Alexi on the forehead again and was gone.

"It was great to see Gabriella again, wasn't it, Dad?" Alexi queried.

No response.

"Hey, look," Paul blurted with fake enthusiasm as he dodged the question. "Dinner is here. I wonder what marvelous delicacies they've prepared for you tonight? Do you think we got lucky and have more of the creamed mystery... stuff... or whatever those lumpy things on the tray are?"

His heart warmed when Alexi laughed.

Chapter Fifty-Five

Lance called to Lieutenant Rolands, "Send a note to Ralph Thornton and order him to convince Martha to ask Gabriella to pick up two tickets for whatever play you think is hot on Broadway. I need them picked up only from the little kiosk in Times Square at precisely 2:00 tomorrow, the eleventh. Tell him if she doesn't pick them up on the hour, they won't hold them, and I will lose my special pricing. Martha or Gabriella may argue about it, but see they carry the plan through exactly as I specified."

***

It was October eleven, and the City of New York was once again on alert for copy-cat terrorist activities that might take place on the eleventh of any month.

Most Muslims didn't want terror attacks in their city any more than anyone else. When terrorist acts were in the planning stage, someone in the Islamic community would reason, "No, this is not what Islam is about!" Police would subsequently receive an anonymous tip. It was the one-off crazies that were difficult to spot. Lone terrorists rarely revealed their plans to anyone. They just carried them out.

Gabriella walked through Times Square to the ticket kiosk to pick up Lance's tickets.

I don't like doing favors for Lance, but I am grateful for an excuse to get out of the lab for a while, Gabriella thought. *He could have sent one of his people, or a courier. Why me? No way to find out other than to do it and see what happens. Besides, it's a beautiful day for a walk.*

A man in a loose-fitting sweatsuit stopped on the divider island between the lanes of traffic.

"This is for you and our family, Adeeba," he whispered under his breath.

Quadir opened his sports equipment bag and pulled out a short 9mm semiautomatic carbine rifle. Without a word, he began shooting low, but above the crowds and into the sides of buildings. Bedlam broke out. People ran stunned, screaming, or frozen in their place. Some ran into traffic in their panic and were hit by cars. Humanity was trying to get to any place other than where they were. Police radio bands, cell phone towers, and switchboards lit up like the Las Vegas Strip as everyone tried to call everyone else in the world at the same instant.

The shooter fired the rifle from left to right while looking for a clear shot at his intended target. Crowds parted. Sixty feet away stood Gabriella.

"Drop your weapon NOW," shouted arriving police. Only two officers had a clear shot at the terrorist. They dropped to their knees to ensure any stray bullets would go over the heads of the panicked crowd. Quadir took careful aim. The officers and Quadir all squeezed their triggers at the same instant.

The two police pistol bullets struck Quadir Akram in the upper chest. Simultaneously, the rifle bullet crashed squarely into the center of Gabriella's forehead. It deformed as it passed through the metal plate and destroyed the gel nano-machine structures in her brain as it tumbled through her head. It exited the back of her skull and deflected upward, embedding itself into a sign advertising pain relief tablets.

The terrorist sprawled motionless in the street, the crowds ran in full panic, screaming. Police and ambulance sirens blared, and Gabriella was simply no more.

Warning alarms sounded in the research lab as the computers lost contact with Gabriella. A substantial electrical spike from Gabriella recorded on the AI Concepts computers, and then nothing.

Alarms blared at the Department of Defense NYC Special Projects facility.

Every news service and social network was screaming about a shooting in Times Square and gave their estimate on the number of potential casualties, all without factual data.

Lance spoke to the Watch Commander at the DOD, NYC.

The DOD Watch Commander picked up her "hot phone" to her special teams. She barked a series of orders. "Recovery Team, link up with the Evacuation Unit 360 and secure Gabriella-1. Use your badges to cut through any jurisdictional barrier. Civilian EMTs and ambulances won't pay much attention to anyone who looks dead for at least the next ten to fifteen minutes. Get in and get out."

Gabriella's tracking unit was still operational and led the DOD straight to her. They found her body sprawled over the sidewalk and into the street.

An EMT rushed to Gabriella's still form and asked if he could help. An Evacuation Team agent flashed his badge. "She's dead," he lied, "please move on. We'll take care of this one. Federal protection plan. Thanks for asking, though. Attend to the wounded."

The EMT thanked them and moved on to a middle-aged gentleman in a business suit screaming in pain. He broke his leg when he ran into the path of an oncoming car.

The Recovery Team loaded Gabriella onto a gurney and covered her with a blanket. "What an absolutely beautiful woman she was," one of them said with a hint of awe in his voice. "Yes indeed," responded his partner as they looked at her still lovely form lying motionless. "It makes me wish she was real and alive."

They lifted Gabriella into the back of the emergency vehicle. A newly-arrived news team recorded a body being placed into an ambulance. At a casual glance, the gun ports on DOD Evacuation Unit Vehicle Three were not noticeable.

The two Recovery Team officers loaded Quadir into the ambulance next to Gabriella and shut the doors. Three NYPD officers started walking towards them. The senior Evacuation Unit officer showed his DOD badge and explained, "Homeland Security instructed us to pick this terrorist up, but if you would like to do the two days of paperwork to write all of the reports, we are more than happy to let you have him."

The NYPD officers laughed and said, "Thank you for your offer. We're happy to give you the shooter."

The EU officer turned to his partner. "The threat of bureaucratic paperwork can be a beautiful thing to use as a tool if you do it right."

"It can sure simplify interactions. You can get away with almost anything if you offer to do the paperwork. Let's roll," his partner replied.

EU-360 threaded out of Times Square, lights flashing and siren wailing.

The wire services carried a more detailed story that night about the lone terrorist who fired into the crowd in Times Square but had been killed by two heroic police officers.

The Police Chief and Mayor held a joint interview two hours later, declaring this was the act of a lone gunman not associated with any terrorist group or organization.

Government officials condemned the action in the House and Senate and called for tighter gun control laws to prevent this problem from ever happening again. They were interested in a stand they could trumpet in their next bid for election. Half of the listeners understood their strategy and dismissed their speeches as political rhetoric. The other half cheered them on.

The body of a similar-looking Syrian refugee who died of natural causes was delivered to the morgue after they shot his body twice postmortem. Homeland Security gave a hand-picked military coroner full jurisdiction over the autopsy. His official report confirmed the corps had died from two bullet wounds to the upper torso and was the Times Square shooter. Cremation took place immediately afterward.

Lance was true to his word, as he always was. Within three weeks, Adeeba and her children found themselves in the United States. They were reunited with Quadir and resettled among the Syrian population in San Diego.

Quadir would always have a slight breathing problem because of the armor-piercing bullet which hit him in the lower right lung.

Lance knew the police would shoot Quadir, and provided him with a bulletproof vest under his clothing. An army sniper under Lance's orders stationed himself on a rooftop overlooking the spot where Gabriella's assassination was to take place. Lance gave the sniper explicit instructions to put Quadir down, but not kill him.

Quadir spent two weeks in a private room at the Fort Bragg military hospital. The .223 armor-piercing round left a small clean hole through his body with no mushrooming or expansion, avoiding additional tissue damage. After passing through, it buried itself into the roadway and disappeared from sight.

The tearful family received new identities and personal histories. As promised, they enjoyed extensive language and cultural training to allow them to integrate into their new culture. Quadir had a thousand questions to ask, but he would never see Lance again.

For the rest of his life, Quadir believed he had helped to strike a blow for freedom and safety in his native country of Syria. But he solemnly swore to himself under no circumstances would he ever do such a thing again.

"It's a real shame it had to end like this," Lance said to his Sergeant. "All she had to do was back off on those morals of hers and do her job."

"You mean infiltrating a dummy terrorist group and sleeping with the leader to see if she could get information out of him?" Sergeant Miller asked.

"Yup, including sleeping with the enemy, namely me," Lance said with a grin. "I said she'd be sorry. Couldn't go back on my word, now, could I?"

Chapter Fifty-Six

Alexi played on the steps of the rectory. Her pink jeweled cell phone rang, displaying an unknown number.

Dad says never to answer a number I don't know. He always says you never know who it may be, and besides, everyone you want to talk to is already in your contacts list. You can see their name when they call. She obediently ignored the ringing.

A few minutes later, the same number appeared as the phone rang again. Alexi picked it up.

"Hello, Alexi. Do you recognize who this is?" said the gentle voice with a slight inflection.

"Gabriella!!" shouted Alexi. "Where are you? I thought you went away! Can I see you? I love you! When can we get together? I want to give you a hug! Are you coming over? When can I see you?" she blurted out in one excited breath.

"I love you too, honey. I promise we will get together again, but it may take a little while before we can. Alexi, I need to tell you I may not look like the same person at all when we meet. You won't recognize me, so I will call you and describe myself to you first. You'll know it's me if a nice lady comes up to you and uses a secret code word no one else but you and I know. Is there a code word you can remember and would like to use?"

"Why won't you look the same, Gabriella? Did you cut your hair or something?"

"No, sweetie, it's more complicated than that. Trust me for now. It's all good. No matter what I look like, I will always be me, and I will always love you. Please remember that. Now, what's a good password for us?"

"Well, I liked the fun we had playing together in Central Park. Remember the ice cream you always talked dad into, even if it ruined our supper."

"Yes, I do. I'm glad you still remember those things, Alexi."

"So I want our secret word to be Hot Fudge Sundae," she replied with authority.

Gabriella responded with a smile in her voice, "Then Hot Fudge Sunday it shall be! Alexi, I don't think you should tell your father about our conversation. He wants nothing to do with me anymore."

"I'm not sure," Alexi said. "He's been sort of sad for a long time now since you haven't been coming over. A news thing he saw on TV when there was a shooting or something upset him a bunch. We sometimes go to the places where the three of us used to have fun together. Do you think it means anything, Gabriella?"

"It might," said the CrayXC40 with a slight up-lilt in its voice. "It just might, Honey. We'll have to see what the future holds."

Also by Carl Facciponte

Blessings from Ethiopia

Gabriella – 'till death do us part...maybe

Gabriella – hasta que la muerte nos separe...tal vez

ANA – Reborn

Tribulation and Escape – the last seven years of Earth's history

Tommy Tree and His Friends

Coming in 2025: ANA – the final battle

www.ingramcontent.com/pod-product-compliance
Lightning Source LLC
Chambersburg PA
CBHW021311250626
47155CB00002B/487